HOKEE WOLF

CLARK VIEHWEG

BLACK ROSE
writing™

ISBN: 978-1-61296-885-8
PUBLISHED BY BLACK ROSE WRITING
www.blackrosewriting.com

Printed in the United States of America
Suggested retail price $18.95

Hokee Wolf is printed in Adobe Garamond Pro

For my beautiful loving wife,
Kimberly; partner, friend, lover and constant inspiration.

ACKNOWLEDGMENTS

My first and second grade teacher, Mrs. Nelson, taught me to read and write. I won a contest for the neatest penmanship in the class. Unfortunately, this was not a trait that followed me beyond the fourth or fifth grade. Still, I owe a big thanks to this wonderful teacher who read a chapter from a book to us each day which instilled within me a desire to read and write. Over the years, I have received many suggestions from friends and relatives to continue with my writing, most notably my sister Adelle Viehweg Miller. Some special thanks are due to Linda Nebon who spent many long hours correcting my horrible spelling and suggesting numerous improvements to my choice of language and phrasing. I owe a debt to all of my wonderful critics who made significant contributions to the story. And finally, my loving wife, Kimberly Viehweg without whose support, encouragement and love this book would never have been written.

HOKEE WOLF

PRELUDE

Pocatello, Idaho, Summer-1963

The kid with long dirty blond hair tied in a ponytail lounged idly against the light pole on the corner of State and Williams Street. The pitiful young man had a sunken chest with acne scars on his face. There were still many open sores on his scarred face. A dirty torn Bob Dylan T-shirt from a 1961 concert at The Folklore Center hung over short denim pants displaying skinny sticks for legs stuck in tattered black canvas shoes. The dirty blond hair framed a bony oblong face with a mere slit for a mouth. It would be easy to mistake him for one of the big losers in life's lottery except for a spark of bright intelligence hiding behind a bored look of indifference. Unless one really looked into the fifteen-year old's eyes, which admittedly was difficult to do given his otherwise unappetizing appearance, it was easy to miss the way he paid attention to everything going on in the world around his corner of the universe. Unfortunately, Officer Brent Morden, not very observant, was totally misled by the youth's sloppy appearance.

Pocatello at that time had an influx of unwashed hippies flopping down at Railroad Park smoking dope, handing out wild poppies while mouthing peace slogans. Unfortunately, the hippie kids had no idea that the colorful wild poppies they were handing out were the same variety grown in Afghanistan to produce opium. The poppies had been planted years ago in the wide US 91 highway borrow pit just outside of town between Pocatello and Portneuf. Some enterprising person correctly assumed that no one in Hicksville would have any idea about the plant's real identity assuming they were simply pretty flowers planted by the highway department. Fortunately, there was not one person in ten thousand who knew that these poppies were loaded and this included the police who smiled and nodded as the poppies were distributed around town.

While the hippie invaders were not violent, local merchants thought of these long-haired, unwashed species of humanity a great nuisance and had insisted that the police get them out of their city. Chief of Police Dwayne Talbot, responding to the merchant's demands, had assigned officers to patrol the downtown streets. Brent Morden, a rookie cop, was walking a prescribed beat to help enforce the city's new policy against loitering when he saw the kid in an obvious hippie shirt with dirty long hair lounging on the corner. Mistaking him for one of the out of town hippies, Brent spoke in an authoritative commanding "God" tone of voice all would-be police officers learn in the academy. A voice that said "I'm God and you're a piece of shit so do what I say NOW!"

"Get off that post and get your ass out of town," he bellowed. As he was saying this Morden pulled the black hardwood billy club from the holster on his belt just to be sure the kid obeyed.

The kid did not even bother turning around to see who was addressing him but instead just extended his left arm behind his back giving Brent the middle finger salute. Infuriated, Officer Morden raised the club over his head intending on striking a blow to the youth's back to move him along. As the club reached its apex and began coming down with the full force an angry cop could swing the young man seeming to sense something going on behind his back suddenly whirled around to see what was happening. Everything happened so quickly Morden was unable to stop his downward blow which struck the kid squarely on the side of his head.

Brent was horrified. The youth fell unconscious onto the sidewalk with bright red blood trickling from his broken scalp. Morden's attack had been unjustified and disciplinary action was certain with possible dismissal from the police force. He quickly glanced around to see if anyone was in the vicinity who might have witnessed the incident. No one was visible. Without checking to see if his victim was alive or dead, Brent hurriedly walked away hoping to be out of sight before anyone noticed a bleeding young man lying on the sidewalk.

*****

Hung Wong, a young Chinese boy from a prominent family was sold into slavery by his brothers in 1895 and shipped to San Francisco. Ostensibly slavery in the United States ended in 1865 with the Emancipation Proclamation but that only applied to the southern slave states. In 1870 slavery became illegal throughout the United States but that did not stop the importation of Chinese slaves to California, primarily young girls for prostitution. Beginning in 1877 and throughout the 1880's California enacted a series of laws to theoretically halt this barbaric practice which unfortunately persists even today. However, it was not only the women who were sold into slavery, but many men were also rounded up in China and sold as slaves in California to help ranchers, miners and even the railroads. Hung Wong was one such man sold into slavery by his jealous brothers, much like Joseph in the Bible.

The Wongs were a powerful family in Lhasa, a large town in the Xizang Province. Located in the southwestern part of China next to the Himalayan Mountains, Lhasa is at the crossroads of traditional Chinese culture and the mystical Tibetan teachings centered on mind control and extraordinary power projection. Hung's father was considered an adept in the arcane practice of Shimbalou, a Chinese version of Voodoo. Hung displayed an amazing talent for Shimbalou at an early age which endeared him to his father while making him an enemy of his two older brothers. Hearing about the slave traders in the area seeking girls and young boys Hung's brothers arranged for him to be kidnapped and ultimately shipped to America.

Hung was purchased off the San Francisco docks by a rancher in Redding. This rancher had over 100 Chinese slaves who were supposed to be working off their slave purchase price before being granted their freedom. Many slaves had fulfilled this contract but stayed on with the rancher until their friends were also free. During this time those slaves who had earned their freedom were supposed to be paid a lump sum at the end of their service. When most of the Chinese laborers had earned their freedom, the rancher held a big banquet to reward the workers serving them a cow he had butchered and roasted over a fire. The meat was poisoned killing all of the workers save four who had been out doing last minute chores. This act of depravity was done in order to save the money the rancher owed the Chinese.

Four workers came to the party late and seeing their friends either dying or dead fled into the mountains. Local cowboys took off after the four capturing and killing three in a nearby meadow. The last escapee, Hung Wong, managed to get free ultimately working his way to Idaho. He worked in the mines of Caribou Mountain until the mines closed a few years later after which he moved to Pocatello. During all this time Hung was careful about displaying his occult powers. He knew from experience as a youth that those who possessed extraordinary powers posed a frightening menace to society at large and were often persecuted. Accordingly, he used his powers very sparingly growing old and tired. In 1963 Hung was an old man tired and ready for the afterlife. Hobbling down State Street towards an old Chinese deli he came across an unconscious youth lying in blood on the sidewalk.

Over the ensuing years, the young man lived with Hung who taught him the arcane practices of Shimbalou. Before old Hung died with nothing to leave his acolyte except his teachings, he sent the boy to an ancient master he knew in India for his final preparation. These were lessons never to be forgotten.

*****

Fifteen years went by and Officer Brent Morden had all but forgotten the sidewalk incident. Occasionally some trivial event or a person on the street caused him to recall the accident, as he preferred to think of the event when life would unhappily thrust it into the forefront of his memory. He diligently strived to erase the memory as quickly as possible whenever it did surface. Many months had gone by without any hint of the memory bothering his conscious thoughts until one afternoon as he was sitting on a stool at the counter of Joni's, his favorite coffee and doughnut shop.

Joni's is a fifties chrome and glass railroad style dining room car complete with Wurlitzer jukebox and Elvis songs in the playlist. Bright neon lights running completely around the building helps it command the crossroads at W. Chubbuck and Hawthorn Roads. One long chrome edged counter runs the full length of the dining room with thirty fire-red padded stools. The old Wurlitzer jukebox featured a whole selection of fifties tunes besides Elvis that kept recycling every four hours. Officer Morden, having finished his hot turkey sandwich, was on his second cup of coffee enjoying a piece of French apple pie listening to Kitty Kallen singing "Little Things Mean a Lot" when his life suddenly took a drastically painful turn.

Glancing up at the mirror on the far wall he saw someone walking by on the sidewalk outside just as that person looked into the restaurant. Their eyes locked in the mirror for just a millisecond, but long enough for the blood to stop circulating in Morden's veins.

Chills ran down his spine and he felt cold all over even though it was the middle of July with the temperature in the mid-eighties. He suddenly gasped for breath before realizing that he had momentarily stopped breathing. Throwing some bills on the counter without even looking at the denominations, Morden hurried outside to locate the man he had been dreading ever meeting again. He need not have hurried.

Charging out of the front door he stopped to look up and down both sides of the street nearly missing the slight form lounging against the wall next to the swinging glass door.

"Looking for me?" a soft voice inquired although to Brent it sounded like someone yelling into a megaphone.

The man still had long, stringy, blond hair and a horribly scarred acne face, plus it appeared that his entry into midlife was accompanied by unusually deep crow's feet and more sagging neck skin than most men his age. He had the same slender body and sunken chest of his youth, but the look in his eyes was even more intense than it had been fifteen years earlier. Although blue, his eyes looked like black marbles with holes drilled for pupils that blasted out a beam of white light scorching everything in its path.

Morden stood frozen as the young man walked up placing his right hand on the officer's right shoulder.

"This is payback, officer, for a lifetime of headaches," he whispered. "I've been looking for you." The words barely registered as intense pain paralyzed Brent's shoulder radiating down his arm to the tips of every finger. Morden's arm began to wither even as the youth withdrew his hand and walked away without a backward glance.

Doctors were unable to find any reason for the paralysis or suggest a remedy. Officer Brent Morden's permanently paralyzed right arm withered to mere skin and bone, rendering him unfit for active police duty except dispatch and light office work. He never told anyone about either of his encounters with the strange young man with the blazing black eyes through which ungodly light seemed to burn whatever the young man chose to look upon. These were secrets Officer Morden vowed to keep to himself.

CHAPTER ONE

Three months later - Lake Henry, Idaho
Near West Yellowstone Tuesday, September 5th, 1978 – 3:30 p.m.

The shallow grave was nearly three feet deep.

A plain pinewood coffin without the top was already in the hole resting six inches below ground level. It was a real coffin from Kendall's Funeral Home. The kind of cheap box used to bury the homeless for which Kendall charged the city and county the regular retail price of a much nicer home for the deceased. It was given away for free because during transport water leaked into the shipping container staining the outside of one panel rusty red. A coffin with a stain which looked like dried blood could not be sold even to the government. It did not matter that it was only a cheap pine box. A friend who worked for Kendall's had told the grave digger about the damaged coffin shipment as a joke while they were drinking beer at a local dive. Learning about this saved the digger the trouble of having to build his own coffin.

Now he stood, with a sunken chest in dirty khaki pants wearing an unbuttoned, blue flannel shirt showing sweat stains under the arms, looking down at the grave. As he was studying the pine box he was wondering, and hoping, that the grave would keep him safe.

The coffin's lid had been modified so that it was an open box with sides four inches deep. The original thin wooden lid had been strengthened on the underside with two inches of Douglas fir giving it extra weight. Sod from the hole in the ground had been used to fill the box-lid, so that when the lid was placed on the coffin in the ground, the surface around the grave hole would be even with the top of the lid.

Several months had been spent searching for the perfect grave site. The location had to be in a remote spot invisible from State Highway 20 somewhere near Lake Henry and accessible by vehicle. It could not be too close to the lake where someone camping or fishing was likely to wander by; yet if it was too far from the lake the timing wouldn't work. A site with grass was preferred to dirt so that there would be no footprints and most of all it had to be a place unlikely to be visited by anyone. All the extra dirt from the grave had been carefully collected and hauled away. Special care had been taken when the original sod had been cut for the grave to be sure that when the casket's lid was in place the seams would be nearly invisible. Apparently, the sunken chest man's life depended upon the grave remaining hidden.

Satisfied that he had done everything possible to ensure that his grave would not be found, the man neatly folded an old green army blanket which he placed in the bottom of the casket. He maneuvered the heavy lid near the grave, straining his muscles against the weight. With much effort, he finally managed to get one end of the lid into the grave on top of the coffin with the other end propped up about ten inches above the ground with a pickaxe handle. With great care, he smoothed the grass all around the grave removing evidence of any disturbance. Once he was in the grave with the lid lowered in place there was to be nothing left which would reveal his resting place.

Glancing at an old Timex watch with a scratched face on his wrist, his eyes confirmed with a sense of knowing that there was still an hour before it was necessary for him to enter his grave. A few yards away was a rusty old 1973 Ford Pinto which had once been bright green but was so faded and dirty that it looked nearly brown with red streaks. Walking over to the car, he sat in the front seat with the driver's door open, drinking water and reviewing old Hung's instructions. It was important to become as hydrated as possible. The next few hours he would be as near death without dying as is humanly possible. He will cease breathing, circulating his last breath of air endlessly throughout his body like he had been taught. His heart will beat once every ten seconds. In fact, if anyone does find his grave it would be assumed that he is dead; and if the wrong person finds his grave he will definitely die. If he is to survive the coming ordeal his body will need all the moisture he can pour into it during the next sixty minutes.

*****

12

State Highway 20, Near West Yellowstone:
Tuesday, September 5th, 1978 – 4:30 p.m.

Idaho State Highway 20 from West Yellowstone National Park to Idaho Falls travels through a forest of tall white pine trees creating a visual image of traveling through a deep green valley. At this time of day, the only vehicle on this stretch of the road was a Ford Class 7 truck with a white 24-foot enclosed bed. Red lettering on both sides of the truck said EDDY'S BAKERY surrounded by pictures of bread loaves, biscuits, cupcakes, cookies and Danish pastries. Ernie was unhappily riding shotgun as he looked over at Frank, the driver and asked, "How much do ya think we picked up today?"

At six foot three inches in height Frank was four inches taller and sixty pounds heavier and considerably stronger than his partner. In the testosterone alpha male dance this made him the de facto leader who could be the driver if he chose, and he so chose. Frank had a big square face with Elvis-style sideburns and bushy eyebrows. Without even giving his riding partner a glance, he mumbled, "They don't tell us peons that kinda stuff, but the day after a big Labor Day weekend, with the largest crowd of the season, I'd guess we're hauling at least two or three million in cash, not to mention all the other stuff."

Even though he was smaller and a few years older, Ernie still had a full head of dark hair while Frank was nearly bald, and in the male mindset Ernie used that fact to make himself feel a little superior. In addition, he was more intelligent and was not running to fat around the middle like Frank, which allowed him to feel even better about himself. With Frank indicating to Ernie how little he valued his company by not looking in his direction, Ernie began to grin. In Ernie's mind Frank was simply a prick and one couldn't be offended by the actions or insults from someone who behaved as though physical strength and size constituted all there was to being a man.

"Too bad we can't take a few samples home with us like we do the bakery goodies," Ernie said just to show he did not harbor any bad feelings. He did not really expect Frank to notice one way or the other.

Still without looking at his partner, Frank mumbled a response although one was not needed or called for. "That kind of thinking can get a man in trouble. I'll be happy when they finally hire an armored truck to make this run so we don't have to haul their stinking money back to the bank."

"I heard the merchants got another armored truck company bid last week although the extra hundred bucks a piece they pay us to make this run is really easy money," Ernie replied. "I'll be sorry when it stops, if it ever does."

The West Yellowstone merchants had been looking at armored car services for a number of years but the cost far exceeded the pittance they paid Eddy's Bakery to haul their money back to the banks in Pocatello. Armored trucks were essentially tanks on wheels which got very poor gas mileage and traveled much slower than regular vehicles. The round-trip from Pocatello to West Yellowstone was already a long drive and the lumbering armored truck added even more hours. Add the price of two men plus the profit any business expected, made the run very expensive. Eddy's made the run daily and besides, who would ever think of a bread truck hauling money for God's sake?

"It's gotta stop sometime," Frank said raising his voice. Hauling money in their bread truck was one of his hot spots. As his face turned red and the big blood vessels in his neck started to pulse he continued, "This is just too fucking dangerous; all this money in a lousy damn bread truck!" The symbolism and metaphors were completely lost between his anger and stupidity. The fear of robbery and possible injury dominated his thoughts.

If either man would have looked in the side mirrors as the truck rolled by the east cutoff from State Highway 20 leading to Henry's Lake, they would have seen a dark clad figure rush onto the highway with a saw horse and sign. A few hundred yards beyond the Lake Henry cutoff, Highway 20 began a slow curve towards the south and Idaho Falls. Both sides of the highway were covered with a thick forest of western white pine making it impossible to see more than a few feet beyond the tree line. As the road curved towards the south it was only possible to see a couple hundred feet of highway in front of or behind the truck. With the truck fully into the turn, an overturned vehicle suddenly appeared in the middle of the road. It looked like a Ford Ranchero had apparently rolled over many times flinging its passengers onto the highway. A black Chevy pickup truck facing Eddy's bread truck was stopped behind the wreck. Its driver was between the wreck and Eddy's truck frantically waving his arms trying to get Eddy's bread truck to stop.

Frank stopped a few feet from the pickup and rolled down the driver's window in order to talk with the man waving his arms.

"Could you guys give me a hand here with these injured people?" the waving man pleaded. There was something vaguely familiar about the man, although later neither Frank nor Ernie would be able to say exactly who it was that the man looked like. The mysterious man appeared like a cross between John Wayne and Errol Flynn, although without identifying features of either one. There was an eerie quality about the Good Samaritan that defied description.

Both men hastily got out of the truck hurrying over to the bodies scattered along the highway. Before reaching the first body they were alarmed to hear the gears in their Ford truck engage as it roared off, passing them on its way down the highway. When the men looked back down on the pavement all of the bodies, the overturned car and the pickup had completely disappeared. They stared at each other in disbelief.

How in the hell were they ever going to explain this? The truth sounded stranger than any fiction, yet neither man could come up with an alternate story that made any sense. Eventually, Chuck Alfonso, a curious highway patrolman wondering about the temporary "road closed" sign leaning on a couple of sawhorses crossing the highway, drove down State Highway 20 investigating the reason for the closure. A half-mile after the sign he came across the two bakery employees walking along the road frantically waving their arms to get his attention. Although highly skeptical after listening to their story, Alfonso radioed for help to search for the truck and the missing money.

Four hours later searchers found the abandoned truck a hundred yards off the highway and five miles south of the spot Frank and Ernie insisted was the robbery site. The money was naturally missing along with the reputed truck thief. Although both men stuck to their stories and ultimately took lie detector tests validating their account of the robbery, they remained under suspicion. The money had simply vanished and a week later the Idaho First National Bank offered a hundred-thousand-dollar reward for any information leading to the arrest and conviction of the person or persons responsible for the heist.

CHAPTER TWO

Two Weeks Later

Pocatello, Idaho's primary claim to fame is the Princess Theatre; the place where Judy Garland was born in a wardrobe trunk, but unfortunately over the years no event has added to that reputation. Established over one hundred and fifty years ago as a railroad hub, it was the principal junction in the mountain states between the east-west and north-south railroad lines. It sits within a day's drive of several scenic wonders such as Craters of the Moon National Park, Yellowstone National Park, Teton National Park and the famous Hells Canyon where Evel Knievel tried jumping the Snake River. While these historic and beautiful sights are within a few hours of Pocatello, the city itself is an ugly sprawl located in an equally unattractive location. Today, although home to over fifty thousand people, the town is considered by many to be nowhere while remaining a crossroads to everywhere. The town was named after a Shoshone Indian Chief who granted the Union Pacific Railroad permission to lay tracks across the Fort Hall Indian reservation. When visiting the area one is awed and intrigued by the abundance of black lava rock that seems to dominate nearly every scene. Questions arise as to when and where all this lava came from and is it safe to be here?

Hokee Wolf is a detective who has an office above the Idaho First National Bank that fronts E. Clark Street just off of S. Fourth Avenue. Because of his location, he was one of the first individuals informed of the reward by the bank but chose to ignore the temptation, focusing instead on his primary interest which was locating errant Idaho State students for their parents. Many students attending the university were farm boys and girls away from home for the first time in their lives and the temptations of the "big city" were often more than they could handle. In addition to the attractions of a big city there lurked the ugly underbelly that exists in most college towns. The principal inhabitants of this seamy side of town are the wolves and sharks that live to prey upon the naive young college students away from the guiding influence of their parents. If the student's parents didn't hear from their darlings at regular intervals Hokee was called to investigate their whereabouts and get them back into the university fold, so to speak. It was easy work and once located, Wolf had a way of impressing the wayward students on the necessity of keeping their parents informed. Over the years, he had heard every sob story by the students and had dealt with drug pushers, pimps, thieves, cons and other low-lifers who preyed on the innocent students. Once Hokee expressed an interest in a particular student the parasites feasting on the trusting farm kids knew enough to leave that person alone in the future. More than one nasty man simply disappeared and eventually the word got around. If "the Wolf" as they called him, said lay off somebody, you damn well better lay off.

"Hokee" is a Navajo name meaning abandoned. His mother was a sixteen-year-old girl named Dawn, who had been part of the Arizona Navajo Indian work force of farmers in Utah and Idaho that were trucked in to help with summer irrigation, row crop cultivation and harvesting. This was before illegal Mexicans came in sufficient numbers to handle the dirty work white kids didn't have time for being tied up with dating, sports and parties. Rather than sleeping in a hot tent with ten other unrelated Indians of both sexes, Dawn opted to sleep outside along one of the irrigation ditches. The air was cooler, it was a lot quieter and she wasn't bothered by the mosquitoes. It was here one night that the farmer responsible for importing this group of Indians found and raped the girl, resulting in her pregnancy. Her half-breed baby boy shamed the unwed mother. Unable to find acceptance in both the white and brown worlds, she threw herself with the baby clutched in her arms from a cliff in the Arizona Navajo Reservation. In falling from the cliff, the young mother either consciously or unconsciously twisted in the air landing on her back, shielding the baby boy in her arms thereby saving his life.

The motherless child grew up unloved and unwanted by either world so he learned to survive by his quick wits, daring acts and strength. In the language of the reservation Indians, an abandoned child is called "Hokee" and the name stuck. Nobody knows how he picked up the additional name of "Wolf" but visually his shoulder-long, thick, black hair now tinged with gray added credence to the name that gave him an allure of invincibility. Although his eyes were dark blue the demeanor projected from within his clean, handsome face gave most people the impression that his eyes were black. As a gift from his unknown father, along with the eyes, he stood six feet three with two hundred and ten pounds of granite hard muscle pleasingly arranged on a lean tough frame. The stories about his strength and fighting ability were legendary and his tenure as an apprentice to a shaman added to that mystique. The allure of his good looks unwittingly made him a favorite bachelor target, sought after by the town's seductive women; both married and unmarried. Despite many chances, Hokee remained unmarried and seemingly uninterested in ever settling down with one woman. No one had ever been invited to his home let alone spend the night with him.

Hokee's office complex consisted of two small rooms. An outer room served as a reception area where the phone was answered by Mrs. Hilda Worthmyer, a 45-year-old widow who had a not so secret crush on her boss. Her primary function was to schedule appointments for Hokee who spent the majority of his time out of the office. The walls in her office were bare with no windows. The only furniture consisted of her desk and chair plus a couple of dented green army surplus filing cabinets. Hilda used to keep a photo of her dead police officer husband on the desk but with a burning crush on Hokee she had relegated his photo to the bottom drawer of her desk. Hokee never indicated that he noticed the absence of her dead husband's photo. Clyde, the dead husband, had been killed in a shootout between the police and several drunken Blackfoot Indians hunting for Hokee's scalp due to a tribal misunderstanding. Giving Mrs. Worthmyer a meaningful job with excellent pay was how Hokee paid a debt he believed he owed the dead policeman even though the officer was killed through no fault of Hokee's. Mrs. Worthmyer did not have children so she had plenty of time to run the office without family duties interfering. Even at 45 she was still a good-looking woman with a great figure, a winning personality and plenty of brains. The office was kept humming and the client list continued to grow partly due to her sunny disposition as well as Hokee's reputation as the city's, and perhaps the state's, best investigator.

Hokee's office next door consisted of a battered wooden desk, a high-backed desk chair in front of a large bay window overlooking Pott's Bakery across the road on E. Clark Street and two well-scarred Hudson dining chairs facing the desk. In the corner on a small table was the office coffee pot with only three cups, Hokee's favorite, an old lumberjack mug picked up from an abandoned sawmill, and two chipped, old-fashioned shaving mugs for guests who weren't finicky. Hilda only drank tea she brought from home in a thermos. On the wall facing Hokee's desk hung a large print of an unsigned painting featuring the head of a wolf blending into the head of a Native American male below the wolf. The Indian was wearing a talisman hanging from his neck featuring a dragonfly. The painting was titled, "We Are All One Family." Most people who visited Hokee's office were too polite to ask about the print but they would all swear the Native American in the painting was a dead ringer for Hokee. The side facing walls each had a painting done by a local artist; one featuring Old Faithful in Yellowstone National Park and the other showed the Grand Tetons in all their majesty.

*****

Two weeks after the reward was announced with still no action on locating either the money or the thief, Hokee was visited by both the local bank branch manager from downstairs and the owner of Eddy's Bakery. Their visit happened to coincide with Hilda's visit to the ladies' room that morning, so they just showed up unannounced at Hokee's office door.

Weeb Dillford, the bank manager, a green eye-shade individual if there ever was one, poked his head into Hokee's room and started the conversation.

"Hey Hokee, could you spare us a couple of minutes?" he asked knocking on the doorframe of the open office door. Dillford couldn't help but notice Hokee's custom-made black cowboy boots and casual Levi denim work clothes. He always secretly admired the good looking Indian with his full head of long black hair and devil-may-care attitude.

"Come on in Weeb, I'm just finishing up a report on one of my missing kids," Hokee said setting a pen and yellow legal pad face down on his desk.

Both men entered the room as Weeb continued, "You know Grant Meekam, don't you? He's the owner of Eddy's Bakery."

Dillford wore a gray three-piece wool suit year-round with trousers that always needed pressing and black shoes that were never shined. His thinning hair was parted almost on top of his left ear in a sloppy comb-over in a futile attempt to hide his balding head. His stomach bulged over a wide black belt and his cheek jowls wiggled as he walked across the room to shake hands with Hokee. Heavy black glasses perched on his nose added to the owlish looking bookkeeper. Meekam was wearing dark cotton slacks with a white polo shirt and brown loafers. His pale complexion and sunken eyes spoke of a man who spent his life indoors rarely venturing into daylight.

"I've never had the pleasure," Hokee responded standing up to greet his visitors. After shaking pasty soft palms with his own calloused work hardened hand he waved at both men to take a seat in the two office chairs facing his desk.

Hokee had a good idea concerning the men's visit but had learned years ago that you learned more and gave away less by letting others carry the conversation. There was no one that called Hokee a close friend, however, everyone on the side of truth and justice would describe him as "friendly". You just never wanted to get crosswise with the Wolf because one of you ended up getting the big hurt, and it was never Hokee.

Dillford and Meekam sat squirming on the edge of their chairs waiting for Hokee to ask them why they had come to his office, but Hokee just sat patiently with that damned stoic look on his face revealing nothing. The two visitors glanced around the office as though they found the décor extremely interesting. Finally, Weeb, the green eye-shade banker broke the uncomfortable silence. Uncomfortable, that is, for the two visitors. Hokee was perfectly happy to sit back watching the two men squirm.

"You, must be wondering why we're here?" Dillford asked.

"Nope," Hokee said his face revealing nothing.

"Well, I mean you must have been asking yourself why we both came to see you?" he stammered not knowing how to respond to this laconic one-word reply.

"Nope," Hokee said. Hokee had a very good idea why the men were in his office but he had learned years ago, that in horse trading it never paid off to say very much.

"What he means," Meekam began as though Dillford had actually said something, "is that we were wondering why you haven't shown any interest in our reward money?"

Now that the official reason for their visit had been established both men seemed to relax and sink a little bit into their chairs. It was almost like they had been anticipating an attack and been all tensed waiting for the blows to begin.

"I've got my business," was Hokee's response.

Weeb and Grant looked at each other trying to figure out their next move. Clearly, they had expected Hokee to make their going a little easier. They knew that Hokee made a good living chasing down missing kids, they just didn't know how good. To them a hundred-thousand dollar reward would be extremely tempting. The truth was that neither man had any idea what the detective's financial status looked like. They assumed that as a small business man in Pocatello he was moderately well off, but certainly by no means able to discount the appeal of a hundred-thousand dollars' easy money. Hokee's casual response threw both men into mental turmoil trying to figure out their next move.

"Ya see," Dillford tried again, "we kinda figured that you being our town's best detective, you would be interested in helping us recover our stolen money."

This comment didn't seem to warrant a response so Hokee just sat stone-faced looking at the two men across the desk waiting for them to continue. By now both men had resumed squirming in their chairs trying to figure out their next move.

After waiting for his visitors to say something Hokee decided to take pity on the duo and get the negotiations underway, "Half."

"Half what?" both men asked in unison.

"Half the stolen money," Hokee said. "I'll find your money for half of whatever I recover."

"But that's absurd," Grant said. "Why should we give you half of our money?"

Fed up with this tiresome couple Hokee decided to end their session with one big speech. "Right now, you've got nothing. A hundred percent of nothing is still nothing. If I look for your money it will be a full-time job on my part and you won't be paying my expenses. When I find your money, I keep half for my time and expenses and give you the rest. That's my offer; if you agree fine, if not there's the door and good day," he said nodding his head towards the still open door.

The two businessmen looked like roosters that had just been in a losing cock fight as they hastily agreed to Hokee's terms. Then after signing his representation contract the two nearly fell over each other in their haste to exit his office. It wasn't until they reached the street that either man was able to take a real breath. Their encounter with Hokee was just too stressful.

Meanwhile, Hokee's next stop would be the sheriff's office.

CHAPTER THREE

Glory-New York City
Two Days Earlier

Gloria Bingham was called Glory by the news crew at WSNY. Some thought it was because she was a glory hog while others maintained it was because the stories she pursued always seemed to cover her with glory. A petite thirty-five-year-old blond, five feet four inches high she barely weighed one twenty fully clothed. Being one of the station's leading reporters Glory only dressed in the latest fashion. She had graduated from NYU with a degree in journalism and worked her way up the news chain with a combination of hard work and occasionally sleeping with someone who could help promote her career. Even so, nobody could doubt that the good-looking blond with a killer body didn't know her business and was good at both eliciting the facts for a story and delivering it in style. It came as a surprise, no make that a complete shock, when Levi Morgenstern the news director called her into his office and handed her a plane ticket to Boise, Idaho.

"What the hell is this?" she demanded trying, but failing to refrain from shouting. Normally restrained and careful with her language this kind of treatment didn't happen to a news star. As the reigning queen of the evening news broadcasts in New York City, Glory was able to pick and choose her stories. It was unprecedented to not only give her an assignment but to send her out of town.

Levi had expected the outburst but couldn't resist the taunting. Gloria always wore expensive well-tailored garments with material on the thin side and when she got angry her nipples hardened, dimpling the otherwise smooth fabric of her blouse. Since she had absolute control on television it was never a problem and she liked the way her clothes accentuated the body she spent considerable hours and money maintaining. Besides, her body was just one of the weapons she used to achieve and maintain her position. Having achieved the desired effect Levi feigned resignation and answered her question.

"I need you out of the station for a few days Glory." His tone suggested that he was sorry for upsetting her but the glint in his eyes said otherwise. "We've had some repercussions on that piece you did about the teacher's union. Probably just empty threats but management thinks you should leave town and there's a story out west that you might develop into something interesting. It's only for a few days, a week at the most," he added with what he hoped passed for an honest smile trying to avoid the shit storm he knew was coming.

"Come on Levi, cut the crap," she said. It was obvious that she saw where his eyes had been focused and knew his ploy. One look at her face and Levi could see that she was about to explode.

"This stinks so bad I can't believe you can even keep a straight face."

"Okay. Look Glory, management is really truly worried that some union nutcase out there might want to do you harm. They feel that a few days to let things cool down is in everybody's interest." Seeing that he had her attention a little sugar seemed in order. "You did a hell-of-a-job with the teacher's piece but it ruffled some feathers. Think of this as a paid vacation. You're close to Sun Valley. Go visit a couple stars. I think Eastwood's got a place there. Stay in a ritzy place. We've even got you a first-class air ticket."

One look at Levi's face and Glory knew that it was useless to argue about the assignment. Levi took his directions from management seriously. If they wanted her out of town she might as well go graciously and at least she was going first class. "What's the story out in Idaho?" she said taking a seat across from her boss.

"From what we know it looks like the merchants in Yellowstone Park were shipping all their cash in a bread truck back to a bank in Pocatello. That's pretty rich, shipping cash in a bread truck. Ya jest gotta love those Idaho hillbillies. Anyway, several million dollars just disappeared. Not a clue. It probably isn't much of a story, but what the hell. Money shipped in a bread truck. Local cops completely baffled. We figure it might be a good filler, and it gets you out of my hair for a few days while we treat you like the princess you are."

She knew he was just blowing smoke, but as one of the network's news darlings the flattery while honest was still grating. Besides, she didn't like being manipulated.

*****

Figuring he had avoided most of the anticipated emotional storm, Levi picked up a half-smoked cigar and proceeded to relight it while Gloria digested the news.

Looking at the ticket for the first-time Gloria noticed that it was for Boise, not Pocatello.

"This ticket is to Boise, not Pocatello," she complained. "How far apart are they?"

"How the fuck do I know?" he said blowing clouds of smoke in the air, "probably a hundred miles or so. We couldn't find a flight from either airport directly to Pocatello. We reserved you a luxury car and you have Cutter, your favorite cameraman, who can do the entire driving if you want. He flies coach."

"You have me leaving in three hours. I'll be getting in at midnight," she continued just to let the boss know how much she was sacrificing to do this gig.

"Nah, ya pick up two or three hours crossing time zones. Sleep on the plane. Stay in Boise tonight. Pick a good hotel. Go on down to Pocatello tomorrow and snoop around. See what you can dig up, should be fun."

"Sure, bumfuck USA ought to be a blast." This came out almost like a snort. "Maybe I can do some serious shopping and pick up the latest hillbilly rags." Standing up to leave she asked, "Are you serious about me taking in Sun Valley?"

"Why not, if you have the time," Levi said. "I've never been there but I hear it's really great in the fall. Mostly just stay out of New York for a few days. If you can get any kind of decent story out of this, so much the better, but that isn't a priority. Although, our big bosses could be really generous at bonus time if you could maybe score one of your brilliant essay pieces out of the trip."

Levi relaxed back into the chair after his blatant bribe, enjoying his cigar as Gloria headed out the door shaking her head.

*****

Just as she left his office he yelled out, "Have a good trip Glory." She merely raised her hand waving an extended middle finger back in his direction causing him to laugh which resulted in a coughing fit. Hearing the boss choking on his cigar smoke brought the first big smile to Glory's face. Maybe Idaho wouldn't be so bad after all; and the ticket was first class.

CHAPTER FOUR

The Deputy Sheriff

The Bannock County Sheriff's Department is located in an old frame building next to a horse pasture about five miles south of Pocatello on 5th Street. The Union Pacific Railroad track is in front just across the highway next to a recently harvested poppy crop and out back a hundred yards across another pasture looms a black lava cliff resembling a tall dark form of the Berlin wall only forty feet higher. Chief Deputy Belingsford working on his third cup of office coffee was waiting for Hokee's visit. Robert "Curly" Belingsford had been a deputy sheriff long enough to acquire a considerable paunch and lose the black curly hair that earned him the name everyone still used although he had been bald as the lava rock behind their office for several years. Benefiting from numerous FBI courses in forensics, crime scene processing, and criminal profiling to name just a few law enforcement specialties he had risen to become the number one deputy and the lead investigator for what had become known as the "Bread Truck Robbery".

Hokee sauntered in around ten and declined the proffered coffee having mistakenly accepted such an offer on previous occasions. Instead of his usual black cowboy boots, Hokee was wearing a pair of deerskin moccasins with elaborate beadwork typical of the Blackfoot Indians. Today his long black hair was pulled back into a ponytail trailing out from under an old faded gray Stetson. Glancing around Hokee noticed that the office had not changed much in the year since he had last visited. They were still using faded green scratched WWII steel army surplus desks, scarred wooden conference tables and office chairs with tufts of padding leaking out of the torn seat covers. He sank into a nearby chair and grunted a greeting towards Belingsford.

"Hi Curly, thanks for the meeting; 'preciate your time."

"No problem Hokee, you know our motto, 'we aim to please Poky's leading detective.'"

"Yeah," Hokee said with a slow grin. "I can just imagine how thrilled you are to have me poking around making you fellows look bad."

"In your dreams, Indian man," Curly came back with a grin of his own. "I guess you wanna look over our files?"

"If it wouldn't be too much trouble," Hokee said, "seeing as how you're holding the folder in your hands."

"Just so you know Hokee, everybody from the mayor and the sheriff plus all of the businesses in West Yellowstone have badgered me to get this case solved. If we had one lousy clue you wouldn't get within ten feet of this file, however, seeing as how we got zip, knock yourself out," he said handing the slim file over to Hokee.

As the chief deputy had said, there wasn't much in the file. Statements from the two drivers along with their polygraph exams coupled with the examiner's report. Both men were telling the truth. The report by Chuck Alfonso, the highway patrolman, didn't add any new information.

A detailed search and examination of the bread truck had yielded no clues. There were no fingerprints, no pieces of torn fabric, no miscellaneous item left behind and no suspects. After more than two weeks the sheriff's department had absolutely zero and no place to look.

Curly gave Hokee a few minutes to digest the files before commenting. "As you can see we have a whole lot of nothing and frankly I don't have any idea where to go from here. How can a bloody wreck with live squirming victims suddenly disappear? Everything we have suggests that these drivers, Ernie Lockhart and Frank Simmons, were somehow involved in the robbery, yet you can see the polygraph results. Both guys came up clean."

"What does your examiner say?" Hokee asked. "I see his report, but you and I both know that a polygraph can be faked."

"Neither of these guys falls in the genius category," Curly said. "I find it difficult to believe either one had the brains to pull this off let alone beat the machine. Sure, it's theoretically possible, but I was here when Mort did the exams and I just don't think these guys have a clue. Mort agrees. As far as the sheriff's department is concerned, Ernie and Frank are victims along with everyone else. We can go pay them a visit if you desire."

"Nah, that's alright," Hokee said. "I think that patrol officer, Alfonso, the one who picked them up on the road gives them a clean alibi. They would need an accomplice to pull off this stunt and your polygraph pretty well eliminates that possibility."

"That's our conclusion," Curly lamented. "Where do we go from here?"

"I was wondering if you could show me the scene and point out where they found the truck," Hokee said standing up and stretching his back out. "I'll even buy you lunch afterward, although looking at your belly I might have to buy you two lunches."

"Hey, I've put a lot into looking this good," Curly grinned. "It might take three or four lunches to help me keep up my strength. Come on, I'll drive since you're gonna spring for a couple steaks and a big plate of shrimp."

Hokee had no idea he was about to experience a personal life changing experience.

CHAPTER FIVE

The Site

Hokee followed Curly out to the chief deputy's green Ford Explorer opening the passenger's door for a couple minutes to let the heat out before climbing in the seat. Curly had the car started and the AC cranked up before Hokee sat down and shifted the seat back making room for his long legs courtesy of his unknown father. A short barrel 12-gauge riot shotgun was sticking up from a holding rack between the driver and passenger's seats. "We gotta make a quick stop on the way up north, shouldn't take but a minute," Curly said. "Reporter from New York called the sheriff who thought it would be a good idea if I talked with her. Maybe get the public interested and scare up a lead." The look on his face made Hokee think that the chief deputy considered the whole thing a waste of time, but when the big boss makes a suggestion it is generally a good idea to follow orders.

"What in the hell is a reporter from New York doing here and why are they interested in this story?" Hokee asked.

"Beats me Tonto. I'm just the dumb white man keeping the peace, saving mankind from savages and working hard to pay off my mortgage."

"Sounds more like ass kissing to me," Hokee said. "Besides you can't tell the difference between a savage and a sausage. Where is this reporter?"

"Staying at the Red Lion over on Pocatello Creek Road," Curly answered. "It's only a couple minutes off our path. She'll be waiting in the lobby. And a savage is one of those mean Mexican sausages with little chunks of chili peppers sprinkled throughout that gives you the runs."

"Sounds like the voice of experience talking. I'll take your word for that one white man."

Curly drove into the Red Lion driveway parking under the hotel's large yellow portico.

"You wanna come in and meet the press?" Curly asked while sliding out from under the steering wheel.

"Nah, I think you can probably handle this city savage all by your lonesome." Hokee said reclining the seat back in order to stretch out and relax.

It seemed like only seconds before Hokee saw the chief deputy walking back towards the SUV followed by a beautiful well-proportioned blond lady in designer clothes and a stout heavyset man with black hair in a butch-cut carrying a camera that looked like it weighed forty pounds. Thick black eyebrows and hunched shoulders gave him a thuggish look tempered slightly by a wry smile. It's a smile that said I know what you think of me but I know the secrets.

As Curly opened the right rear door for the reporter Hokee got the idea that they were going to have traveling companions and put his seat back into its original position.

"Hokee, this young lady is Miss Gloria Bingham from New York," Curly said making the introduction. "Miss Bingham, Hokee Wolf." Nodding to the other side of the vehicle as the door opened, "The gentleman with the camera getting in the other side is Donald Cutter, Miss Bingham's cameraman."

Hokee nodded at the two newcomers without comment. He was not sure what was happening and was unhappy for the intrusion, but it wasn't his call. He settled back into his seat waiting for an explanation which he knew would be forthcoming.

"When I told Gloria that we …"

"Please Deputy, call me Glory," she said interrupting Curly's explanation. "Gloria just sounds too old womanish; don't you think?"

"Yes ma'am, I mean sure Glory. Anyway, as I was explaining, when I told Glory we were on our way to the robbery site she insisted on tagging along. I couldn't see any good reason why not," he said. "Besides, I thought it only right that she gets to see Pocatello's number one detective in action for herself," Curly continued with a wicked grin for his old friend.

Knowing he didn't have a vote Hokee just grunted and with a blank face revealing nothing refused to be baited into making a comment the reporter might use against him later. Tipping the battered Stetson over his eyes he leaned back in the seat as though taking a nap.

Glory, insistent on getting some kind of response from the silent detective asked, "Is he always this talkative?"

"Nah, sometimes he puts three or four words together in a whole sentence. You know these reservation Indians, they didn't get much schooling,"

Although Hokee's expression didn't change Curly could feel the heat coming off the big man's body and knew he had gone one step too far. The chief deputy knew that Hokee had a graduate degree from Utah State University in philosophy and had far more education than anyone in the sheriff's department. At one time the detective had planned on a career in teaching until an unfortunate romance turned him in another direction. When the occasion demanded Hokee could speak the King's English as well as the best educated Oxford scholar, although few people ever got to experience that side of his personality.

In an effort to calm the storm building up in the passenger's seat Curly quickly addressed the reporter before she could ask any more questions. "So, Glory, what really brings you to our beautiful town; surely a little robbery isn't that big a deal back in the big city?"

Glory was prepared for the question. "Truthfully, I needed a break from the usual big city happenings and a bread truck doing double duty as an armored car that gets robbed is an unusual event. My editor thought it would make an interesting story for our readers."

Although he didn't make any visible response Hokee had to suppress a verbal snort as Glory provided her answer. In his experience, anybody starting a sentence with *truthfully* was saying anything but the truth. If it really is true you do not have to advertise. Not that there might not be some truth to the statement, but in the detective's mind that was not the real reason for her presence in Pocatello. While her motive for being here was not of any real concern he was curious about the true purpose of her visit. If it ever became important to know there was no doubt in the detective's mind that he could discover the truth.

"Speaking of the robbery," Glory continued, "what can you tell me about what actually took place?"

As the miles of lava plains gave way to rolling hills of pine forests Curly and Glory discussed the robbery. It was obvious that Curly was impressed with the beautiful New York reporter and anxious to please her in every way possible. Since most of the details had already appeared in the local press there really was no reason to withhold any information. After all, it was not like the sheriff's department had any idea about what actually took place.

Meanwhile, Hokee leaned back in his seat with the Stetson over his eyes tuning out the conversation. He was putting himself mentally into the scene trying to figure out the exact sequence of events and how they all fit together. In his world, everything had a cause and effect. If one saw the effect, there must be a related cause. It was up to the observer to determine the exact cause and so far, the only tangible evidence was the effect. It was in his ability to find hidden causes that the detective had established and maintained his reputation. There was no doubt in his mind that given time he would find the root cause of the bread truck robbery as well as those responsible. That was the main reason for wearing moccasins today. He felt more in touch with the earth through the thin layer of leather beneath the soles of his feet. It was as though he could actually feel energy and vibrations rising up from the earth's surface. This was why it was so important for him to visit the actual site of the robbery as well as the location where the bread truck was abandoned. By being there he would be able to actually feel the events taking place and have much more information about the cause. There is a rhythm to events and situations. Everything is related in some way to everything else. There is harmony in the universe. If you really pay attention you will discover that the car's horn honking in the street, the dog barking up the hill, your oven timer starting to ping and the crying baby in your arms are all in some kind of syncopated rhythm. It is man's task to discover those hidden chords making celestial music.

Hokee was startled out of his meditation when Curly slowed down to pull off the road and then stop by a long slow curving stretch of Highway 20. Hokee had become so engrossed in reliving the robbery details that time seemed to have vanished. It was actually a relief to discover that two hours had gone by and he had not been required to participate in entertaining the reporter or her cameraman.

"Well, here is where the bread truck was stopped," Curly said getting out of the Explorer and pointing to a spot on the highway.

"For about a hundred yards back down the way we came," he continued pointing, "is where the wrecked cars and bodies were supposed to have been and up the road just around the corner is where the saw horses were placed with the road closed signs."

Glory discussed the scene with her cameraman and had him start filming the site although the only thing visible was a highway lined with tall straight pine trees. It was beautiful country and the day was spectacular. The sky was a brilliant deep blue, the air was crystal clear September mild as only the fall season in Idaho can produce with the clean scent of pine; the kind of day you just wanted to stop and enjoy being alive.

Hokee walked up the road to where the saw horses had been placed examining the borders on both sides looking for any clues that might have been missed by the sheriff's men. He then walked back down to where the bread truck had been parked and on to the site where the injured and broken bodies had been located. At one particular spot, he knelt down putting both hands on the highway and closed his eyes.

"Whatcha got Wolf?" Curly asked. "Find something useful?"

"I don't know what was here," Hokee responded. "There is some kind of energy. I can only tell you that it wasn't human."

Hokee continued walking down the highway stopping every few feet to place his hands down on the dark pavement feeling for energy. Glory walked along the side of the road watching Hokee as he examined the highway.

"What kind of name is Wolf?" Glory asked the detective. "I don't think I've ever known anyone else with a name like that."

"The wolf is a carnivorous mammal that usually feeds on the flesh of weaker species," he responded without a trace of humor or glancing in her direction. "In my case I prefer to hunt other predators."

The terse pointed reply was slightly frightening silencing any further questions.

Walking back to the Explorer Hokee called out to Curly who was looking for tracks on the other side of the highway. "Okay, I'm done here deputy; let's go see where the truck got ditched."

As everybody piled back into the SUV, Glory desperately wanted to ask Hokee what he had discovered but for one of the few times in her life she actually felt intimidated. The detective's gruff unsmiling exterior and quiet dedicated concentration unnerved her usual outspoken reporter behavior. She was used to the male species responding to her sexy figure by falling all over themselves to please her and she actually dressed to inspire their attention. Yet in spite of the fact that she was nearly one hundred percent positive Hokee was not homosexual he had barely noticed that she existed. She experienced a great relief when Chief Deputy Curly asked Hokee if he had learned anything useful at the robbery site.

"All I can tell you for sure is that the robbery occurred exactly where you stopped," Hokee said. "There is still a great deal of energy all around that place, especially where the wrecked cars and mangled bodies were supposed to have been located. The energy is not human; at least not a living breathing human. I'm still trying to figure out exactly what it is that I experienced. Something happened there. I just don't know what."

CHAPTER SIX

Back in Pocatello

The one room basement studio was neat and clean although the green hide a bed couch was faded and had rips in the cushions. The small Kenmore refrigerator had rust spots down one side and the toaster oven sitting on the worn cabinet countertop was missing the door handle. A tiny closet, next to what the landlord called a three-quarter bathroom, but most people would call a joke, held a couple pairs of faded Levi pants, three long sleeve patterned wool shirts, one worn brown suit coat and a pair of dirty sneakers with holes in the toes. The bathroom consisted of a rust stained toilet jammed in next to a tiny wash basin hanging from the wall. A blue shower curtain featuring painted yellow fish hung on a rod barely covering the small door. A screen-covered drain in front of the sink would handle the shower runoff if the water was only turned on half way. Otherwise water spilled over into the main room wetting the one decent object in the entire apartment; a hand braided rug the tenant had purchased from a second-hand store.

In the center of the room was a Formica table where the red and white checkerboard design had been worn completely through in many places, although today the table was completely covered with stacks of money separated in various denominations. Hundreds were stacked along one edge with fifties, twenties, tens, fives and ones marching across the table like soldiers in formation. At one end was a pile of papers including checks, credit card receipts, money orders, traveler's checks and miscellaneous items representing other currencies. Sitting in the only chair, a stainless-steel tubular with a torn padded yellow seat cushion and solid wood back was the sunken chest man with a stringy blond ponytail. He had just finished counting and recounting all of the money in each stack. The figures from each denomination were jotted down on a piece of yellow paper and each column had been totaled. The final total of all the real paper money came to $3,289,488.00. He had not bothered counting the coins which were still in bags lying under the table nor had he bothered with all of the extraneous paper. He was undecided as to whether or not to try and sell the bundle of extra paper to someone he knew who could probably fence the stuff or just burn the whole fricking pile. Trying to peddle that kind of paper could only mean trouble and three million dollars in real money was more than enough to satisfy his needs. After all, how much vengeance does one man need?

*****

Lake Henry

Curly drove the Explorer back down Highway 20 almost five miles before slowing down and pulling off to the side of the road. A dim trail could be seen off to the right between the white pines where grass had been flattened and tire tracks pressed into the bare brown earth. "The truck was parked back in here a ways," Curly said. "We'll walk so we won't add any more disturbances to whatever signs might still be readable."

"This is far enough away from the robbery site so the truck drivers couldn't hear the truck pull off the highway," Hokee said. "Pretty smart."

"Yeah, and the truck was also far enough off the highway that it couldn't be seen by any passing traffic," Curly responded.

Glory was busy with Donald showing him the trail and tire marks she wanted him to film. Hokee was still waiting to hear the cameraman say something but apparently, the photographer was happy taking orders and didn't need to express an opinion about what the senior reporter wanted him to shoot.

As they neared the clearing Curly hung back letting Hokee move ahead alone as he knew that the detective wanted to get a feel for the place without any interference. When Glory came marching past intending on following Hokee, Curly grabbed her arm forcing her to stop.

"Wait here," he said in a tone that told the reporter she had better obey. "Let's let Wolf have some time alone before we go blundering in messing things up worse than they already are. If there's anything to be found, Hokee will find it. That's why he's wearing moccasins; they give him a better feel for the earth and what it can tell him."

Donald finally caught up to the pair and the three of them watched Hokee work the scene. Watching the big man work was like watching a sushi master prepare an exotic seafood wrap. Every move was deliberate, precise, thoughtful and exact.

It was easy enough to see where the truck had been parked and after studying the ground for a few minutes Hokee located where a small car had been parked and then backed up next to the truck in order to transfer the money. After a few minutes, he moved slowly around the clearing and the three watchers could feel the energy radiating from his body. He finally stopped almost in the center and stood perfectly still with his eyes shut. From their position at the edge of the clearing Curly and his companions were able to catch a tiny glimpse of blue on Henry's Lake between the pines over the Indian's left shoulder. After another couple of minutes Hokee began walking in small expanding circles studying the ground. After about five more minutes he stopped and called over to Curly.

"Hey Curly, do you have a shovel or pry bar in the back of your Explorer?" he asked.

"No, the closest thing I have would be my tire iron," the chief deputy replied.

"Okay, that will do. Would you get it please?" Hokee said.

"Is it okay for us to come over there now?" Glory asked.

"Yeah, just stay back about five feet until Curly gets here with the tire iron. I think I may have found something."

Motioning to her cameraman Glory said, "Come on Don, let's go see what the big detective has found for us to shoot. So far all we have are some fascinating scenes of a highway, scintillating shots of pine trees and spine tingling pictures of the earth. If anything more exciting shows up I don't think our viewers will be able to take the heart pounding suspense."

Hokee was tempted by her sarcasm to say something about her coming along was her own idea but he knew that saying it out loud would only net him grief. Besides he was still trying to figure out exactly what he had found. While waiting for Curly to get back with the tire iron Hokee could not get past the idea that he was looking at a grave; but what would a grave be doing here?

Coming as close as she dared Glory asked, "What have you got Hokee? I can't see anything."

"Don't come any closer just yet, but if you look here," he pointed to an invisible line on the ground, "you can barely make out a cut in the sod. The grass has been carefully raked back over the cut to hide it from any observers. That's why I need Curly's tire iron. There's something down there beneath the grass and dirt."

"I can't see anything," Glory said. "How on earth did you ever spot that in the first place?"

"I felt it first, and once I knew something was here I just kept looking until I found it. In a sense, it really found itself."

Glory did not even try to understand that last statement. It made absolutely no sense to the seasoned investigative reporter. "Well, if something really is there then I'm impressed," she said. "Maybe you really are the big deal your deputy friend seems to think you are."

Once again Hokee had to bite his tongue. He wanted to tell her what a big mouth she had but he knew that would only make the situation worse. Avoiding a response, he squatted down and started separating the grass looking for a spot in which to use the tire iron he could see in Curly's hand as he came back into the clearing.

Motioning the chief deputy to stop Hokee held out his hand for the tire iron. With the tool in his hands Hokee squatted down and began gently probing the earth along the nearly invisible seam of cut sod. Satisfied with one particular spot the detective shoved the iron into the ground a few inches until it struck something hard. Hokee worked the tire iron back and forth a few times twisting it until the iron slipped down another couple of inches into the earth. Then using the top of the iron as a lever he pulled back on the handle slowly raising up one side of the buried casket lid.

"Hey Curly, give me a hand here," Hokee said.

Curly squatted down beside Hokee who showed him where to put his hands. "Try and hold this up," Hokee commanded, "while I move to another spot."

Moving to his left a couple of feet Hokee repeated his move with the tire iron getting leverage in a different spot. As the coffin lid was raised a few inches Hokee put his foot on the tire iron holding it down while grabbing the underside of the lid with his hands. Instructing Curly to assist, together they lifted the lid grabbing around until they were able to remove it completely revealing the coffin below.

"Well, what do we have here?" Curly asked. "It looks like a grave with an empty coffin."

Glory had Donald start filming as they both moved in gaping at the open hole.

"What's with the hole?" Glory wanted to know, asking the question to either Curly or Hokee.

"What do you think Wolf?" Curly answered. "Did the thieves originally hide the money here, and why?"

Hokee had jumped down into the open coffin and was holding the pick ax handle when he answered.

"I don't think so. I'm not real sure what went on here but I have a very strange feeling. The energy in this place is all wrong. Something really weird happened in this coffin. I've got to visit an old shaman I know to help me understand what I'm feeling. Hopefully then I can give you some answers."

"Is that a real coffin?" Glory asked.

"Yeah, it's just a cheap pine box, but it's a real coffin," Hokee said. "These coffins are usually what they use to bury the homeless whose bodies remain unclaimed. You can see how the lid was modified to hold the original sod. Whoever made this didn't want it to be found. We were just lucky."

"From where I was standing Hokee, it looked like you made the luck happen," Glory said with admiration in her voice. It was becoming apparent that over the last few minutes the girl from New York had developed a sincere appreciation for the detective's capabilities.

CHAPTER SEVEN

Wolf's Place

The Snake River rushes past Pocatello ten to fifteen miles west and north depending on which part of the city is used to measure the distance. Made famous in a movie by Marilyn Monroe and Robert Mitchum, the producers used the local Indian name for their production, *The River of No Return*. Many years later a stuntman named Evel Knievel would unsuccessfully attempt to jump a motorcycle across another section of the river called Hells Canyon. A desolate forbidding lava plain of uninhabited and uninhabitable tortured, broken, black rock covers several hundred square miles. Lava flows are common throughout southeastern Idaho. A massive large uninhabited lava flow begins in the area between Pocatello and the Snake River extending a hundred miles north, west and east. Uninhabited means that the plain is uninhabited except for coyotes, antelope, snakes, other wild creatures and Hokee Wolf. There are many who would argue that Hokee was just another wild creature.

To call Hokee's home a house is technically incorrect, but neither is it a cave. It's sort of something half-way between and partly something else.

When hot lava was flowing over this vast plain thousands of years ago, it was not a smooth flow like you get when pouring well mixed pancake batter onto a grill. The lava flow would start and stop in fits and jerks much like lumpy unmixed batter. This made the lava depth uneven allowing some sections to cool down more rapidly than others. Those sections that had cooled down a little became an impediment to hot flowing lava from later ejections causing the newer hot lava to flow around the cold lava creating voids and holes. There are millions of bubbles in the lava where thin shells of lava cover large voids. These thin shells look like solid rock but most are too thin to support a human's weight. When walking the fields, it is essential to test each step. Walking onto one of these bubbles could mean certain death if the lava breaks dropping you into deep pits lined with jagged rocks. This layer of thick uneven treacherous lava rock is one of the main reasons several hundred square miles of southeastern Idaho is the home of nothing but wild animals, occasional tufts of parched grass and intermittent patches of scattered sage brush. Today the plain is full of caves, holes, voids and tunnels most of which have never been found. Walking and exploring this wild country is not for the faint hearted and most people have sense enough to leave the country to the critters that live there. After all, the land isn't fit for any practical commercial value and it sure as hell ain't all that pretty; unless you are drawn to bleak, harsh, uninhabitable landscapes.

After his one failed try at romance Hokee went to the Fort Hall Indian Reservation for a little counseling from a shaman he had lived with for several years when much younger. After spending a few hours with the heartbroken young man in a sweat lodge, the old shaman suggested a snake walk. For his walk Hokee was told to find the vast lava plains to the west and walk through the plains for ten days. He was promised by the shaman that this walk would cleanse his soul and give him back his spirit making him whole once again. He was to take nothing with him except his trousers, a knife and moccasins.

Hokee was desperate so he accepted the shaman's remedy leaving the next morning. This ten-day journey became an epic story by itself but along the way Hokee found the place he wanted to live in for the rest of his life.

This lava plain is not a smooth flat landscape. There are no mountains or deep valleys, just undulating heaps of lava that cracked as it cooled creating a surface that had deep fissures with sharp edges. The rough, broken terrain makes walking difficult and impossible for driving a vehicle, or even a man on horseback. By the end of the first snake walk day Hokee's moccasins were in tatters and his feet were bleeding. He was desperate to find some place on this God-forsaken plain to stop and give his battered feet a rest when he literally stumbled into one of the lava voids. Actually, it was more like a large fold as hot lava slowly oozed around a solid block of older hardened lava creating a large empty hole in the lava field.

The bottom of the void was almost forty feet below the lava plain and was solid earth. The void was almost 450 feet long and about 300 feet wide with clumps of dry grass, a few sage bushes and towards the north end there was a small grove of willows. Willows meant water and Hokee couldn't believe his luck. Who would have ever thought that out here in the middle of a broken hostile lava field one would find water?

Hokee had stumbled onto the east side of this void in the lava plain. He could see that from the south end there was more of a gradual slope to the walls whereas from his location the walls were nearly vertical. Although the walls were steep they were also very rough, providing numerous hand and foot holds that made a descent to the desert floor possible but difficult. It would have been much easier if his feet had been in better shape. Hokee was anxious to get to the bottom of the void and find the water so he climbed down the side ignoring the pain in his feet.

When he got to the grove of willow trees he was amazed to discover a small stream of water flowing from the mouth of a hidden cave. The small stream wandered about twenty feet onto the desert floor before disappearing back into the ground. There is a famous story about a really large river that disappeared into the lava fields someplace near Arco, but Hokee had never been there and didn't know if it was a true story. But, this stream was real and Hokee sank to the ground at its bank with relief and thanksgiving.

He went flat on his face into the stream drinking like an animal quenching his thirst then turned over and sitting up put both feet into the stream soaking his bruised and cut-up feet. Looking around at his surroundings, a vision of this large enclosure transformed into a fantastic Garden of Eden filled his imagination and at that instant he decided that this would be his permanent home.

Naturally the water drew in all kinds of desert animals including antelope. Hokee fashioned a spear using his knife and a branch from the Willow Grove. Before the sun sank below the black lava he had an antelope skinned and the meat roasting over a fire. He began working the hide in order to fashion a new pair of moccasins and a shirt. By the time, he left the enclosure nine days later his feet were healed, he had a new pair of moccasins on his feet, an antelope hide shirt plus an extra pair of moccasins hanging from his waist. The wound in his soul had scarred over and the pain was gone but there was a void in his heart that might never be filled.

This particular section of the lava plains belonged to an old homestead back along the Snake River and the current owners were delighted to sell a few hundred acres of worthless lava plains to the stupid Indian for almost nothing. From the owner's perspective, the land was worthless and anything they could get for it in exchange was a gift.

The first thing Hokee did was find an old dump truck he could purchase cheaply and began hauling in dirt and gravel for a road. Having obtained easements across the lava plains from the Bureau of Land Management and the State of Idaho he slowly filled in the crevasses across the plain building a ten-mile one lane road from the county road along the Snake River to the void where he was going to build his house. Where his road began Hokee put up a strong iron gate with provisions for a chain lock, however, over the years he stopped using the lock as nobody ever bothered opening the gate to drive down the road. They knew there was nothing down there except one crazy Indian who nobody wanted to anger. He had no neighbors and didn't share his address with anybody. Very few people outside of the police and fire departments knew that the crazy Indian living out in the lava flats was Pocatello's leading detective.

Glory Bingham was determined to find Hokee and learn more about this big quiet detective. She had quizzed Deputy Curly Belingsford who had volunteered practically nothing. Curly knew about Hokee's penchant for privacy and was not about to violate his friend's solitude. Glory ultimately found herself at the police station downtown where one of the officers with a withered arm tending the desk was happy to provide the sexy New York reporter with a detailed map of Pocatello and the surrounding area including the road to Hokee's place. Admittedly the officer had never been down the road but he was confident that Hokee had a house somewhere out on the lava plain that was accessible from his private road. A few minutes later after stopping for a cold six-pack of beer the intrepid reporter was staring at the gate at the beginning of Hokee's lane; a long ten-mile stretch of a single lane private road.

Driving down Hokee's road across the barren lava plain Glory began to wonder if this was such a good idea. Anyone who went to this much trouble for privacy really didn't want to be disturbed. The one-way road discouraged visitors. If they happened to meet Hokee on his way out there was no place to turn around and that could be a very long backup drive. Actually, Hokee had built a small turnout at every mile of road which allowed cars to pass each other but as they remain unused weeds and brush eventually obscured them from view unless you were really paying attention. Try as she might, and the reporter in her had a vivid imagination, it was impossible to find anything in this region to make a person want to live here. After traveling nine miles on this desolate lonely road and still no sign of a residence she began to worry.

There was no place to turn around and she had come too far for backing up to be an option. She had no choice but to proceed and the apprehension continued to grow. Just as she was about to totally lose her composure the scene suddenly changed taking away her breath.

The lip of a gentle downward slope suddenly appeared at the bottom of which was a sight so unexpected and dramatic as to make her stop the car and gasp in astonishment.

At the bottom of a short downgrade was a small valley full of different varieties of pine trees and cacti completely enclosed by a black wall of lava. The trees were arranged in graceful geometric patterns intermingled with colorful rock gardens featuring rocks from all colors of the rainbow. Between the rocks at exactly the right distance for grace and symmetry were clumps of native grasses and fragrant sagebrush. In the exact center of the clearing was a large circular driveway surrounding a fifteen-foot waterfall and fountain made from black and red lava stone. At the very north end of this dramatic lava walled garden was a large adobe style house front complete with brilliant red begonias hanging from the center of graceful Spanish arches. Behind the arches a wide porch was terminated by ten-foot high windows. The adobe front looked like a typical large Spanish ranch house except that the short sides of house terminated at a forty-foot black cliff of lava rock. Obviously, the house must be inside of this cliff. Just as she was beginning to regain her composure she noticed something else. Standing at the foot of the gentle sloping driveway leading to the bottom of the valley was a large gray wolf Glory could swear was as big as a Volkswagen van. She couldn't turn around and yet the wolf was blocking the entry into the circular driveway around the fountain. She sat there with her foot on the brake wondering what to do when she saw Hokee exit from what appeared to be a hand carved door in the center of the wide porch. He stepped out to the front of the porch and made some kind of hand signal recalling the wolf that trotted back to his side.

Flooded with relief Glory continued down the driveway parking on the inner side of the fountain closest to Hokee.

There was no sign of greeting or welcome. No words were spoken. Hokee simply stood like a carved cigar store Indian with a blank look waiting for Glory to explain herself. The wolf stood by his side facing Gloria and the car.

Climbing out of her rented Cadillac Glory was filled with dread; an Indian named Wolf standing next to a real four-legged version. What in the hell was she thinking?

"Is that a real wolf?" she asked knowing the answer but feeling compelled to ask just in case.

"Yep."

She suddenly remembered that Hokee was not a big talker and getting any information was going to be like trying to find water in the Sahara.

"I thought wolves were extinct in this part of the world," she said trying to start a conversation.

"They are."

Hokee still had not changed his expression nor had he moved and Glory was beginning to wish she had listened to her intuition and never started on this journey to visit the detective.

"But..." she paused suddenly at a loss for words. Hokee finally took pity and let her off the hook.

"His name is Shilah; means brother." This was said with a solemn straight face as though describing a relative, say your grandmother. "I don't know where he came from. An old shaman gave him to me a few years ago when he was just a few weeks old. We sort of learned to live together as I built this place."

Brother, she thought. *He has a wolf he calls brother and his last name is Wolf. There has to be a story here. I wonder if it is one I will ever get to know?*

"Yeah, a brother," she quipped. "I can see the family resemblance. It must be the gray hair," she continued attempting a smirk but ending up with a smile. "I picked up a cold six-pack and was wondering if we could have a beer together and talk for a few minutes," she asked beginning to regain her composure.

"I have a few minutes," he said. "We can sit on the porch," he added turning around and going over to a handmade chaise lounge in the shade. Looking closely one could see that the patio furniture had been crafted from native woods by someone with patience and skill. Hokee waited for Gloria to get her beer and join him before sitting down.

Gesturing with his hand he waved her to join him in another lounge close by as Shilah plopped down at his feet.

Glory handed him a cold Coors before sitting down. She had debated for several minutes about what beer to buy before settling for the rocky mountain brew thinking that was as west as you could get. She was disappointed to be sitting outside as she was dying to see the inside of this most unusual place, but she wasn't sure how to go about inviting herself inside. This big, silent, handsome Indian radiated male testosterone like a marquee movie star yet he seemed so composed, so self-assured and so completely private. There was no way to get inside yet she was determined to try and find a way.

"I was really impressed by the way you found that casket today," she said trying to get a conversation started.

Hokee just gave a small grunt of recognition that she had spoken without changing the expression on his face.

When it became obvious that she was not going to get any response from her initial observation she tried another angle. "Have you been a detective for long?" she asked.

"Long enough," he said.

"You know," she said in frustration, "a conversation usually has two people talking. You barely say anything."

"Hey lady, you're the one wanted to talk, so talk." Hokee still seemed to have about as much expression in his words or face as an Idaho potato.

Sensing that the only way she was ever going to get the big detective talking was to be straight forward and honest so she started over.

"Okay look, I was sent out here by my boss to get me out of New York for a few days. One of my stories riled up some folks back home and the powers that be thought I should get out of town until things cooled down. This bread truck robbery is unusual and they were hoping maybe I could make it into a human-interest story as a kind of filler on a slow news day. Since you are the only one with a clue as to what is happening I was hoping maybe you would give a girl some insight into the case."

Hokee smiled in spite of himself. He had known her story in Curly's car was mostly bull and was quietly pleased that he had been right. Glory saw the smile and wondered what she had said to bring it about? At least he was showing some emotion.

"Deputy Sheriff Belingsford pretty much told you everything there is to know about the case," Hokee said.

"Yeah, he showed us where the robbery took place. He showed us where the money transfer took place and he told us how much money was stolen. Other than that, he is just blowing his horn. He doesn't know anything," she said taking a long pull on the beer and pulling a sour face. Beer wasn't really her thing but she thought sharing a beer would be a good way to break the ice and get the taciturn detective talking. Too bad she didn't know Hokee hated beer as well, all beer. He was a single malt guy by preference although during the week he usually settled for a good blend. Glory looked over at the detective trying to figure out some way to get him to open up.

Hokee wasn't sure what the attractive reporter with the dynamite body was doing on his porch and he was becoming uncomfortable in her presence. He knew enough about himself to understand his discomfort arose because he found the lady attractive. It had been several years since he had allowed those feelings in his life and he wasn't sure how to handle the situation. Because he had been badly burned in a relationship when he was a young man his tendency was to shy away from any kind of emotional involvement with the opposite sex. The woman sitting on his porch was someone he could easily find himself getting involved with which made him very uneasy. Knowing she was only here to get a story and go home made his decision easy. He would give her what she wanted and get her out of his life as soon as possible.

"Look Glory," Hokee said, "I really don't know any more than Curly has already told you."

"You found that grave," she responded. "You must have some ideas about what that was all about."

"That is puzzling," he admitted. "I am just about to go visit the old shaman who gave me Shilah. I have a few ideas but it is way too early for any kind of definitive analysis. Tell you what. Give me the telephone number where you're staying and I'll give you a call just as soon as I know something useful."

"How about I go with you to visit the shaman?" Glory pushed.

There was a long pause while it looked like Hokee was actually considering this possibility. In actuality he was trying to find the right words that would keep her from continually pestering him to allow her to accompany him or asking for additional information.

"That isn't a good idea," he responded reverting back to that stoic unreadable face and voice. "It's a long drive and I have several errands I need to take care of along the way. Afterward I'll probably be taking off for parts unknown following the information I collect. No telling when I'll be back. Just give me your number if you want me to contact you afterward," he said standing up letting her know he was preparing to leave. The brusqueness of his voice and movements left no room for further negotiations.

Glory was feeling miffed but what could she do? She had felt the big man's interest in her but she also detected the steel resolve behind his refusal to let that interest sway his emotions. Deciding to retreat and live to fight another day she tried one more gambit to get a peek inside of his house. "Okay," she said standing up with a big smile while using every trick she knew to appear as provocative as possible. "I know when I'm being brushed off. But before I go, could I please use your restroom. It's a long drive out here and back and with this beer and all...."

Hokee wasn't fooled by her request but there was really no polite way of refusing. But before giving in to the New York charmer he couldn't resist having a little fun. "I usually go behind the tree over there," Hokee said pointing. "That's the one Shilah prefers as well." He said this with a straight stern face and Glory thought for just a second that he was serious. The look on Glory's face was worth the joke. It was priceless; a mixture of frustration, total despair and bewilderment. Then he broke out into a big grin. "Sure," he said. "Come on, I'll show you. There's a bathroom just off my living room."

Hokee led her inside where she gasped, losing her breath for the second time as she got a good look at the entry and living room. Her mouth was literally hanging open. The floor was a mosaic of colored tile featuring the picture of a big gray wolf with snow on its back standing on a rocky ledge overlooking a valley of snow covered pine trees. Each wall featured a colorful hanging Navajo blanket. There were several large oversized chairs made of hand-carved wood with cushions made out of both leather and material woven into an Indian pattern. Scattered around next to the chairs were several end tables and a large coffee table also made from hand-carved wood. The workmanship was excellent. The furniture had been made with the same pride and craftsmanship as that on the patio.

Catching her breath Glory couldn't help exclaiming, "Wow!" In a voice full of wonder she asked, "Who built this floor and all this beautiful furniture?"

"It's just some old pieces of scrap wood I threw together," Hokee replied without expressing any kind of proprietary pride.

The bathroom is over here," he said pointing to a door off to her left.

Glory wanted to just stand and feast her eyes on the scene for a few minutes but she could tell Hokee was not happy with her inside of his house so she quickly made her way to the bathroom.

Hokee waited for her by the front door and as soon as she came back out from the bathroom opened the door signaling time for her to leave giving her no opportunity to see the part of the house that went into the mountain. As they were leaving the front porch Hokee said something she found very revealing.

"You are the first person to not only visit here, but the only other person besides me to ever step into my house." As though this revelation opened some kind of door he continued, "If things work out I might invite you back for a special Wolf dinner," he said surprising himself as well as Glory, while giving her his first really sincere smile. "Of course, you do know that wolves are carnivores, right?" he added with a big white-toothed grin.

The unusual announcement plus the warmth of his smile reached Glory in a way she thought was no longer possible. She found herself immensely attracted to the big handsome man with the dark hair and piercing eyes. It was with real regret that she walked to her car preparing to leave. Hopefully the offer of dinner was real and would actually happen, although as she thought about it, what exactly was a Wolf dinner?

CHAPTER EIGHT

The Shaman

Watching Glory drive away Hokee thought about his offer for dinner at his place. Where in the hell had that come from? Standing there confused and uncertain he wondered if this was really a good idea and what had possessed him to make such an offer? It certainly wasn't something he had been thinking about while she was supposedly in the bathroom. He'd been burned by an early college romance when the girl's father discovered that his daughter was dating an Indian and sent the girl back east to live with her grandparents forbidding any further contact. He had been deeply in love with Shareen looking forward to their life together. When the girl meekly obeyed her father's wishes and never contacted Hokee again he was deeply wounded. He never again let himself get emotionally or seriously involved with another woman. He had all the hormonal urges of any healthy male and from time to time found a female companion who didn't demand a commitment in order to share a bed but he was very careful about who and when.

There was no question that the sexy reporter from New York was pushing all of his buttons and he could tell the girl was interested in him, but that could only be because she wanted information and, he thought to himself, *was it really wise to continue developing a personal relationship?* He was a proud Native American and she was a sophisticated New Yorker on a paid holiday. He was not at all sure that she was the type of woman to share a bed without wanting something in exchange. Shaking his head to get rid of thoughts about the woman he brought images of the open casket back into his mind and started framing questions he would ask his old shaman mentor Why-ay'-looh, the Silver

Fox.

Why-ay'-looh was a Blackfoot shaman living on the Shoshone Fort Hall Indian Reservation. When Hokee was still a teen twenty-five years earlier, he had met the Silver Fox who recognizing something special in the young lost boy brought him into his Hogan as an apprentice. Since Hokee had no known living relatives there was no one to either approve or disapprove and the young boy was flattered to be chosen by the highly respected medicine man. At the time Hokee thought the shaman was an extremely old man considering his smoky dark wrinkled skin, silver hair and hunched back. Over the years, the old shaman with a wizened face and sparkling eyes had not changed in appearance while Hokee had grown into a large handsome tall square-jawed man with several university degrees and a prosperous business. Why-ay'-looh was disappointed that his apprentice had chosen to be a detective rather than a shaman, but on the other hand, he considered Hokee to still be a young man who might someday consider changing his profession.

Why-ay'-looh alone knew about Hokee's considerable wealth and knew that should he wish to do so the detective would never have to work another day in his life. This was primarily the reward for saving Narveen Olsen from kidnappers, the daughter of Wesley Olsen, Idaho's wealthiest businessman who owned one of the world's largest construction companies doing business all over the planet. Olsen was extremely happy to get his daughter back unharmed and so impressed by the detective's skills he had insisted on giving the young man ten million dollars, a fact unknown to everyone except the old shaman. Hokee tried to decline the generous reward but Olsen had insisted. Investing his windfall carefully it had multiplied over the years allowing Hokee to pick and choose his cases taking only those that appealed to his curiosity or in the case of missing students a desire to aid the defenseless.

Silver Fox's Hogan was a square, dumpy, low roof, one-room house built primarily of lava rock. The twelve by twelve one-room shack had a small electric burner resting on a square black rock, an old army cot along one wall with a bright colored Indian blanket, and a small shelf directly over the burner which held a coffee pot, a tea pot and a few mismatched drinking mugs. There was a gallon jug of water on the floor beside the burner and one rickety wooden chair placed by a small square, eighteen-inch handmade table. For the four years Hokee had lived with the shaman he had slept on a rug covering the dirt floor with only a blanket to keep him warm. Close to the Hogan was a rock sweat lodge with a canvas opening fronted by a fire pit surrounded on three sides by stacks of wood and lava rock. A fifty-gallon barrel rested on six-foot high sawhorses next to the sweat lodge. The barrel was fitted with a hose attached to a shower head to help purify those about to undergo a sweat lodge journey. The barrel was filled daily by Indian children anxious to earn the old shaman's respect not to mention the black liquorish hardtack candy he gave them which seemed to always induce a feeling of euphoria in the children.

Hokee had tried to give the old shaman money over the years and provide him with a new house with modern conveniences but Why-ay'-looh had flatly refused every attempt to let Hokee improve his station in life. The old shaman was content to live his life as it was structured.

The Hogan had no window and only the one door. No running water and the outhouse was fifty feet behind the back wall. Water came from a community water tap a hundred yards up a slight grade towards the trading post. Light came from an oil lantern hanging from the low ceiling. Upon entering the Hogan, whether for the first or hundredth time, you were immediately struck by the smells and the walls. Each wall except for the small space right above the electric burner was covered with shelves spaced six inches apart filled with little colored apothecary bottles, small cardboard and wooden boxes plus tiny bundles of dark unidentifiable herbs, twigs and weeds. Every visitor to Why-ay'-looh's lodge first observed these shelves stuffed with the shaman's pharmacy while at the same time one's senses were overwhelmed by the combined scent of the hundreds of different herbs and spices. It was a smell that reminded you of something from a very distant past regardless of the age you happened to be now. The memory while faint, was persistent but there was no one spot in the mind where a particular memory could be found. It was the scent of a million ancient fires burning sage, sandalwood and cedar. It was the smell of incense mixed with rose water and lavender petals. It smelled of peace, tranquility and love. It was the odor of mystery, suspense and magic. Above all it was the scent of security, peace, and serenity.

Hokee paused at the door to Why-ay'-looh's Hogan. It had been at least two years since his last visit and he was feeling a little ashamed. The old man had been very good to him over the years and deserved to have more respect. Hokee knew the shaman never left his home and really had no means of travel. If there was any visiting to be done it was up to him to make the effort to go visit his mentor. Somehow the time just seemed to vanish and a few months became a couple of years. Knowing he couldn't put it off any longer Hokee took one last look at the wooden owl to make sure it was facing away from the door.

If it faced inward, it meant that the shaman was occupied and did not wish to be disturbed. Seeing that the way was open Hokee pulled on the bell cord setting a string of tiny bells jiggling announcing his presence.

He waited nearly a full minute before he heard the shuffling inside and the door was finally opened. The old shaman looked the same as ever, like ancient darkened leather topped with thin silver hair; bent and stooped over, however, the light in his eyes was as bright and strong as ever.

"My son finally found a reason to visit," he said by way of greeting. "I've been expecting you for several hours."

"Hello father," Hokee replied. "You probably already know that I was simply stalling because of my embarrassment. I should have come by several times in the past couple of years."

"Yes, you should have," the old Fox said, "but you're here now and even if it is for business I'm still happy to see you."

"And you too father," Hokee said with affection. "How come you never age?"

"Oh, I age alright. Outwardly I'm like many wild creatures that never change their appearance but gradually slow down until nature takes its course. I'm getting to the point where nature's creatures that feed on the old and infirm will be making their way into my Hogan soon. Until then, let's smoke the pipe and tell me what it is I can do for you."

Why-ay'-looh had an elk antler he had hollowed out and fitted with a stem making a peace pipe although in his shaman's practice he called it the Revelation. After smoking the pipe his visitors were able to reveal their real problems and ask for the help they actually needed. This was the shaman's way of getting his guests to relax and open the door to their subconscious desires. While Hokee was no longer someone that needed this form of inducement to open up with his old mentor it had become a habit to share the pipe and a cup of special herbal tea. After the ritual of smoking and taking a couple sips of a very stringent bitter tea Hokee explained the reason for his visit.

The old shaman was sitting on his bed while he listened to Hokee who sat in the chair nearby describe his perplexing problem with the grave, the disappearing accident victims and missing money. After the detective was finished speaking the Silver Fox was silent for several minutes while Hokee sat patiently waiting for an answer to his questions.

The old shaman let himself flow into that sacred place deep in his subconscious mind where all is connected and every path intersects. The pipe

51

smoke and tea made the journey easy and having traveled this path thousands of times over the years the old Silver Fox knew the terrain well. Like his namesake, he hid among the millions of disconnected thoughts waiting for the right moment in which to pounce on a fleeting passing thought related to his quest. For the uninitiated and untrained this landscape can be overwhelming and frightening with its cacophony of sensations, endless unknown boundaries and eerie silence.

In order to succeed in any particular quest one must remain focused, intent, determined and patient. Letting down your guard for even a second might be the one time that the object of your quest passes through your consciousness. A few moments in this unfamiliar and uncharted territory can be pleasant. Anything more takes considerable energy, stamina and willpower to avoid becoming lost and disoriented. The price of success is often very painful.

After a considerable time, the shaman began, "I believe you are dealing with a doppelganger," he said. "In ancient Egypt they were called 'ka'; my people called them 'Devilaal', the son of the devil, just like the Hindu."

"I thought doppelgangers always looked like your double," Hokee said.

"Generally that's true, but there are certain evil practitioners of magic who can teach you how to create a doppelganger to look like anyone, or anything you choose. You can even use doppelganger energy to create images in another person's mind. For instance, you can make someone see a car accident that wasn't there."

As Why-ay'-looh was telling Hokee about this aspect of doppelgangers he had a faraway sad look in his otherwise bright eyes. It was as though he was seeing things that he wished were not possible to witness.

"Where would you ever go to learn how to do this?" Hokee asked.

"I was told by my grandfather that a long time ago there were a few such men who knew how to do this black work in our own land but I know of no one who has ever seen or heard of it being practiced recently. Perhaps someone over in the mid-east, maybe India or Tibet would know this practice. That's where I would look."

After he finished with this advice the old shaman lay down on his cot and closed his eyes. It was obvious that the ordeal of seeing these visions in his head had been very wearing. Hokee leaned over kissing the old man's cheek while whispering in his ear, "Thanks father, you rest and I'll see you soon."

Why-ay'-looh waved a feeble hand in farewell without opening his eyes. As Hokee left the Hogan, he thoughtfully turned the owl around facing inward.

CHAPTER NINE

Pocatello

He was smart enough to know that he couldn't go out and buy a flashy new car or spend money frivolously on fancy clothes, a better apartment or even buy a new television. Anything that suggested a change in living style would draw attention and he was determined to not get caught. On the other hand, what good was three million dollars if you couldn't use it to live better? The only solution that presented itself was to leave Pocatello and move to someplace where he was not known. While he didn't particularly like that idea there was really nothing keeping him here. Friends? He didn't have any. Family? All dead. Sure, he was familiar with Pocatello; he knew all the alleys, backstreets and dope pushers. He knew where the prostitutes lived and where they worked; not that he had ever paid any of them. Being basically a night person he often met them at a diner in the early morning as they either finished for the night or gave up looking for a john. It sometimes happened that one would invite the pockmarked loner home for a freebie. The bottom line was no one would really miss him if he left Pocatello and if he disappeared in the right way no one would ever come looking for him.

This brought to his mind the question, what was the right way to leave? In order to avoid suspicion, he would have to tell his landlady that he was thinking about leaving town and would be giving up the studio, but what would be his reason? As he thought about where he might want to live it suddenly dawned on him that he already had the perfect excuse for leaving town; his headaches.

The robbery had aggravated his headaches beyond belief. In spite of Hung Wong's teaching his body was only now getting back to normal. Creating a doppelganger is much harder on your real body than anyone can imagine. The damage caused to your body is directly proportional to the energy you utilize in creating your illusions. Furthermore, your doppelganger begins to have a life of its own and the longer it stays in existence the more difficult it is to make it disappear. If you put too much energy into the doppelganger you may never regain control. In extreme cases, doppelgangers have been known to kill their creator in order to have an independent life. Of course, they don't realize that as soon as they kill the one responsible for their being they automatically kill themselves. No one ever said doppelgangers were smart.

Sure, the cold winters aggravated his headaches and he had been thinking about moving to southern California for several years. Come to think of it his headaches sounded reasonable enough to be true and would probably satisfy his nosy landlady. God only knows, the move probably even had some merit. Now the question was how could he use the money to get a vehicle reliable enough to get him to California and move his meager belongings without arousing suspicion? He had to have a plausible explanation if asked and his inquisitive landlady was sure to pry. The small disability checks he received from the state each month paid for his lodging and simple lifestyle, but it surely wasn't enough to buy a new car. The only explanation seemed to be he had to get a temporary job; some kind of work that would allow him to purchase a car. This might take a few weeks, but then he wasn't in a real hurry. The money wouldn't spoil and the anticipation of all the things he would buy once he was free of this town would make the time go quickly.

With that thought in mind he went out for a paper and the want ads anxious to find some kind of job.

*****

Glory

Glory was pacing her suite at the Red Lion fretting about her next action. The walls of her room featured large colored photos of Hells Canyon, Ketchum and Sun Valley in the winter and summer plus stunning shots of the bleak Valley of the Moon. Each photo was professionally presented in a black and gold pattern frame with a two-tone double layer mat providing depth which made each scene enticing; something you just had to want to see for yourself. The carpet, wall covering and bedspread all complemented the pictures helping to focus the attention of anyone in the room on the dramatic photos. What made it difficult for the tough New York reporter was that she knew she had the freedom to go visit any or all of the scenes, on the boss's money even, and yet here she was pacing around in her room like a caged tigress.

She just couldn't get the big handsome detective out of her mind. She could see him relaxed in his homemade lounge chair on the veranda of his unusual house drinking beer. She wanted to know more about him, what made him an incredible detective; she wanted to know more about his house and what made him tick? In her mind, this unusual investigator made a far more interesting story than the robbery of a bread truck carrying bags of dollar bills. While the robbery story had its merits, and was certainly worthy of a couple minutes' air time if they could ever find all the missing pieces, it didn't have nearly the depth, complexity, texture and curiosity factors going for it that Glory saw in the Wolf. The name itself was intriguing enough to focus her attention on his background. She knew he was both intelligent and educated, although it was his instincts and operating procedures that held her interest. What made him choose to be a private investigator and why did he choose to live so far away from humanity in a cave all by himself? Well, he did have a real wolf-brother for companionship. It was only when she was thinking about him and her visit to his house that she came to realize he really did live in a cave; just like a real wolf. This sudden insight was almost scary. What in the hell was she getting herself into?

And then there was the shaman; his mentor. What was that all about? Glory would have paid almost any price to accompany him on the visit to this mysterious teacher from the past. She didn't believe that a Navajo shaman lived in the vicinity, but she was unfamiliar with both western history and the makeup of any local Indian reservations so she wasn't sure of herself. On the other hand, Hokee had never said where the shaman lived. Who was this shaman and how does he figure in Hokee's life? This question along with all of the other intriguing unknowns kept the reporter pacing the room trying to figure out a strategy for finding answers. The only person who seemed to have any real knowledge of Hokee was Curly and he wasn't talking. She decided that until the Wolfman called, if he called, all she could do was some independent research at the library. Being a trained and aggressive investigative reporter in her own right, she knew a few things about investigation. Her first stop would be the public library for back issues of the local papers and anything she could find on the Hokee Wolf Detective Agency. Then she would pay a visit to his office to see what might be learned there. After learning the library's address and checking out a map on where it was located she picked up her bag containing a notebook, pen and pocketbook on her way out the door. As it was closing behind her she caught a fleeting glimpse of the Sun Valley photo in the summertime and wondered again at what she was doing? She could be off relaxing and enjoying a mini all-paid vacation and yet here she was on the way to the library to actually do some work; although not strictly related to the story she was supposed to be investigating. It must be something in the water she mused while walking to the concierge to ask for a taxi; she could have had Donald drive her around in their rented Cadillac but that would entail too much explanation. Better to just go it alone.

Pocatello's main library is a large, two-story soot stained yellow brick building located on South Garfield Avenue. The entrance is an A-frame bay vestibule with an air lock to keep out the cold winter air. On this bright pleasant September afternoon, the inner doors were wide open and Glory sauntered inside drawing glances from men and women alike. Used to being ogled at she took it all in stride, but after a few moments became uncomfortable as the patrons and library staff alike continued to stare at her as she walked towards the help desk. She was nearly at the desk before she realized the reason for all the gawks. Dressed in the latest high New York fashion her clothes stood out like an elephant in a herd of sheep. "To hell with them," she muttered to herself. "Let 'em gawk." Approaching the desk, she asked for information on back issues of the local paper, The Idaho State Journal, *IT'S ALL ABOUT YOU.*

The library had the past ten years of the journal on microfilm. She spent the next three hours searching past issues for any information on Hokee, Hokee Wolf, Hokee Wolf Detective Agency, Hokee Wolf Investigations and just plain Wolf. The last term yielded more information than she really wanted but none of it was about the man bearing the name. Other than that, she discovered his name in numerous stories over the past ten years glorifying his accomplishments as a detective and investigator but almost nothing about him personally other than some vague references to his age, actually unknown but somewhere in his late thirties-early forties, and his residence, presumably someplace in Bannock County although there was never an address or description of his dwelling.

Swallowing her pride, she went back to the information desk and asked Judy, the assistant librarian if she could help her find out any personal information about the private investigator, Hokee Wolf? Judy smiled in that conspiratorial way women have of sharing secrets and said, "No and I don't know anyone who can help. If you find out anything would you let me know?"

she added with a wink.

Studying the attractive New Yorker dressed in clothes she would kill to own the librarian said, "I've been dying to get to know the man for years, but outside of his investigative practice no one seems to know anything. I do believe he is single, not gay and not involved with anyone. That is all simply my unverified belief, sorry." She actually looked sorry and Glory felt a twinge of pity for the bookish looking librarian who apparently carried a torch for the town's handsome unattached number one detective. She wondered what the girl's reaction would be if informed that just yesterday she had shared a beer with Hokee on the veranda of his most unusual house. Deciding it would be just plain cruel she thanked Judy for her help, minimal though it was, and left the library no wiser than she was before.

After calling her hotel only to discover there were no messages for her, damn; she decided to treat herself to a great dinner. The River Gorge Steak House had been mentioned in one of the flyers in her hotel room so flagging a taxi she soon found herself seated in front of a large picture window looking down into a steep gorge. If there was a river down there it was invisible but still the view was breathtaking. The dinner was excellent but the pockmarked busboy with dark penetrating eyes made her uncomfortable. She would like to have stayed for an after dinner drink but as the middle-aged busboy began cleaning up her table, he looked into her eyes and she actually felt a twinge of fear. The black holes in his eyes seemed to be burning with some kind of fire. The light pouring out was almost painful to witness and definitely unnerving. Silly to be afraid of a busboy, however, an after-dinner drink back in her hotel suite suddenly seemed like an excellent idea. Leaving the restaurant, she wondered briefly what it was about that man that gave her such a fright.

On the taxi ride back to her hotel she forgot about the frightening busboy resuming her questions and thoughts concerning Hokee. How was she going to learn about him and who was he exactly? It seemed pretty obvious from his eyes, facial structure and build that he was not a full-blooded Indian so who were his parents? How did he come to live in Pocatello and why was such a learned and talented man a detective; or was he more of an investigator like herself? She briefly wondered if the similarity of their professions was her attraction for him, but dismissed that thought almost immediately. His self-confidence, easy grace and masculinity were the main attractions; it didn't hurt that he was also incredibly handsome. No, she decided, her investigations were developed in order to tell a story. Hokee investigated in order to solve a mystery and perhaps undo or prevent a wrong. Her motives were almost entirely career driven while his business seemed to be more humanitarian, not that he was averse to making money. For the first time, she wondered if it would be possible for a New Yorker, a sophisticated investigative New York journalist, to ever live in a place like Pocatello, Idaho? The answer that immediately came to mind was a resounding NO! Not only no, but hell no! Okay then, what's the big interest in Hokee and how come she gets the first date jitters at just the thought of him inviting her to a Wolf dinner? She was still pondering this question when she ordered a drink from room service; Bols gin and tonic with a twist. If you don't have Bols then Tanqueray would do nicely instead.

CHAPTER TEN

Glory's Dinner

Hokee arrived back home near sunset with a lot on his mind. Before pouring a single malt scotch and sitting down to contemplate his next move Shilah was given a jackrabbit from a small refrigerator he kept outside on the veranda for just such occasions. Usually he let the wolf run into the lava flats and catch his own meals but today he had asked his friend to stay home and guard the house. Getting back late meant that the prime hunting time was over and it might take several hours for the wolf to catch a meal. Hokee often went out hunting with Shilah whenever the refrigerator supply of rabbits got low so that when a hot case made him late getting home he could feed the wolf without waiting up all night to make sure his friend got dinner.

While Shilah was busy tearing into his meal Hokee decided on a St. Magdalene single malt neat and sat down to enjoy a scotch while considering the next move. His first sip reminded him why he went to so much trouble importing such an expensive luxury. With only 408 cases made annually the cost of his annual case would have been prohibitive without the money he had made and invested. As the complex smoky aroma filled his nose and the amber liquid warmed his mouth Hokee thought about doppelgangers. What kind of person would even be interested in creating such an entity? Where would you find such a person in Pocatello? Where would someone living in Pocatello go to learn how to create and use this energy? And the million-dollar question, actually in this case the three-million-dollar question, was why?

It obviously had to be someone local who knew about the Eddy's bread truck money delivery contract. That information was not widely known outside of the merchants in West Yellowstone, Eddy's bread truck employees and certain people at the bank. That still included a fair number of people and people do talk. In addition, there was the local armored truck service who Hokee knew for certain had made several bids to take over that money run. The problem was that the West Yellowstone drive was a long distance, armored trucks got very bad gas mileage and safety rules plus the insurance bonding company demanded two individuals per truck. When all of the expenses were added plus even a small profit the contract was much higher than Eddy's charged since they already had a truck in West Yellowstone anyway. For the bread company, the extra money they made hauling the West Yellowstone cash receipts was pure gravy. There was just no way the armored truck service could be competitive. Was it possible for the armored truck company to stage this robbery in order to secure the contract? Sure, it was possible, but the company was highly insured and the owners plus all of its drivers were bonded. Hokee had performed many of the background checks himself for the insurance bonding company. Probably not the armored truck people, but it wouldn't hurt to investigate.

Since it more than likely was not someone in the money hauling profession trying to secure more business, Hokee decided to leave the "why" question and concentrate on the "who". Perhaps it was someone with a grudge or someone looking for a big money score; or possibly both. It was obviously someone who knew the bread truck was hauling money and someone who knew about doppelgangers. Learning enough information about doppelgangers to actually create the kind of false images used in the robbery probably meant someone traveling to the mid or far east to find a teacher. The local library would not contain sufficient detailed information to enable that kind of mastery.

After talking with Why-ay'-looh, Hokee was convinced that nobody locally possessed sufficient knowledge to teach the powerful version of doppelganger mastery demonstrated in the robbery, so that meant travel. Perhaps he should visit all of the local travel agencies to determine who had visited the Far East in the last fifteen to twenty years. With a direction and plan for the following day's activities, Wolf called Shilah for a head rub before he went off to bed. His pet had the option of sleeping inside but usually chose the great outdoors sleeping inside only during the biting cold of a hard winter.

Hokee spent the next morning visiting each of the city's four full-time travel agencies who had survived competition from the failed start-ups over the years. He had learned that there was always someone new getting into the business for a few weeks or months, thinking about all the travel discounts they could get, but not realizing that travel still took money, plus an office that was a hungry "cash cow" requiring constant feeding. Trying to locate these former would-be travel agents seemed almost certainly to be a waste of time, so Hokee spent his time with those agencies that he thought might produce something positive. This was not to be the case. Although the agencies did have the names of several people who had traveled to the far and mideast during the years in which Hokee was interested he was able to eliminate everyone on the lists very quickly. Too old, too rich, too secure or simply too feeble.

After calling his office manager to check for any particularly pressing matter, such as a desperate parent who had lost track of their darling child, Hokee stopped for a quick lunch at Granny's Shack. Granny featured real down home cooking in an actual shack next to a railroad switching yard. The eatery had been around for nearly forty years and Granny now in her late seventies still showed up for work every day supervising the menu and workers. It was while eating Granny's world famous pot roast that Hokee had an idea for his next investigative action.

Thinking he would start fresh tomorrow he gave some thought to his promised dinner with the New York reporter. He was attracted to the sexy beautiful lady and she was smart, pushy and talented. The question was what in the hell had been behind his impromptu invitation and should he actually go through with the dinner. Preparation would not be a problem. Hokee had been cooking his own meals most of his life and had become somewhat of a gourmet cook, at least for western fare. The more he thought about it the easier his decision became. She was an investigative reporter. Let her help with the investigation. If she actually produced anything useful it could only help and while she was off investigating his case it would keep her out of his way. After finishing his pot roast and final cup of coffee he used Granny's phone to make a date for tonight's dinner.

Digging the paper out of his wallet with her local phone number, Hokee called the front desk asking for Gloria's room. He was actually surprised when she answered, expecting her to be out hounding someone looking for information. Her voice sounded just as warm and well-modulated on the telephone as it did in real person.

"Hello, this is Glory."

"Glory, Hokee. Are you still interested in dinner?" Hokee kept it short as usual.

Glory paused as though somewhat in shock, "Absolutely, I'd be lying if I said otherwise. I figure that's the only way I'm ever going to get a story out of you." Her candor took Hokee by surprise and for a moment he was speechless.

"Are you still there?" she asked.

Recovering quickly Hokee responded, "Yeah, just figuring out the time, how about seven?"

"Sounds perfect, can I bring anything?"

"No, it's all taken care of. Remember how to get here?"

"Sort of, but I still have my map. It won't be a problem," she said hoping that was true.

"Great, see you tonight," he said hanging up terminating the call. Farewell speeches were not in his repertoire.

On the way home Hokee stopped by a rancher he knew who grew rabbits for sale. Picking up a couple he drove on home and began preparing dinner.

After cleaning and skinning the rabbits the rabbit skins were stretched over a wire coat hanger frame for tanning at a later date. White rabbit fur made excellent trim for all kinds of garments. The entrails went into the outdoor refrigerator for Shilah. Nothing on Hokee's property went to waste. He cut up the rabbit into sections before rinsing, drying, oiling and then dredging each piece in flour seasoned with salt and pepper plus a variety of herbs grown in his own herb garden. Shilah watched every move hoping something would fall on the floor that he would be allowed to rescue. After browning each piece in a large Dutch oven with a couple tablespoons of butter, he added a full cup of sherry and let the meat simmer while sautéing some shitake mushrooms, a little chopped garlic and white onion. After the mushrooms were cooked he added them to the meat with a full can of Campbell's mushroom soup, a half cup of shredded carrots, a handful of chopped celery and a touch of red pepper sauce. With his famous, at least famous in his own eyes, rabbit stew simmering on the stove he made some homemade biscuits from scratch to sop up the rich gravy. This was accompanied by a traditional Caesar salad with raw eggs also purchased from a local farmer. After storing the salad in the refrigerator to keep it crisp he raided the wine rack deep in the back of his cave for a decent bottle of Cabernet. Finding he still had a couple bottles of BV 1968, he decided to sacrifice one on the New Yorker. She probably only drank white wine, but that just wouldn't do with rabbit stew.

While the biscuits were baking Hokee settled back for a well-earned glass of single malt. Sitting on his veranda he watched the afternoon shadows creep up the side of Caribou Mountain nearly sixty miles to the east. He was only able to see the top one-third of the mountain over the rim of his shallow valley. It was a view he never tired of watching. Today he relaxed as he often did when observing the shadow play on the side of the mountain named after Caribou Jack who discovered gold there nearly a hundred years earlier. He wondered whatever really happened to all of the Chinese miners when the New York owners suddenly closed the gold mine back in 1898? The original Caribou Jack's claim was purchased by a group of New York investors who hired the Chinese railroad workers. They were discharged by the railroad after driving the final spike in the transcontinental railroad at nearby Promontory Point in 1869. At one time the Chinese Caribou mining camp was the largest community in the Rocky Mountains. Mining was halted in the late eighteen hundreds and local rumor has it that the Chinese miners were all herded into the mine which was then closed by dynamite sealing the workers inside, thereby saving the owners considerable money. No one ever dug out the mine entrance to prove otherwise.

The biscuits were cooling and Hokee was enjoying his scotch on the veranda when Glory drove down the slope into his yard. As she was getting out of the rental Hokee couldn't help but notice she was sporting a form fitting pair of jeans and a tight blue V-neck sweater accentuating the upper part of a well-toned beautifully proportioned body. Keeping his mind on business was going to be more difficult than he wanted, but the detective was determined that he would not let lust overcome his good sense; although, my God, she was a sexy lady.

"Hey Hokee, I see you're relaxed in your favorite chair," she quipped walking towards the veranda carrying a small package and swinging her hips just a little more than was necessary.

Hokee stood up to greet his guest with a wry welcoming smile. "Hi," he said, "just admiring the setting sun waiting for my dinner guest." He purposefully ignored that little voice in his head that said; *that ain't all you noticed.* Remaining focused and reserved as possible he continued, "Can I fix you a drink before dinner?"

"Sure, Tanqueray and tonic would be great if you have it. If not any gin will do," she answered handing him the package.

"What's this?" he asked taking the paper sack wrapped package.

"Just a token of appreciation for the dinner," she responded with a million-dollar smile of her own.

Opening the package Hokee found a bottle of 21-year-old Glenlivit. "How did you know I drink single malt scotch?" he asked with a puzzled expression. Try as he might he could not remember ever discussing his whisky preference with the lovely lady from New York.

"Hey Hokee, you are not the only one who knows how to investigate," she answered with a mischievous grin on her face. Although he asked the same question a couple more times throughout the evening she refused to give him the answer.

"Well, thank you very much. This costs a lot more than my dinner but I will enjoy it. Why don't you take a seat while I fix your drink," he added motioning to the chaise lounge next to the one he had been occupying as she drove up. "I've got some gin in the house someplace."

"I'll just tag along and watch you work if that's okay with you," she said anxious to get another close look inside of his house/cave.

Since they were going to be eating inside anyway Hokee invited her to come inside while he got some fresh ice from the freezer to fix her drink. Feeling free to take a real close look for the first time, Glory almost gasped at the simple beauty and symmetry of Hokee's kitchen and dining area.

The floor was a mosaic of black and red polished flat border stones arranged in a stunning pattern. Inside of the border; yellow, green and white stones formed a complicated triangular design wherein each triangular segment seemed to be three dimensional drawing the eye towards infinity. The triangular segments began at the edge of the room curving in towards the center of the room in a spiral reminiscent of our galaxy. The size of each triangular segment grew increasingly smaller as the spiral grew tighter and tighter until the triangular patterns also seemingly disappeared into infinity. Hokee's kitchen was laid out around this pattern with a triple sink made of polished black granite. A long smooth work surface made of the same black granite ran from the sink to a black sub-zero refrigerator. The black granite countertop rested on a base covered with turquoise gems. Glory had never seen so much turquoise in her life. Across the kitchen was a commercial black gas range and oven combination with various pots and pans hanging from long hooks on either side attached to the ceiling. The other wall contained an open-faced handmade rock cabinet illuminated from inside with indirect lighting. The cabinet was made of polished red rock with black shelving for his dishes. Two drawers at waist height held his silverware and cooking utensils.

The other side of the kitchen opened into his dining area which was actually part of the cave. Indirect lights illuminated a curved polished wall featuring a desert scene from the vantage point of a gray wolf laying at the edge of a cliff high on top of a mountain. The desert stretched out below in a panoramic view of the desert at sunset featuring all of the colors in Hokee's kitchen. Whoever the artist was he or she had captured the spirit of Hokee's wolf; perhaps the spirits of the Wolfman himself. In fact, the wolf in the picture actually looked like Shilah, his pet wolf. The viewer seemed to be seeing the desert valley below through the eyes of the wolf. The power in the picture captured your soul drawing you into the landscape to the point where you could almost hear the breeze blowing across the mountain and smell the hot afternoon air rising from the desert floor.

Although Glory made her living with words, none came as she was caught up, first in the floor of his kitchen and then the painting. She was startled when Hokee nudged her shoulder handing her the gin and tonic.

"Shall we go outside and see our own sunset while we have our drinks?" he suggested.

He turned and walked out, leaving Glory who reluctantly took her eyes from the picture and meekly followed behind, still shaken by the power of her experience.

"When she was safely seated and composed Glory couldn't help but ask, "Who designed your floors and painted the picture in your dining room?"

"I believe I told you last time you were here that you are the first and only person who has ever been in my house." His answer seemed even to his own ears to be a little sharp, so he tried to ease the sting by continuing, "In another lifetime I thought of becoming an artist but 'life' kind of got in the way. Funny how that happens, isn't it?" he answered without smiling. Taking a sip of scotch, he relaxed back into his chair catching the final rays of light glancing off the top of Caribou Mountain. "Here's to you Jack," he whispered tipping his glass towards the mountain, "whoever you were."

For the second time in a matter of minutes Glory was again stunned beyond words. How could this Indian, this detective/inspector what-cha-ma-callit possibly paint such a powerful picture? She was already convinced that he was no ordinary man; in fact, she had come around to believe that he was not only an incredible detective but a very talented artist as well? Needing time to digest this revelation she chose another topic. Hearing Hokee's quiet toast she had to ask, "Who's Jack?"

Hokee explained how the ancient prospector, mountain-man had literally stumbled over the gold on Caribou Mountain and later sold the claim to the New Yorkers who still owned most of the mountain, although there had been no mining for nearly eighty years.

After listening to the story while sipping her gin, Glory asked, "Can you tell me what you learned from your shaman friend?"

By way of an answer Hokee asked one of his own. "What do you know about doppelgangers?"

This caused the inquisitive investigative reporter to pause and think. "I'm not sure; I don't believe I've ever heard the word."

"You're not alone. It isn't a common word in the English language and we don't get a chance to use it very often. If you are going to continue working on the bread truck robbery you might want to bone up on the topic," he continued with a smile making his eyes twinkle, causing Glory to get those funny romantic warm feelings while appreciating his good looks even more.

"Okay," she said playing his game. "What is a doppelganger?"

"A doppelganger is an energy-being, sort of like a hologram, created by, and from, the mind of an individual to represent himself, or herself, to other people in order to perform certain tasks," he said taking another sip of scotch.

"And that's what happened in the bread truck robbery?" she said. Glory's intelligence and quick mind impressed Hokee as she made the connection and saw the relationship to the known events of the robbery and the explanation of doppelgangers.

"Yeah, more or less. Come on in while I set out dinner and I'll explain a little more," he said getting up and extending a hand to Glory. "Shilah, you wait out here boy, I'll feed you later," he said as they walked inside. The large gray wolf didn't even move from his resting spot next to Hokee's chair. Carrying their nearly finished drinks inside Hokee ushered Glory to the table while he went to the oven for his stew. She had been so taken by the power of the wall painting that she completely missed the handmade table. The table top was inlaid with a variety of different colored woods matching the same spiral pattern formed in the floor. She couldn't imagine the hours such a masterpiece would take to complete. The Indian woven placemats and silver place settings perfectly complemented the table and room. Where did this unbelievable man get such decorative talent to go along with everything else he had working for himself?

*****

66

While Glory was lost in her examination and appreciation of Hokee's artistry he was busy serving up rabbit stew with a side plate of warm sheepherder's buttermilk biscuits and butter. Glory had no idea what she was being served but the aroma alone was enough to make her mouth moist. This was followed by a crisp Caesar salad straight from the refrigerator. After setting the meal before his guest he poured each of them a glass of Cabernet.

"Ma-bu-hay," Hokee said raising his glass to Glory. "Long life," he added as they clinked their glasses.

Glory looked at her plate trying to decide exactly what it was she was eating and couldn't make up her mind. In some ways it looked like a chicken, but then again it wasn't. But oh, the aroma coming from her plate, she had never smelled any food that made her mouth water so much. She watched Hokee use his fork and a piece of biscuit to secure a chunk of meat and some of the stew juice so she copied his movements. The aroma was not deceitful. Glory had never eaten such mouth-watering food in her life. And the Cabernet was out of this world. Say what you would, this Indian sure as hell knew how to cook.

"Do you mind if I ask what I'm eating?" Glory said. "It's so delicious that I'm afraid of making a pig of myself, but I would like to know what it is; but only if it won't make me sick," she quickly added.

"Baby wolf," Hokee said teasing. "I told you we were having a wolf dinner." Then seeing the horror on his guest's face he quickly confessed. "Actually it's rabbit from a friend of mine who raises them," he replied watching for her reaction. "These are not the same rabbits that I feed Shilah," he explained in case she thought they were eating dog food; although come to think of it she didn't know what he fed Shilah so the whole subject was unnecessary.

"Wow!" she said. "I've seen it on the menu at some exclusive restaurants but I never had the nerve to order it. I didn't know what I was missing."

The dog food thing didn't exactly register as Glory didn't know the difference between jack rabbits and domestic rabbits raised for eating. The evening progressed through homemade banana nut bread made with caramel and coconut topped with chokecherry jelly that was equally unique. As they were finishing the last of the wine Glory got back to the doppelganger.

"You said you would explain a little more about the doppelganger," she prompted.

"Remember when we were on the highway I said the energy felt all wrong?" he said.

"Yes, I didn't know what you meant though," she responded.

"Creating a doppelganger that does not look like the creator takes a lot of time and practice. Being able to simultaneously control the mind of others so they see an image that isn't there adds still more dimensions of difficulty. One has to master several disciplines. In ancient times an adept would lay down his body and shut down nearly all of his body's functions. All of his energy would be focused on creating the illusion of another human being, a doppelganger. The adept would see through the doppelganger's eyes and use his own mind to control the doppelganger's movements. In this way, the adept could have the doppelganger perform any and every kind of hideous act without being personally involved. While the doppelganger was active, the adept was very near death and usually had a very trusted servant stand guard over his body, keeping it from harm. A doppelganger is not human and the energy it leaves behind, although having human characteristics, is strange and often has an evil or dark component."

"Is that a for real creation? I mean, can people actually do that?" Glory asked completely bewildered.

"My mentor told me that he knows of no one in the United States with this capability today, perhaps a century or two ago, but he believes it might still be taught in the mid or far east. After my own studying, I believe it can still be found in the Himalayas, probably near Tibet." After thinking about the statement he had just made Hokee continued proving once again the subtle nuances of his mind that make him a great detective. "I suppose it is always possible that someone who has been taught this black art migrated to the United States."

"How does one go about finding out about such things?" Glory wanted to know.

This is where Hokee had wanted the conversation to go from the beginning. "The library," he answered. "And that is where I would like you to go tomorrow, providing you want to participate," he said with another of those enigmatic grins that drove her crazy. "After all, you are an investigative reporter," he added still grinning.

"Okay, I'll bite," she said faking a frown that pulled down the corner of her eyes giving them an oriental look, altogether very sexy. "What am I doing in the library?" she asked.

"Sometime during the past fifteen to twenty years, someone in Pocatello checked out a book on occult practices, mysticism, arcane religions or paranormal phenomena. We need to know who." He added the "we" making it a joint investigation knowing that being inclusive had a better chance of getting her cooperation.

"So," she said with a sly grin, "while I'm doing the grunt work in the library what's Pocatello's claim to investigative fame going to be doing?"

Trying in vain to hide his own grin Hokee replied, "There have been three people involved in what I would call paranormal events in Pocatello during the past couple of years. I want to look them up and see what happened in their lives. We can get together tomorrow night for a drink at your hotel and exchange notes if you're agreeable."

"You've got yourself a deal buster," she said this time with a real smile lighting her face. "So, the coffin in the ground was this adept's way of protecting his body," Glory concluded just to wrap up the topic.

Once again Wolf was amazed at the flexibility and quickness of Glory's mind.

"That's what I believe happened. It fits the circumstances and it just feels right. Our thief could not afford to have someone stumble on his nearly dead body while he was out robbing a bread truck."

Dinner was over and Glory couldn't think of any more questions to ask without sounding stupid. She had been trying all throughout dinner to think of a way to get a tour through the rest of Hokee's house. Sensing the evening was coming to a close she brazenly asked, "Would you show me the rest of your home? This is the most fascinating residence I believe that I have ever visited." Hokee had been expecting the query all night and would have offered if she hadn't asked. "Sure," he said after draining the last of his wine. "Let's start over here by the outside door," he said, motioning to a door so cleverly concealed by the framework that it blended in perfectly with the solid rock wall. This door led to what Hokee laughingly called his backyard. It was really just a shaded gravel courtyard with a permanent sweat lodge behind a rock fire pit. A pile of lava rocks was on one side of the fire pit next to a neatly stacked pile of wood. Seeing the sweat lodge Glory just had to ask.

"Do you use your sweat lodge very often?"

"At least once a week," he responded. "For me it's a form of meditation. I use it to reconnect with mother earth and her creations; and a few other things." As he spoke his countenance had a serious no-nonsense expression that did not invite further questions.

Behind some low growing shrubbery, Glory caught a glimpse of a large propane tank. Going back inside, Hokee took her around a sharp corner in the dining room and into a short hall leading to the single bedroom. It was a massive room of solid lava rock soaring more than thirty feet high. Wall hangings of various Navajo designs covered every wall up to about twenty feet. The floor was a duplicate of the dining room except that the colors were reversed. The border was of various colored stones and the inward spiral was black and red with a white rock outline. She was not surprised that the king-sized bed was another homemade masterpiece with the headboard made of inlaid wood much like the dining room table. A simple white down comforter covered the bed which was stacked with a variety of colored pillows. Recessed reading lamps were built into the wall above the headboard illuminating the room with a soft glow.

"Where do you get your electricity?" she asked. "I didn't see any power poles on the drive out here this afternoon."

"There is an underground river just behind this wall to your left. That wall is not part of the original cave. I built it to match the rest of the room but if you listen carefully you can hear the running water. The river is almost entirely silent. It has a laminar flow. The only reason you can hear any water running is the small diversion leading to an offshoot flow that allowed me to discover this place. This is how I am able to grow all the plants outside plus live here. The stream has sufficient energy to power a number of electrical generators originally built for diesel trucks. I have an electrical room off to the side with twenty twelve-volt batteries that are kept fully charged by the generators. Everything electrical is twelve-volt direct current. I have plenty of power and lights to do anything I want. A professor at Idaho State designed the system for me."

"Well, you certainly are self-sufficient," she lamented to herself thinking that the last thing he probably needs in his life was a woman. "Well, I guess it's time I was getting back to my room. Tomorrow is going to be a busy day."

Much to her chagrin Hokee agreed. "Yeah, let me show you out and turn on some outdoor lights," he said leading the way back through the house to the veranda. Pausing at the beautiful carved doors leading to the outside, he hit a switch that turned the outside into a brilliant bowl of light. The entire valley was alight much like football stadiums. Glory couldn't believe how bright it was.

"Wow, you weren't kidding when you said you have all the power you want. How do you get it so bright?" she asked. "It's the headlights from trains. Ever notice how bright they are? They're blinding. Anyway, I can't run them for more than an hour or two, I just turn them on when a lion or some other predator comes slinking around. Shilah lets me know when it's time to turn them on. Safe driving," he said opening her car door.

Disappointed to be leaving without at least some show of affection she held out her hand to shake goodbye, "Thanks for a wonderful evening and the sensational meal. I don't think I've ever tasted anything so good in my life."

"My pleasure," he said giving her a firm handshake. There was an impulse to hold her hand a little longer than necessary and he felt it might be welcomed but being unsure he let his hand fall away. "I'll call you tomorrow afternoon about getting together to compare notes," he said.

There was real angst in his emotions with a desire for a more personal relationship with the beautiful sexy reporter but his shyness kept him from acting on impulse. Hokee headed back towards the veranda. Perhaps it was just as well. Women had only been trouble in his life and while he missed making love, the consequences were usually not worth the hassle; although, there was something special about that girl from New York. Maybe he would have to reconsider. But that was for another time.

He was already thinking about the three people he was going to be looking up tomorrow as he waited for Glory's car to top the ridge on her way home before turning off the lights. While getting a rabbit out of the refrigerator for Shilah's dinner he wondered what kind of an approach he could use to get people talking about the terrible event that had transformed their lives.

CHAPTER ELEVEN

The Three

During the past two years three possible paranormal events registered in Hokee's mind. Nearly two years ago, Judy Negranti had suffered a sudden paralysis on the left side of her face. Judy had been a world-famous opera singer slated to be Pocatello's next Judy Garland. She was only thirty-five and climbing the world's operatic ladder, rapidly becoming one of the leading divas of her time. With a major performance scheduled in New York's Lincoln Center, Judy had agreed to a rehearsal billed as a benefit for local Pocatello charities. The Mystique Theatre had been sold out for weeks billing Pocatello's own operatic star the lovely and talented Judy Negranti. Judy was backstage in her soundproof dressing room preparing for her entrance by performing a few warm-up voice exercises when her left eye began twitching. Thinking it was simply pre-stage jitters, although this was not a usual occurrence, she continued with the warm-ups only to have the twitching grow worse until ultimately the entire left side of her face became paralyzed.

Naturally the concert had to be cancelled disappointing her many fans. The local papers reported that the medical profession could not explain the sudden paralysis which ended her promising career. A stroke was ruled out, as the only part of her body affected was the left side of her face, making it difficult to speak properly and of course sing. The last thing Hokee remembered reading about Judy's condition was a report speculating on a paranormal event of some kind. Possibly a hex or curse by a bitter jealous rival. While no sane rational person actually took the paranormal speculation seriously it made for titillating gossip. Hokee was wondering if they ever determined the cause of her paralysis and if it had any connection to his case?

Judy lived on Park Lane up on the east bench with her husband Lester Worthington. Les owned the local Ford dealership making serious money selling Ford pickups to the local farmers. Judy taught singing lessons to a select group of young ladies whose voices promised rewards if they were willing to sacrifice the work necessary to develop properly. Most started out religiously but gave up settling for mediocrity after discovering just how much work it took to become a master. One out of a hundred would stick with it for a couple of years before giving up and joining a startup band as lead singer. After two years Judy was still waiting for that one in a million with the talent, determination and will to become a real opera star. She lived on and taught hoping that one day she would discover such a girl.

Hokee searched his brain trying to remember a mutual acquaintance. While he enjoyed the theatre and even took in an occasional ballet performance he had not developed a taste for opera. He did have a couple of recordings at home that he played from time to time but had never been to a live performance. While he had rescued many young men and women whose parents undoubtedly moved in Negranti's circle he didn't know this for a fact. In the end, he could see no alternative but to make a cold call.

Wearing hand tooled cowboy boots, a neat pair of pleated black slacks and white shirt with a black leather vest Hokee decided to just go knock on the door and play it by ear. For this visit Hokee let his hair hang loose framing a strong chiseled face many called handsome and most women looked at twice. Seeing his reflection in Judy's front window as he walked towards her door, Hokee decided if he couldn't charm his way inside he didn't deserve being called Pocatello's number one investigator and detective.

The door was opened by the lady herself still looking beautiful, serene and thoughtful. She rarely smiled as it emphasized the paralysis on the left side of her face. She had learned to speak with barely moving her lips, much like a ventriloquist, "Can I help you?"

"Good morning Madam Negranti. My name is Hokee Wolf; I am a private investigator looking into the Eddy's bread truck robbery on behalf of the bank involved. I have great admiration for your talent and know that neither you or your husband are involved in the robbery in any way, but I hope you may be able to help me with my investigation. Would you spare me a few minutes of your time?"

Hokee gave her a sincere smile hoping to persuade her to let him in for a few minutes. He had genuine respect for everyone like her who had achieved the level of mastery he knew she had commanded at one time. Confronting her with sincere appreciation for her accomplishments was not difficult.

"Yes Mr. Wolf. I recognize you from your frequent pictures in our paper. You have made quite a name for yourself." It was obvious she was suppressing a smile so as to not distort her face.

Hokee was embarrassed by the acknowledgement and was momentarily speechless.

"Well madam," he said regaining his composure, "my own accomplishments hardly compare to the excellence you achieved in your career." Hokee knew he was risking her displeasure by mentioning something that she may well want to forget, but he could not accomplish his goal in seeing her if he was reluctant to bring up the topic.

Acknowledging his compliment with a slight bow she waved him in. "Come on in detective and tell me what is on your mind," she invited.

After exchanging pleasantries for a couple of minutes Hokee got right to the point. "My investigation suggests that there was some paranormal activity associated with the bread truck robbery. I remember reading a couple of years ago that someone suggested your paralysis might have a paranormal source. My desire is to see if there is any connection?"

At this ridiculous suggestion, Judy was unable to suppress a smile even though it distorted her beautiful face. "Oh detective, I'm afraid you have wasted your trip. You see, last year I went to Stanford University in Palo Alto where they have developed a new imaging technology called CAT scanning. I've forgotten what the acronym stands for, something about computers I think, but it is able to take extremely detailed images of the head. They discovered that a small blood vessel inside of my brain exploded, damaging that area of the brain controlling the left side of my face. The doctors seem to think it might be a genetic weakness of some kind which showed up in my life because of my singing. You know us singers; we like to use our cranium as sounding boards. Apparently, my high notes ruptured an already weak blood vessel. There was nothing paranormal about it. I'm sorry if that is bad news."

"Quite the contrary," Hokee replied. "I'm delighted that you discovered the source of your problem. Perhaps someday medicine will be able to reverse the damage. I know the opera world would be delighted to have you back on the stage."

"That is not even in my dreams Mr. Wolf. I cannot spend my life hoping for a miracle that may never happen; but thank you for the kind thought."

Having learned what he came to discover Hokee thanked the lovely lady for her time and information before leaving to try the next lady on his list. He was saving the police officer for last, since he knew that Morden was lying and getting the truth could take some difficult arm twisting. It might not be a pleasant experience for either man.

Joyce Kimball was one of Pocatello High School's leading cheerleaders in the spring of 1977. Baseball gets a later start in Idaho than in other parts of the country due to the weather but the athletic department still fields a team even though a lot of the spring workouts occurred in the basketball gym. The five Ram cheerleaders, Ram being the high school mascot, led by Joyce didn't care what they were cheering for as long as they could strut their stuff, show off their great figures in skimpy costumes and attract boys. In late April when the weather was finally cooperating with some pleasant days the Pocatello Rams were playing the Idaho Falls Tigers. It was the bottom half of the seventh inning with the score tied at 5-5, the bases loaded with two out when Johnny Bishop came to bat. Johnny was the leading batter on the team averaging 475 and the home crowd was going nuts. Joyce was leading a cheer waving her pom-poms screaming her lungs out when she collapsed on the ground clutching her chest. She was unable to breathe and soon fainted for lack of oxygen. A doctor in the stands rushed to her side and began artificial respiration. An ambulance was called and she was soon strapped on a gurney with an oxygen mask on her face. It was later determined that her lungs had collapsed and she was never again able to participate in any strenuous physical activity.

The local papers carried the story and photo of her lying on the ground being administered to by someone performing artificial respiration but they could never report the reason for her problem. The medical profession called it a mystery. With no new information, the story died after five days having first been relegated to page ten in the Idaho State Journal. The last story carried a speculation that the cause of her mysterious ailment had a paranormal association similar to what had occurred several months earlier at the Mystique. This story also disappeared from the news with no further information regarding the source of Joyce's problem. Hokee could see no relationship to his bread truck case but any possible paranormal event should be investigated.

Joyce Kimball, the former cheerleader, still lived with her parents in a shabby house with an unkempt yard on the west side of town in a rundown neighborhood. Her father was a truck driver, home only a few nights each month. Her mother did some waitressing for Pete's Diner on weekends and probably moonlighted at times at the world's oldest profession. She visited a couple of truck stops on a semi-regular basis often getting home later than it would take to have a meal and visit with her friends. If Joyce knew of or suspected her mom's extra-curricular activities, it was never mentioned. Unable to do much in the way of physical activity besides walking slowly, due to her breathing problem, she spent the majority of her time alone in her bedroom reading books or watching one of the four television channels she could access with rabbit ears. The rabbit ears had to be adjusted for each different station which was a real pain so she spent most of her time reading. She was on a physical therapy program which was supposed to help increase her oxygen intake and stamina, but Joyce lacked the discipline to keep up with the required work. At the present time, she had given up on life, existing mostly in a vegetable state.

Walking up the cracked sidewalk to a sagging front porch, Hokee had to remind himself not to judge. While he had overcome a miserable childhood, and succeeded by sheer will, he knew that life had also cut him some serious breaks. Without his mentor, God only knows what would have become of him, so he was careful in his judgment of others. He had to knock on the door a couple of times before he heard shuffling inside as someone came to answer the door. Joyce finally opened the door looking peaked and weak in a pair of soiled pajamas breathing extra heavy. It was still possible to see the beautiful young girl who had been the leading Ram cheerleader less than two years earlier but she was hidden under a layer of grime and unhappiness.

"Miss Kimball, my name is Hokee Wolf and I would appreciate just a couple minutes of your time if you wouldn't mind," Hokee said wearing his sincere smile and acting like mister humble.

Joyce no longer considered herself beautiful or desirable. Unafraid of being raped or molested she did not even hesitate to wave Hokee inside saving her precious breath for when she was comfortably seated on the living room couch. Hokee was waved to a nearby easy chair. Puffs of dust escaped into the living room air as he sat down.

"What can I help you with Mr. Wolf?" she asked slowly wheezing all the while.

"I am investigating the bread truck robbery that happened a few weeks ago. You may have heard or read about it in the papers?" Joyce merely nodded in the affirmative.

"It appears that the robbery had some paranormal aspects to it that are troubling. At the time of your breathing attack there was some speculation that it might have some paranormal origins. My interest is in finding out if that is true and if so whether there could be any possible connection to the robbery."

As he was speaking he saw Joyce shake her head in the negative before he had even finished his statement. He had considered a relationship between Miss Kimball's incident and the robbery to be highly improbable but it was still necessary to eliminate the possibility.

Speaking very slowly one word at a time in order to avoid the wheezing sound Joyce provided the answer Hokee had been waiting to hear.

"It was not anything paranormal Detective. I had what the doctors called a spontaneous pneumothorax. This is a rare medical condition in which a small area in the lung that is filled with air, called a bleb, can rupture, sending air into the space around the lung. I had pneumonia as a child which severely weakened my lung tissues. Unfortunately, I didn't realize that my cheerleading activities would aggravate this condition causing my lungs to collapse."

"Oh, Miss Kimball, I am so very sorry to hear about your condition. I was hoping you might be on the mend. Is there anything that I can do to help? You are still a beautiful young lady with a lot of living to do," Hokee paused trying to think of some words of encouragement he could offer Joyce without appearing insincere or sounding foolish.

"No, but thanks for the kind words Detective Wolf," she said in her slow wheezing delivery. "My doctor tells me that a new type of oxygen treatment is available that might help strengthen my lungs. He is getting the equipment so I will be able to start treatment next month. We are all keeping our fingers crossed," she finally finished, giving Hokee her first real smile.

"Well, I certainly wish you the best of luck young lady. I know that positive attitude can only help make things better. Thank you for your time. Please don't bother getting up to show me out. I'll be thinking about you," he said while standing up and walking to the door. Giving her a big smile and a wave goodbye he opened the door closing it quietly behind him as he left.

The third case was someone Hokee knew personally. His work put him in contact with Pocatello law officers on a frequent basis and he had met Brent several times both before and after his injury. Officer Brent Morden had shown up with a withered right arm a few months back and when asked about what happened Hokee could tell Morden was dishonest when he claimed ignorance. The official story was that it was the sudden onset of some mysterious malady that the doctors were unable to diagnose, however, Hokee suspected there was a lot more to the story. Since it was really none of his business he had never pursued the matter. With nothing more to go on than a hunch and believing there was someone in the area capable of using paranormal powers, Hokee thought it worth pushing the officer a little to see what really happened.

Driving back into town Hokee tried to think of some way he could crack Officer Morden. Threats and intimidation would probably not be effective. The source of his disability was clearly not something he wished to discuss. This indicated to Hokee that either Morden was injured while off duty and was afraid to admit if for fear of losing some kind of health or disability benefit, or he was injured while on duty doing something irregular or possibly illegal, which would get him suspended or fired. When in doubt, Hokee's rule was "go with the truth"; although it never hurt to insinuate that you knew a lot more than you were saying.

*****

Brent was on duty at the front desk when Hokee got to the police station. Suggesting that he would buy the officer lunch in exchange for a few minutes of conversation, Hokee was able to arrange for a meeting at Jake's Grill in forty-five minutes, just down the street a couple of blocks. He had time to drop by the office and check for messages and give Hilda a little encouragement. She seemed to be a little sad the past few days and Hokee was smart enough to understand the reason. Glory had been to the office and no doubt the love-struck widow was feeling not only jealous but insecure. While Hokee had no desire to stimulate any kind of romantic relationship with his office manager and had been extremely careful to keep their relationship professional, he also knew that everyone could use a pat on the back occasionally, especially employees. This is something many managers fail to comprehend. Stopping by to tell Hilda what a great job she was doing wouldn't take much time and could help improve the office atmosphere considerably.

Having done his good deed for the day, Hokee was sitting down enjoying a cup of Jake's specially blended coffee when Brent Morden slid into the opposite side of his booth. Hokee had already decided to eat first while participating in small talk creating a relaxing atmosphere. He wanted Morden to like him, but more importantly trust him sufficiently to tell the truth about his disability. They each ordered Jake's special hot roast beef sandwich, clearly the best lunch in town and although a bit pricy, it was well worth the extra couple of bucks. Several people over the years had tried to buy and/or bribe the secret to his sandwich but Jake was steadfast in his refusal to discuss the issue. He always prepared the meat and sauce himself so his help could not learn his secret and sell it to a competitor.

With lunch winding down Hokee mentioned the robbery and asked Brent if the police had any new developments. He already knew that the police didn't know beans and had no clues but it broke the ice for his discussion.

"No," Brent said. "We really don't know what transpired in that robbery. So far nothing makes any sense."

Brent did seem confused and bewildered wondering where the detective was going with this conversation.

"I've discovered how the robbery took place," Hokee said by way of exciting the officer's interest. His intent was to subtly suggest a willingness to perhaps exchange some information.

"Really," Morden responded. "I'd be interested in hearing about that."

This was exactly the response Hokee wanted. "It was done by a doppelganger."

Clearly Officer Morden had no idea what a doppelganger was. "I have never heard that word before," he said. "What is a doppelganger?"

"A person can learn how to shift the energy from their body into another body or form. This other form or body is called a doppelganger. In addition to creating the illusion of a real being, the doppelganger can cause other people to hallucinate and see images that are not real. All of this activity is directed by the person creating the doppelganger who sees through the doppelganger's eyes while providing the mental direction."

"Wow! Is that really possible?" Brent asked.

"According to my sources that is the only way the bread truck robbery could have happened," Hokee responded. There was nothing to be gained by telling the officer that his sources were simply one old Indian shaman.

"Well, it's no wonder we haven't been able to find any clues," Morden said.

"Yeah, a doppelganger doesn't leave behind much evidence. And that's what I want to see you about Brent," he said using the first name hoping to inspire more camaraderie. "Clearly this was a paranormal event and I'm trying to link this to other paranormal events that have happened in Pocatello over the past couple of years. Your injury falls into the paranormal category and while I know you have been reluctant to tell anyone exactly what happened, I also know that you have not been telling us the truth Brent. I really need to know what happened to your arm. I promise that I will not divulge anything you tell me without your express permission."

Officer Morden was fighting for composure. He knew that Hokee would know if he continued lying about his injury; on the other hand, he was embarrassed to disclose the action that resulted in the use of his right arm.

"Do you really think there might be a connection between the robbery and my injury?" he asked simply to buy a couple more seconds to frame his answer.

"I honestly don't know Brent," he said. "But I think it's worth investigating, don't you?"

Morden hung his head in shame at the thought of his action, but after a few moments looked up and facing the detective decided to confess. "Years ago, I used my night stick to whack someone I presumed to be a hippie loitering on the streets. Unfortunately, it was a local kid who turned around just as I was striking a blow with the stick. The club hit him on the head knocking him unconscious. I looked around and seeing nobody just took off leaving the boy bleeding and unconscious on the sidewalk. Not too long ago I ran into him on the street. He laid his hand on my shoulder and said 'this is for a lifetime of headaches'. My arm immediately grew very hot and instantly became paralyzed. Over the next few weeks it just withered away. You can see why I have been ashamed to come forth with the truth and I'm going to hold you to your promise about nondisclosure."

"No problem. Can you give me the boy's name or at least a description?"

"I never knew his name. He is a slender man with a sunken chest. As a teenager, he had really bad acne and today his face is badly scarred. He's approximately thirty-five and probably about five ten or so weighing around one fifty. Kind of stringy blond hair in a ponytail the last time I saw him. I'm sorry but that's the best I can do Hokee."

"Thanks Brent. I appreciate your candor. That sounds like our guy alright. Now all we need is a name to go with the description."

Officer Morden was anxious to go walk off his anxiety and frustration and Hokee was happy to see him go. He wasn't going to learn anything more from the sorry officer and he needed time to think of his next action. How was he going to learn the name and address of this pock-faced man?

CHAPTER TWELVE

Getting Away

Being a busboy at the River Gorge Steak House didn't pay that well but he did get to split tips with the waitresses and the steak house attracted affluent customers. Unfortunately, Pocatello was not a town with big tippers but the job still provided an income which was all the cover he needed to satisfy his suspicious landlady. For a down payment he planned on saving everything he earned using state disability money for living expenses. He figured a couple of weeks and he could go buy a used car. It didn't have to be fancy or expensive. All he needed was reliable transportation for a three or four-thousand mile trip. There he would dump the car and fly away someplace to enjoy his wealth.

He was already reading about various countries in the Caribbean Islands and South America. St. John was appealing. It was a U.S. territory and they spoke English. On the other hand, St. Lucia was an English-speaking country and was outside of U.S. jurisdiction. From what he could gather reading about the countries in the library his money would set him up for life in either country. All he had to do was get there without leaving a trail.

He would buy the junker under a false name. If he paid cash, he would not have to show any income or provide job information.

As far as his landlord or neighbors were concerned he would claim to be making monthly payments if the issue ever came up. He was not really that friendly with anybody but some people were just naturally nosy so it paid to have a story handy just in case. He liked that idea. That way when he abandoned the car it would not be traced back to him. Now all he had to do was figure out how to buy an international airplane ticket under an assumed name. He would need a passport.

It was time to start visiting graveyards looking at grave markers. He needed a name at the right age, yet a name that would not attract attention. He had to get the state to reissue a birth certificate so he could get a driver's license and passport. He was spending the hard currency obtained from the robbery for all of his incidentals as often as he could. He didn't dare cash it in all at once but if he only spent a few dollars at a time no one would notice and it saved on the folding green stuff which he could carry so much easier. He had already dumped all the traveler's checks and miscellaneous credit slips by putting a small amount in different dumpsters spread around town. There was no use leaving anything behind that would indicate what had happened to the bread truck money.

With his plans for the next couple of weeks in place he was able to relax and begin thinking about living his life in modest luxury. About damn time, he concluded.

CHAPTER THIRTEEN

Comparing Notes

Hokee spent the rest of the day at his office answering phone calls he had been ignoring while reviewing new requests for his services piled on his desk by the widow Worthmyer. There were several requests from both sexes to spy on wayward spouses, work Hokee did not do, and a couple of possible industrial espionage cases that might be interesting but not nearly as lucrative as recovering the stolen bank money. There weren't any emergency issues such as a missing student that required immediate action for which he was grateful. In the middle of a major criminal investigation he hated to have his attention diverted by some wayward child who had gotten into trouble; the only type of case that in Hokee's mind warranted special attention.

Hokee called Glory's room at the Red Lion leaving a message for her to meet him later on for dinner at the Quail Run, the in-house restaurant at her hotel. Although a bit pricey with small portions the food was decent and meeting there saved everyone some hassle.

He was seated in the rear corner sipping on a Macallan, the only decent single malt the restaurant stocked, when Glory entered. She was wearing a white linen pantsuit that although completely modest, managed to display the voluptuous figure underneath, causing all eyes in the room to track her entrance. Hokee felt himself being aroused, but with iron willed self-control he brought his mind back to business, waving to attract her attention. The motion wasn't needed, as Glory had spotted the big detective as soon as she entered the room, feeling herself drawn to the handsome man. His white shirt and black leather vest stood out like a red rose in a basketful of white lilies. Hokee stood up as she approached his booth giving her a hand to help her get seated.

"I hope your day was productive," he said by way of introduction keeping his emotions safely in check.

"The first thing I discovered is that there is a hell-of-a-lot of occult books that mention doppelgangers," she said. Sitting down she wondered if there was any possibility that Hokee would offer to fix her another dinner at his house. She was looking for any excuse to spend more time getting to know Pocatello's leading detective.

"And I am being rude, sitting here sipping on my scotch without offering you anything to drink," he said smiling an apology just as the cocktail waitress arrived.

After Glory had her drink and they exchanged a few pleasantries she gave him a rundown on her investigation. Basically, only a handful of people seemed interested in the topic of doppelgangers and not many names were on the list. The Pocatello Library system used checkout cards kept in a folder glued to the inside of the book's front cover. When the book was checked out the librarian stamped the card with the date the book was due back next to the name of the person checking out the book. This card went into the library's "active book file" under the book's name. The book's due date was also stamped on the card's folder inside of the book's cover so the person borrowing the book would know when it was due to be returned without a penalty. Unfortunately, once a library checkout card was full of names it was discarded and a new card was inserted into the folder. None of the books Glory found had cards going back fifteen years. Some of the books only had two or three names on the current cards but that didn't tell anything about past history. The library had no way of recovering who had checked out any particular book in the past unless their name was on the card in the book. In other words, her research had been in vain.

Hokee told her about his visits to the big three as he called them saving Officer Morden for the last. As he was describing Morden's arm and how it became injured Glory remembered that this was the officer who had given her directions to Hokee's home. When he had finished describing his day Glory asked, "What do we do now?"

"We find the acne scarred, sunken chest man with long, stringy, blond hair," Hokee said sounding confident. Glory wondered how he could sound so positive when they lacked any substantive clues as to the man's identity. It was then that she remembered her meal at the River Gorge Steak House.

"You know, I ate at the River Gorge Steak House the other night," she said. "The busboy was a middle-aged man who made me feel really uneasy. He had these penetrating dark eyes that were really frightening. Now that I think about it, he fits the description of the man you said Officer Morden described. We could get his name from the restaurant; perhaps even catch him at work. I just feel in my bones that this is the man we are looking for."

"What do you say we go over there for dinner and check it out? I was planning on eating here but if you can tolerate another meal there we could finish our drinks and head on over to the Gorge. I wouldn't mind some of their prime rib tonight myself."

"Yeah, let's do it. I liked the food. The busboy just made me uncomfortable but with you along I won't have to worry," she cooed with a seductive smile.

The clock in Hokee's custom-built Ford Bronco XLT 4x4 read 5:45 when they pulled into the steak house parking lot.

Hokee drove his truck to the far end of the lot in order to keep the sides of his gleaming dent-free vehicle from being banged.

It was just pure bad luck for the detective duo that the busboy was just arriving to begin his evening shift when he noticed the shiny Bronco being parked on the far side of the lot. This drew his attention and he stopped and watched as Hokee helped Glory get out of the truck.

He remembered the beautiful woman from the other night and while he didn't know anything about her, the fact that he made her uncomfortable had registered on his mind. He was not expecting to see her again and for her to show up this soon after she had scurried out of the restaurant rang an alarm-bell in his awareness. The fact that she was with the detective who was instantly recognized was a double warning to his survival instincts. Sensing that their visit to the steak house was not simply to enjoy a relaxing dinner, he decided the prudent course of action would be to disappear. He had used a fake name and address to obtain the job so there was no way the detective would be able to find him through the restaurant employee register. Regardless of what his landlady might think it was time to hit the road. Good thing she didn't know his real name either, not that it would probably matter since he wouldn't be using any of the names used previously.

Tomorrow he would buy a used car and after making some excuse to his landlady would hit the road. By the time Hokee and the girl found out who he was, if they ever got that close, he would be long gone leaving no trail for anyone to follow. He had everything necessary to make a clean escape except for identity papers stored at home in his closet. The paperwork he would take care of tonight. He didn't want anybody else to know his new name, but sometimes you had to take a chance. The lady giving him a new name would know what the name was and people talk, everybody does. Maybe he might be able to do something about her memory after she provided him new documents.

Hokee and Glory did not notice the slender ponytailed man in black pants and white shirt slinking around the far side of the restaurant. By the time Hokee helped Glory out of the truck and they headed towards the restaurant's front door the busboy had disappeared. They were promptly seated by a window with a magnificent view as the hostess fussed over Hokee like he was a movie star. Glory had to suppress a grin as she knew firsthand just how little the Wolf man cared for the opinions of others or any kind of adulation. As far as she knew, the only opinion he really respected was that offered by his shaman friend, who she would love to meet but deemed highly unlikely, as Hokee kept his private life, well, private.

They were nearly through with their dinner when the manager stopped by their table to inquire after their meal which was excellent as usual. Hokee was devouring the end-cut of the prime rib roast, his favorite selection while Glory was happily doing the same to a slice cooked very rare. Hokee wondered why she even bothered having the meat cooked as it looked pretty bloody, but he decided to keep his opinion to himself.

As the manager was visiting their table Hokee asked him if he had a middle-aged man with a ponytail working as a busboy. "We're supposed to," he replied, "but he didn't show up for work tonight. He was supposed to be working the evening shift starting at six. He's only been working a few days but has been reliable until now."

Hokee saw the disappointment register in Glory's face. They were both hoping to end their search tonight at the restaurant.

"Would you give us his name and address?" Hokee asked. "I'd like to ask him a couple of questions."

The manager frowned as he replied, "Normally I wouldn't give out our employee's private information Hokee, but since it's you, his name is Holden Walker. I'll have to get his address from the office. I'll be right back," he continued while walking away quickly.

"Dammit," Hokee said after the manager left. "We got here just a little bit before six. I wonder if your busboy saw us drive into the parking lot and decided to take the night off?"

"That's certainly possible," Glory said. "He probably knows who you are by sight, and if he saw us together, with me coming back to the same restaurant after just eating here, he might have wondered what reason we could have for coming here for dinner. It isn't like this is the only good restaurant in town, is it?"

"No, you're right. We might have scared him off."

Just then the manager returned and handed Hokee a piece of paper with Holden's address. "Here's the address," he said while managing a smile. "I have a hunch this may not be his real name or address, but when it comes to busboys we usually just make sure they are clean, know how to dress and are respectful of our customers." It was obvious that he didn't like what he was doing but his admiration for Hokee persuaded him to go along with the big man's request.

"Thanks Jake," Hokee said with sincere appreciation for the manager's willingness to bend the rules. "I'm really grateful. Let me know if I can ever do you a favor sometime, please."

"Sure Hokee, I hope this helps whatever it is that you're trying to do. I just might take you up on that offer some day," he concluded with a real sincere smile this time before walking away.

"What do you say we go check out an address after we finish our dinner?" It sounded like a question but Hokee meant it as a suggestion which Glory interpreted correctly.

"I'd be scared to death going over there alone," she confessed. "However, you have a way of making a girl feel really protected and I would love to tag along," she said with a twinkle in her eyes. She was flirting shamelessly but if the big galoot wasn't going to be more aggressive it wasn't beyond the sophisticated New York reporter to take the lead. Hokee's response was the barest hint of a smile before finishing the remains of his dinner.

It didn't come as any surprise to Hokee that Holden's address turned out to be fake and with a little more investigation they determined that the name was also bogus before calling it a night.

"I am going to need a few hours to decide on my next course of action Glory," Hokee said before dropping her off at the Red Lion. "I'll give you a call after I figure out where to go from here."

Glory debated with herself about inviting Hokee up to her hotel room but there was something in his demeanor that warned her that this was not the time; perhaps later, but definitely not tonight. It was obvious the private investigator with dark brooding eyes had his mind elsewhere. She would have given a lot to know what he was thinking. Never in her wildest imagination would she have been able to guess Hokee's next action.

CHAPTER FOURTEEN

Getting Away

HELL, SHIT, DAMN! That fucken nosy reporter and mister private asshole investigator; together, going into his restaurant. That could only be bad news. She was just there the other night and he suspected that she was uneasy around him for some reason. Coming back this soon could only mean that he was a suspect in her mind and possibly the big Indian as well. Too damn bad. He was going to have to move sooner than he had expected.

He hadn't expected Pocatello's famous detective to have any interest in the robbery even though it had been mentioned prominently in the local papers. He was never worried about the Pocatello police or county sheriff's office. They couldn't catch a cold even if they went barefoot in a blizzard. That Indian guy was a whole different problem. He seemed to have some kind of sixth sense voodoo about things that ordinary people lacked. With him in the hunt it was time to hit the road.

Oh well. Shit. They wouldn't learn anything in the crappy restaurant that would do them any good and by the time they did get a handle on him, as if they ever could, he would be long gone. *Adios baby, hasta la vista and good bye.*

He had to get away sooner than expected and to hell with the landlady. He could feed her a line and chances were pretty good no one would ever find out she was his landlady. And even if they did what could she tell them? Nada. She didn't even know his real name.

His first impulse was to buy a car and just drive away, but soon changed his mind. He wouldn't even buy a car in Pocatello. He would just take the bus or train to Utah someplace; probably Salt Lake City or maybe Ogden. Buy a cheap car there. Maybe use some of the stolen bank cash plus write a check with his savings. That wouldn't be unusual. Besides the checking account was in another fake name and he had to drain that account anyway.

One of his useful talents was negotiating and finding a sleazy used car dealer willing to take an under-the-table cash transaction for a junker would be easy. Hell, it would be like erasing somebody's mind or making a salesperson miscount the change they returned. Now all he had to do was get some fake IDs and he was out of here.

In every large city, there is a seamy underbelly and while Pocatello would not be considered large by many accounts, its underbelly was probably equivalent to many of its larger sisters. This was due to a combination of factors.

First of all, it was a railroad crossing town with tracks going north and south plus east and west. It was a major switching hub that employed a lot of extra railroad workers to take railroad cars from east-west bound trains and reload them onto north-south bound trains and vice-versa. This meant that most railroad crews also changed here, meaning even more helpers were needed. Most of the porters and many of the switcher laborers were African-Americans, giving Pocatello one of the largest black populations in the Rocky Mountains.

Pocatello is very near Promontory Point where the Union Pacific railroad tracks running east and west met for the first time; known as the home of the famous Golden Spike. This had caused several thousand workers to be stranded in the area, mostly Chinese from the west coast branch, but also several Irish and Polish workers from the east coast line. Following the railroad gangs and their weekly pay checks were the hustlers, pimps, prostitutes and pick-pocket artists along with all the railroad cooks, big game hunters and boot-makers. They were all stranded in Pocatello as well.

Then there were the Indians from nearby reservations. They were attracted to the bright lights of civilization compared to the dreary res-life and were easy victims for the hustlers. This led to all kinds of violence and interracial disharmony.

Added to this volatile mix was the University and its population of farm boys and girls who although bright and industrious, were as naïve as the new born lambs many of the kids helped birth.

Walking the streets of any city provides an education that you can only get by walking those streets. If you walk all hours of the day and night while covering each section of town, you become familiar with the rhythms of each neighborhood. You know who is usually up late at night and who leaves for work early in the morning. You know where the good kids live and where nasty kids play. You know where the homeless hang out and where they feed. And ultimately you become familiar with the seamy side of town.

Every town also has its dark secret places where even the police are reluctant to venture. Some are even so uncivilized that the police are never seen there. They are seldom called, and if they are they do not respond. Pocatello does not have any neighborhoods quite this dark and ugly; but some areas are close. Here is the underbelly of society where you find the pimps, prostitutes and pickpockets and all those who prey on the healthy; and it is here that you find the person who can provide fake ID documents.

Victoria Alquest, (Vicky to everyone who knew her), had been an exotic dancer who often moonlighted in woman's oldest profession whenever she was offered the right proposition. She used a stage name Crystal for her dance act and the johns she serviced. Women in her profession often use fake names for a variety of reasons and this can necessitate the use of forged papers. Vicky got burned once by using a purchased ID that had been poorly made, so she taught herself how to make better looking papers.

Her friends in the same business discovered that Vicky had this talent and started using her services. As the demand for fake papers grew so did her talent and accomplishments. By the time our thief came needing her services she produced some of the most authentic papers in the west. You could get driver licenses, birth certificates, passports or any other kind of paper, if you could pay the price. Her talent was known throughout the dark side of Pocatello although you never met her without first being vetted by several of her closest associates. Having traveled in the dark underbelly of Pocatello most of his life, our thief easily passed through her checkpoints. All he needed was a new name which was easily found. He was almost on his way to a new life.

CHAPTER FIFTEEN

Moonlight Walk

Driving home after dropping Glory off at her hotel, Hokee was preoccupied with his late evening plans. Whenever he was stumped on a case he reverted back to the time he lived as an apprentice shaman. Why-ay'-looh had taught his young acolyte how to get centered in order to find order and harmony in the universe. Of all the techniques and ceremonies Hokee knew to achieve this state of balance his favorite method was a nighttime walk in the lava fields. A good sweat helped unravel tangled thoughts or to tune into other realms where the minds of others might be found, but solitude in the lava fields opened his mind for other mental possibilities.

Walking through the lava fields in broad daylight is considered foolhardy by many and dangerous by everyone. Walking across the forbidden landscape in the dark was considered insanity. The uneven texture of the broken fields contained thin crusts that would break underfoot sending the unwary into deep pits lined with jagged rocks like spears. There were loose rocks everywhere that turned or rolled under a person's weight, throwing them onto jagged outcroppings or dumping even the most careful hiker into a deep crevice capable of breaking legs, arms and ribs. These dangers prevented most sane individuals from attempting any kind of trek across the plains, even in daylight. Hokee was not of the mindset to be bothered by what most people considered sane. For him, these late evening walks through the treacherous black rocks were a form of meditation. The focus and attention required to navigate safely through this dark hell sharpened his mind. Every time he paused for a break, images and thoughts relating to the problem that had him stumped flooded his brain providing avenues of exploration applicable to the case.

Thoughtful preparation was Hokee's prelude for a successful walk. The evening walk began with an hour of meditation followed by a cleansing sweat in his custom-made lodge. With a combination of sage and cedar incense-infused steam from pure water, the heat waves carried him to the outer edge of consciousness where pure thought originates. It is here in the distant absolute dimensions of time and space that Hokee's mind became empty of all previous thought.

For him the preparation ritual for this nighttime walk was another form of meditation. His clothing was extremely important. His pants were made of heavy canvas difficult to tear. High-topped leather shoes had extra inch-thick soles of rubber that would withstand the sharp-edged rock and were great for gripping the uneven terrain. A thick cotton and nylon long-sleeved shirt and tough leather gloves completed his outfit. Hanging from his waist was a Colt 45 with extra clips snapped onto the holster belt. While the lava fields were hostile for humans they were the home for many forms of wildlife including bobcats, an occasional badger and even cougars all capable of inflicting serious damage if cornered.

Grabbing a thick, six-foot long oak walking stick and a waterproof four-cell flashlight, Hokee signaled to Shilah that they were ready for their adventure. The ever-alert wolf had observed his master's preparations and knowing what they meant, he was anxious to begin. The wolf seemed to come alive on these hikes through the lava plains. Rabbits, weasels, ground squirrels, snakes, antelope and even coyotes roamed the area, providing the carnivore with a smorgasbord of scents and the opportunity for many exciting chases. Hokee let his friend roam freely knowing that the wolf would more than likely flush out any animal that posed a threat. Never in his previous journeys through the plains had he been required to shoot his pistol, but having it available seemed prudent. Better to be prepared and not need it than find yourself cornered by a frightened wildcat without your gun.

The canyon wall twenty yards west of Hokee's house and directly opposite the fountain was curved, hiding a crack unobservable unless you were standing in exactly the right spot. The crack was barely wide enough for Hokee to squeeze through turning sideways while working his way to the top of the plains. Coming out of the dark crevice, he was faced with the challenges that had led him to make this difficult and dangerous hike.

There was a partial moon in a bright starlit sky with just enough light to make the distorted shadows indistinguishable from the dark lava rock. The flashlight was an option, but it restricted his vision to the narrow tunnel of light while requiring him to focus his attention on the light beam. He preferred to let his senses and intuition guide his feet. Thinking about the walk, instead of just being, could prove fatal. With every step, there was the possibility of landing on the thin crust from a lava bubble that could send him plummeting into a hole with jagged sharp rocks below. Stepping on a rock that could break off or roll would send him flying downward. On one of his previous walks he had stepped into a hole that caught his boot, and it took him hours to work free without damaging his leg. If he were to get stuck or seriously injured anywhere on his walk, the possibility of being found and rescued before the lava plains claimed his body were practically zero. Hokee knew all this, which is what made this particular form of meditation so appealing. Without impeccable attention to his senses and surroundings his walk would most likely end in disaster. He had to fully trust his intuition and inner guidance in order to proceed safely.

In previous excursions, he had mapped the terrain that was close around his house, so tonight he had chosen to extend his exploration into uncharted territory. Trekking across the lava fields is not a straight-line maneuver in any direction. One step is up and to the left with your next step down two feet to the right, or up another foot further to the left. You are constantly going up and down, left and right when crossing the lava fields stretching for miles in every direction. Although he had explored the lava fields for many miles in every direction, Hokee had not found any other open area that approached his canyon in size. He had discovered several smaller openings where animals of several varieties had staked a territorial claim. On this outing he stayed clear of these known valleys, hoping to avoid an unpleasant encounter. He wasn't worried about his or Shilah's safety but he didn't want any kind of confrontation where he had to kill an animal if it could be avoided. After all, this was their home and he was the interloper.

Moonlight excursions have historically provided man with haunting, frightening and terrifying experiences. Distance, color, space, time and shape can all become distorted. Time seems to lose relevance turning into infinity. Seconds become hours and hours can seem like seconds. Not only are the eyes fooled by the moon's seductive, mysterious lighting, but the other senses are equally distorted. The faintest sound can be amplified many times sounding like a small rocket coming from an indistinguishable direction. You begin hearing mundane sounds, such as the sole of a boot scraping across a jagged lava rock that sounds more like fireworks on the 4th of July. And then there are those faint little crackling sounds that are more like a sigh or whispered murmur that seem to come from every direction. The old Indians used to say these sounds were the spirits of their dead ancestors buried under the lava. Hokee thought it might be the lava fields shrinking in the cool night air. Whatever the source for all of those eerie nighttime sounds, it was not a place for the faint of heart.

Meanwhile, your nose isn't left out of the night air's plethora of scents. Heat from the sun gives the lava field a uniform scent of blistered rock during the day. As the hot rocks cool down after sunset this scent is replaced by what seems to be hundreds of different scents. Animal spore and hair are the most prevalent, with each species contributing their own unique smells. And the dry grasses, scrub bush and chilled air all combine to overwhelm the senses. No wonder that Shilah loved these moonlight walks since it is canine paradise.

An hour and a half into their walk Hokee found himself in territory he had never trekked. Without any warning, he found himself in a very deep, narrow crevice comprised mostly of dangerously sharp edges. The lava plain appeared to be at least eighteen feet above his head with no obvious method of ascent. The crevice held him in a tight vice-like grip, making it impossible to turn around or even reach the flashlight in one of his side pockets. His solid oak walking stick had become useless and had to be abandoned. The deep, narrow fissure blanked out almost all available light that made it nearly impossible to see. Lesser men would panic at this stage risking entangling themselves in the jagged rocks so that escaping could be impossible. Hokee simply closed his eyes and relaxed, to let his mental intuition and primal senses work out an escape plan.

There was never any doubt in his thoughts that he wouldn't get out of this tight bind. It was, in fact, when all forward movement became totally restricted that the answer to his questions regarding the ponytailed busboy leaped into his mind. It was so obvious he almost groaned, while being filled with gratitude for this insight. Normally he would have given himself a back-pat for another successful hike, but under the circumstances the impulse for self-congratulations was postponed. Now all he had to do was get back home without wrenching a leg or breaking his arms. Sensing that there was more maneuvering room below his knees, Hokee slowly began wiggling himself down the rock walls. The heavy canvas clothes helped to keep his body from being completely torn up and inch by inch he squirmed downwards, eventually shredding his clothing in the process.

Finally, Hokee was flat on his stomach with sufficient lateral room for him to reach the pocket containing his flashlight.

The light revealed an almost level plane extending about two feet on both sides and running off into the distance beyond the reach of the flashlight beam. It was only about eighteen inches in height but sufficient for Hokee to crab crawl. The question was then should he keep on going forward or turn around and try to retrace his path. From his present position, it would be difficult to turn around plus trying to follow the exact route that brought him here would be very difficult if not impossible. Still, he had made it this far so theoretically he should be able to go back the same way. On the other hand, he could just keep on going and hope for the best. The crevice might open up providing an escape route to the top of the plains or it could eventually squeeze down to a point where he could not move forward or backward. He had no idea where Shilah was; probably up on top of the plain somewhere chasing rabbits or looking for his master. It didn't matter as the wolf would be of no help in his present situation and might even be a distraction. After taking a drink of water from his thermos and considering the possibilities, Hokee decided to go forward; somehow the thought of retracing his steps seemed too much like being defeated. He might get stuck and lose his life, but it would be on his own terms, not out of fear.

He squirmed and wiggled forward inches at a time using his elbows to lift and drag his body over the jagged surface. His left hand was holding the light as he used his right hand to help ease his body past the snags that constantly grabbed at his clothes. After what seemed like hours, the crevice narrowed and grew thinner making forward progress almost impossible. Hokee was no longer able to reach his canteen for water and was barely able to squeeze ahead inch by inch. Frustrated he was beginning to think he had made a mistake by proceeding forward rather than turning around and retracing his steps when he had the chance what by now seemed like hours in the past. He paused to catch his breath and consider his plight. As he relaxed his mind and body he became aware of a new sensation.

The confining lava crevice he was squeezed into had a distinct odor different than the rock and dust he had been inhaling for the past few hours. It took a few seconds before he recognized the smells.

Mountain cat.

And water.

Hokee was disappointed in himself for taking so long to recognize the scent. Living with Shilah meant that cats naturally avoided the area around his home and Hokee seldom ran into the feline species during his investigative work. Also, wild cats give off a more pungent tangy odor than the domestic variety and it was a wild cat scent that Hokee now detected. Since he only recently detected the odor it meant that the source was somewhere ahead. It was a "good news, bad news" situation. The good news was that the tight crevice he was in probably opened up if he could squirm ahead for a few more yards. The bad news was that he was probably headed into the cat's den. The present tight constrictions meant that there was no way to reach the gun down at his waist. If this was a cougar, which was likely, and if the cougar had a cub which was very possible, the mother would be ferocious in protecting her young. If Hokee crawled head first into a mother cougar protecting her cub, one swipe of the cat's sharp claws could rip off half his face. Given his situation there really was no option. His only hope was to move ahead and hope for the best. Now he thought, where was Shilah when he was really needed?

While pausing to consider his next moves, Hokee thought about the ponytailed man who had paralyzed Officer Morden's arm with a single touch. He had been preparing his mind, knowing that when he met this man face-to-face he would need all of his shamanistic training in order to combat whatever powers the man possessed. This same training would be tested now in the minutes ahead if he came face-to-face with a cougar in her den.

Could he summon his totems to help him under these circumstances? Perhaps this was the real reason for his moonlit walk in the lava fields -- a chance to exercise powers he had almost forgotten.

Snaking forward over sharp jagged spikes, Hokee was now shredding both his clothes and skin. He needed the crevice to widen soon or he could bleed to death from the sheer number of tears in his flesh. What did the Chinese call it, "death by a thousand cuts", or was it the Japanese? God, he was getting dopey and weak from the loss of blood. The smell of his own blood mixed with cat scent grew steadily stronger as he struggled forward. He could feel himself growing weaker as his blood flowed from several deep wounds. He found himself wishing he could wrap up the cuts to stop them from bleeding and drink some water to help restore his blood supply. He was becoming afraid of stopping to rest, believing that he could never get his body moving again. He thought about his first trek into the lava fields many years ago, when he was on a vision quest to heal his troubled soul. Then, as now, he was bloody and sore, thirsty and about to give up, but somehow he persevered and discovered the cave that became his home. Believing that his fate was not to die deep underground, alone and forever lost to the world above he kept pushing himself to the extent of complete exhaustion. It was just when all of his physical resources were completely depleted that the bottom fell out of the crack he was following. With one last grunting heave forward the upper half of his body was now dangling out in black space.

CHAPTER SIXTEEN

The Cavern

Hokee used his flashlight to explore the open space he was hanging in to discover there was a gap of about twenty feet between his location and the continuation of his ledge visible on the other side of the opening. He was not surprised to see a mother cougar across the void crouched on a ledge protecting her cub. Shining his light downwards he could see water fifteen feet below. It appeared to be a stream although it was flowing very silently with barely a ripple on the surface. The quiet river sliding by in the black lava rock gave the cavern a spooky, other worldly feel; like walking through a cemetery at midnight under a half-moon partly shielded by clouds. The river looked like liquid mercury, better known as quicksilver in southeastern Idaho.

For uncounted centuries, this underground river had worn the sides and bottom of its lava river bed smooth reminding Hokee of Navajo Tears; a glistening, smooth, black rock found in the Arizona desert near the Navajo reservation. The silent flowing river below Hokee looked sinister with its unknown depth that made it look like a ghostly apparition. Hokee's flashlight could not penetrate the smooth surface which reflected light around the cavern as though it were a mirror.

The cavern seemed to be about twenty feet high and roughly fifty feet in diameter forming a crude oval. The air was cooler than the crevice Hokee had been squirming through and slightly damp from the river, making the cat odor even more pronounced.

The rock wall below Hokee and the water was like all of the other surfaces he had encountered, cracked and buckled with protruding jagged edges.

Descending to the water would be an easy climb but then what? He had no desire to confront the mother cougar on the other side, assuming he could cross the water but he really didn't want to kill the cat. On the other hand, staying put was not an option and he really needed to pay attention to his bleeding. Using his arms as braces against the sides of his prison, Hokee pulled his legs out of the crevice he had been crawling in and climbed down the wall towards the water, watching for the cat's reaction as he moved. Five feet above the water a protrusion jutted out just enough to enable him to sit down dangling his legs over the edge. The cat was crouched ready to pounce but was holding back watching for a more immediate threat.

Relieved at being able to finally move freely Hokee placed his light in a nook to free both hands. Off came his shirt and using a knife he cut off long strips to bind his cuts. In between wraps he drained the canteen of water knowing that he could replenish it from the stream running silently below his feet. Occasionally he would look at the big cat sitting on the ledge across the stream ten feet above to see what she might be planning. Apparently, she was waiting to see what kind of threat Hokee posed. The big cat was crouched and ready to spring but Hokee doubted she would try and jump the stream; on the other hand, he didn't want to give the protective mother any more reason to feel threatened. He was about as close to the mother cat as he could get without provoking an attack. After draining his canteen and binding his wounds, Hokee could feel his strength returning. It was time to figure out his next move.

There appeared to be three choices although in practical terms he really had only one choice. Hours later he belatedly realized there were really four choices.

Returning back through the narrow crevice that brought him here was a possibility but Hokee wasn't at all sure he would be able to survive the tortuous crawl. His ragged, torn, bloody body couldn't take much more abuse.

Upon examining the cavern he was in, he could see that the silently running river had at times carried considerably more water. The water had worn smooth the sides and the roof of the channel in which it was flowing. There was a good four feet of clearance between the river and the rock ceiling above. Could this be the same river that ran in the back of Hokee's cave and was it possible to ride the river back home? Surrounded by black lava rock and with the river reflecting his light beam it was impossible to see the bottom of the river. Could he take the river back to his cave? Were there any waterfalls or hazards along the way that could impede his progress? The water was undoubtedly very cold and he wouldn't survive if forced to spend many hours surrounded by ice cold water.

The river bottom was undoubtedly as smooth as the sides. If the river was not too deep it might be possible to walk along the bottom, but even if he could wade in the river, losing his footing was a distinct possibility. In that event, he might be swept along to a certain death.

The third possibility required Hokee to cross the river. Undoubtedly the big mountain lion poised on the ledge over his head had an entrance to the cavern on the other side of the river. In order to find this opening he would have to kill the mother cat and possibly her cub. Killing such a beautiful creature was not a pleasant thought although dying here deep underground was even less pleasant to contemplate. If Hokee knew for sure he would be able to squeeze through the cave opening on the other side of the river that provided access for the mountain lion, he would have seriously considered removing the cat. Since he had to get into the river either to follow it hopefully back home or to reach the other side he decided to let fate make the decision.

Hokee carefully made his way to the river's edge then stuck his hand in to gauge its temperature and speed.

Cold. Numbing cold. Paralyzing cold.

Fortunately, the river's flow was gentle. The channel's ceiling was much higher above the river than it had appeared to be from his previous perch. Knowing that the lava plane was basically flat he didn't expect there to be any significant waterfalls or rapids between his current position and his home cave, maybe two or three miles downstream.

If the river would carry him home, he could be treating his wounds in a matter of minutes. And if so, he would have a whole new backdoor to his cave and the possibilities for future exploration seemed endless. He was suddenly filled with enthusiasm and confidence. The apprehensions which had seemed so debilitating only minutes earlier faded along with the aches and pains previously paralyzing his body.

An essential survival item stowed in one of his many pants pockets was a Mylar thermal blanket. This thin three-inch square package only a quarter of an inch thick held a six-foot square sheet of mirrored Mylar capable of retaining over ninety-eight percent of a person's body heat when properly employed. However, Hokee had no intention of using it as a thermal blanket.

The only spot within sight providing a reasonable place to sit was the protrusion he had sat on while bandaging his legs. He climbed back up and sitting down began unlacing his boots. Off came the boots and socks followed by his belt and pants. His gun was going to be a problem and he didn't want it with his boots as he needed all the flotation he could get. He finally decided to just leave it on the rocky shelf where he was sitting. He wouldn't need it in the river and if he failed he would never need it again anyway.

If his hunch was right, he could always come back later and retrieve the gun. It was one of his favorites.

Setting his clothes to the side, he unfolded the Mylar and placed it on his lap. The boots went in the center side by side with his socks and folded pants on top followed by his empty canteen and shirt remnants. The Mylar was carefully folded around his package using the reverse paper-funnel fold (the fold people often used to make funnels out of folded paper). Doubling over the top fold three times there was sufficient bulk for his belt to provide a tight cinch. Hokee now had a homemade float. The air trapped in his boots, canteen and clothes would provide a certain amount of buoyancy and hopefully the air would not escape before reaching his cave.

This was all the physical preparation he imagined making; everything else depended on his shaman training.

He already knew that the river water was very cold. Under normal circumstances it would drain the body of heat within a few minutes resulting in hypothermia. Before that you begin hallucinating, muscles spasm, then locking the body's joints, causing the body to shut down. All the blood then goes to your brain which sends you into a coma, from which it is almost impossible to recover. Shamanic training includes a meditation and breathing exercise designed to generate excess body heat. Devoted practitioners are capable of being left naked outside in freezing weather and then drying a wet, freezing blanket thrown over their shoulders. Hokee had never been subjected to this test and had not practiced breathing this heavy in many years. Could he summon back the skills required without practice?

The chilled air inside of the cavern was already causing his body to sprout goose bumps the size of rain drops. Closing his eyes Hokee began humming an ancient chant to set the cells in his body vibrating. Once he could feel the vibration in his toes he began the long, slow, deep breathing he had learned from Silver Fox. Within a few minutes, sweat was beginning to run down his forehead and cheeks. While maintaining his slow shamanic breathing Hokee opened his eyes and gingerly made his way down to the water carrying his float in one hand and his flashlight in the other.

At the water's edge, he took one last deep breath while looking briefly at the cougar perched above. The big cat was still tense but seemed to have settled back with a curious look watching the strange man. Holding the float out in front of his body with both hands, Hokee jumped into the river without giving himself another chance to reconsider.

CHAPTER SEVENTEEN

The Walk Home

Cold....Cold.....Icy cold. Goose bumps peppered his body like small bubble-wrap blisters and his muscles clenched into tight knots.

The cold shock almost paralyzed him, driving all of the air from his body in an explosive burst as he sank to the river's bottom.

Although he had raised his outer temperature by shamanic breathing the pores of his skin were open, allowing the cold to invade his body at a faster rate. His battered and bruised body wasn't responding to the mental command he normally exercised over the physical. This was partly due to his infrequent practice but mostly due to fatigue and injury. He sensed that without the shamanic preparation he would already be a dead man.

Before jumping, Hokee had bent his knees slightly in order to act as shock absorbers if the river turned out to be shallow. Although the river was only about five feet deep he was almost totally submerged before his bent legs came in contact with the river bottom cushioning his descent. He knew that the water was probably between 45 and 50 degrees Fahrenheit but it felt like 25 sucking the heat out of his injured body at an alarming rate. He knew he had just used up a great deal of good luck as he stood up, gasping for air and filling his lungs with the cool cavern air tinged with the ripe taste of cougar.

He had managed to keep his flashlight above the water and using both hands pulled the float into his chest while raising his legs to see if his homemade float would keep him above water. It seemed to be working, although he had to completely submerge the entire package in order to get sufficient buoyancy for floating. Since he could stand upright with the water only a little over mid-chest, he didn't need to use the float. He could walk on the river's bottom which would help burn up some calories restoring much needed body heat. Even walking, without some extra precautions he could die of hypothermia if he didn't get out of the river within a couple of hours.

The river was flowing gently providing a little push which allowed Hokee to walk without slipping on the smooth rock bottom. The lack of sunshine had prohibited the growth of moss or algae which would have made his footing treacherous. The lack of any sound was encouraging as it meant that there were no significant waterfalls or rapids ahead posing an additional hazard.

Shining his light for a final glance at the big cat still perched on the ledge overhead, he silently saluted the protective mother before facing the river to begin walking downstream. He never once gave thought to the fact that he was totally disoriented and did not know in which direction his home was located. He just started walking, letting the water push him along saving his tired and bruised muscles while preserving energy. Once he found a smooth walking gait Hokee renewed his shamanic breathing to keep the cold water from draining his natural resources. Circulating each breath throughout his lower body rapidly raised the temperature of his legs and chest. It is well understood by the yogis in the Far East that our breath has nearly unlimited power. They teach that there is sufficient energy in one breath to last a person an entire lifetime. In Hokee's own practice he had trained himself to stop breathing for over thirty minutes. Once he was over the initial cold water shock and learned the river's hidden secrets of depth and speed, Hokee was able to relax his mind and focus on restoring his body's normal rhythms.

Playing his light along the walls of his underground passage Hokee wondered what had caused this underground channel. The river made many changes in direction and although some of the river bends were very sharp the river still barely made a sound. In studying the water flow around one such bend he discovered that over time the water had formed grooves in each bend giving the river a quiet laminar flow much like you see in those silent waterfalls in many upscale shopping malls.

After walking for over an hour Hokee stopped for a breath and to consider his situation. There was no way of knowing how far he had traveled from his house originally but his best guess was between four and five miles in a straight line. No telling how far he had crawled or how many turns he had made in the narrow crevice before reaching the underground vault with the cougar's den.

With the many turns made by the river it was equally impossible to know how many miles the river traveled from the cavern to his house, assuming it was the same river. Surely there could not be two underground rivers this close together in the same lava field, could there? If this was not his river he was really screwed. If it was his river, how many miles before he reached the cave and home?

He had been underground a little over six hours. It was now daylight outside and Shilah would be wondering what happened to his master? While Hokee could usually go for a couple of days without sleep or normal rest the recent experiences had sapped his strength. He was nearly spent but there was no possibility of quitting. To quit was to die. His only alternative was to continue pressing forward. It was with this thought that he had a sudden mental flash of a possible tragedy. Where was forward?

What if he was going in the wrong direction? Suppose his house was upriver from the underground cavern. Was this even possible?

He had brought no compass and had absolutely zero sense of direction. While crawling in the jagged fissure he knew there had been several twists and turns. He had no idea how far he had actually scrambled and crawled before reaching the cavern. He really had no idea in which direction the cavern lay with respect to his cave. In addition, he had no idea as to the actual course of this river. It could travel several miles towards the Snake River before turning back towards the mountains in the east. Presumably his cave was somewhere between the water's source and the Snake River; but initially he had assumed that this river was flowing south while the Snake River actually flowed to the north. Everything seemed counterintuitive.

Hokee had been so confident originally in assuming that he had been crawling downriver, but suppose he had been crawling upriver the whole time? In that case, he was walking away from his cave towards an unknown destination.

These were sobering thoughts and Hokee knew his life now depended on making the correct decision. If he continued following the river's flow for another one, two or possibly even three or four more hours without reaching his cave he would know for certainty that he had chosen the wrong direction. Already spent and without any food it was highly unlikely that he would be able to turn around and walk back upriver to the cougar's cavern and however far his cave was in the other direction. However, if he turned back now he just might make it to his cave if it was upriver. What to do?

Think. There must be some clue. Nothing came to mind and Hokee knew he had no recourse. He had to meditate and get into a shaman state. That was the only way he could make the correct decision. The decision and his life were going to be entirely up to his spirit guides.

Hokee carefully opened his float in order to remove his shoes. Balancing everything to keep if from falling into the river meant he had to hold his float and most of its contents between his teeth while removing the shoe laces. He carefully repacked everything, refolding the float. Fortunately, his flashlight was waterproof so it didn't have to go into the float. Tying his shoelaces together he had a string over six feet in length. He fastened one end to the belt holding his float together and the other end was tied to his wrist. When everything was secured, Hokee forced the flashlight under his belt before turning it off. The blackness surrounded him immediately. He still closed his eyes and began a ten-minute cycle of deep breathing. After getting his breath totally regulated and his body fully oxygenated Hokee sank to the river's bottom releasing the float which tugged at his wrist.

The peace was incredible. The only sounds were the beating of his heart, the whisper of river water gliding around his body and the flow of blood coursing through major arteries. Hokee's favorite spot to meditate was the lonely rock outcropping captured in the mosaic tile work in his living room floor and the picture on his dining room wall. It was an actual spot high above the Arizona desert not too many miles from where his mother had taken her own life. Hokee went to that spot now in his mind.

Hokee felt the water flow around his body, but even that soon disappeared. All alone on the top of his rock he felt the sun warming his body while inhaling the warm mountain air carrying a hint of cedar carried by the breeze from the valley below. Hokee watched a hawk circling below while it hunted for a meal before putting his mind towards solving his current problem. Which way to walk in the river?

Surprisingly, it turned out to be the wind that gave him the answer. He had expected to see his wolf that normally came and provided an answer to his quest. But today it was the wind. Carrying the subtle hint of cedar, the wind reminded him that there was no hint of cat smell in his cave. That could only mean that his cave was upriver from the cavern. Otherwise the river current with its small breeze would carry a hint of the wild cat down to his home.

This was a "good news, bad news" situation. He now knew which direction to go in order to return home; unfortunately, it was all upriver in the other direction.

Standing up and resuming normal breathing Hokee retrieved his flashlight to check the time. He was shocked to discover that he had been on the river bottom for a little over sixty minutes; a new personal best. His shamanic breathing meditations always left him feeling refreshed and relaxed. Today's session was no different even though it had been conducted in cold water at the bottom of a river. Facing upriver Hokee began trudging homeward against the current. The only way he knew how to survive the long struggle ahead was to put his body on remote control and focus his attention entirely on the moment of now. Breathing in, breathing out, left foot, right foot; all time is happening right now. This moment, this step; there is no other time.

While living in the moment walking upriver the cat cavern's sudden appearance came as a surprise. Going against the current caused the water to make soft rippling sounds as it flowed around his body. This plus the light alerted the cat to his coming and passing. Hokee noted the cat in passing but his relaxed demeanor and focused attention barely caused the cougar to stir. It watched him slide pass with barely a glance.

Although his body was torn, battered, bruised and his energy depleted, Hokee trudged on one step at a time. In that quiet spot beyond our mind and its incessant chatter lies the center of our being and this is where Hokee called home. From this source of being Hokee felt connected to everything in the universe. He was the water in the river. He was the lava rock channel in which the river flowed. He was even the cat and her cub as well as the scent they gave off which is what was saving his life. Here he could observe his body struggling to stay upright while slugging away upriver against the current. There was no doubt that his body would continue to function until he was safely back in his cave. How much damage would need to be repaired, if repair could even be accomplished, was another thing entirely. In this case, there was no other choice. Proceed forward or die. The homeward trek might be the end of his life, but that was still to be determined. At this moment, he chose to live and that meant driving his body beyond its endurance. One more step, and then one more step, and then one more step.

There is no "time" in the moment of "now"; so Hokee had no idea how long he had been walking upstream when he became conscious of the river channel getting wider and the ceiling receding ever higher. His senses all came alive and Hokee knew from some inner awareness that he was entering the back of his cave. The edge of a wall he had constructed to enclose his bedroom appeared in the light, removing any lingering doubt he might have had. Hokee was home.

Dropping his float bundle at the river's edge Hokee stumbled into his home and went outside to check on Shilah. Glancing at his watch he noted the time was well past one in the afternoon. He had been underground for nearly twelve hours. It seemed like twelve years. Shilah was standing guard at the front door and jumping up, stood on his hind legs putting his fore legs on Hokee's shoulders nearly knocking the weary traveler down as he began licking his master's face. After ruffling the hair on his wolf's head Hokee went back inside, stripping his wet shorts as he walked. While Shilah watched, he took a long hot shower letting his muscles soak in the heat.

Before starting his shower Hokee had begun to fill an inground hot tub with warm water into which he added a bundle of special herbs. A mixture of sage, cedar, fenugreek, liverwort, sandalwood, dandelion root, various minerals and salts all mixed with peppermint and lavender essential oils. A fifteen-minute soak in this old shaman's healing mixture would speed the healing of the cuts that laced his entire body. After soaking and drying off he made a light paste of the peppermint and lavender essential oils with powdered clay and minerals which he rubbed into each tear of his skin. Satisfied with his medications Hokee flopped on his bed ready for rest.

The final thought in his mind just before drifting into a deep slumber was that he knew how to identify the ponytailed user of doppelgangers.

Tomorrow.

CHAPTER EIGHTEEN

The Hunt Begins

Hokee slept until early evening before dragging his weary body out of bed for another hot shower. Sitting on a stone bench built into the shower stall, Hokee let the steaming hot water run down his body for several minutes soaking in the heat and reviving aching muscles while speeding up circulation to his damaged skin. After several minutes in the shower while doing his shaman breathing, Hokee stepped out feeling alive and capable of functioning; maybe not at 100 percent but 50 percent of Wolf was better than a 100 percent of the average person.

Firing up an indoor grill built into his countertop Hokee threw on a steak while whisking four eggs for an omelet. After shredding some sharp cheddar, he diced a few mushrooms and some yellow onion. Melting some butter in a well-seasoned cast iron skillet, Hokee added the onions and mushrooms letting them get tender then turned his steak, putting a few dabs of butter on the seared top letting the butter melt into the meat. He added the seasoned egg mixture to the skillet with onions and mushrooms before putting another few dabs of butter on his steak. When the omelet was ready to turn Hokee flipped it over expertly then added the cheese before folding it onto his plate. Forking his steak next to the eggs Hokee carried his plate over to the table where he had already placed a half loaf of fresh bread and dish of butter.

While taking his time enjoying breakfast, lunch or dinner depending on how you considered those meals, Hokee thought about his nocturnal journey and the insight acquired concerning the ponytailed busboy. The only real clue he had to work with was the coffin. True he was looking for a small, sunken-chested older man who wore his blondish streaked hair in a ponytail, but trying to find that single person in Pocatello was like looking for white rabbits in a snow storm. It takes pure blind luck to stumble on a rabbit hiding under a bush in falling snow which deadens the sound making it hard to startle game. There is nothing to flush the rabbit out of its hiding spot and the same principle applies to finding one person among thousands walking the streets of a big city. It's just too easy to hide long hair under a cap and wear clothing which alters your appearance. The person he was looking for could appear to be a young boy or old man from a distance and it would be impossible to get a close-up view of every single individual in town. But the coffin he had found came from a mortuary or funeral home. It was obviously a low-end factory model probably purchased by the county to bury their homeless indigents or a really poor family unable to afford the upscale metal boxes. If he could find the mortuary that had provided the coffin buried near Lake Henry, there was a good chance they could identify the person who ultimately ended up with the box. The bread truck robber probably never expected the coffin to be discovered, at least not until long after he had left the area.

Hokee thought about calling Glory. Now that he was starting to feel human again thoughts of the beautiful well-dressed journalist from New York stirred his blood making him wonder about his real motives for thinking about inviting her to join in a search for the culpable funeral home. He was long past the fear of rejection, but still felt shy around females that attracted his attention. It was difficult to find the correct words to express his thoughts without feeling foolish. He didn't want to appear presumptuous, yet still wanted to let the woman know he was interested in more than idle conversation. He was pretty sure that Glory found him attractive as did most of the females in his life, still how was one to know how much of their supposed attraction was real and how much was faked in order to manipulate his emotions? That was a conundrum he was never able to solve. His usual method for dealing with flirtatious females was to ignore their signals by pretending to be uninterested. The problem with Glory was that his interest was real and he was pretty sure she already knew it.

Much as he would love to see Glory he didn't want her to see him in his present condition. Although he was feeling nearly human, his body and arms still showed significant damage although his herbal medications were speeding the healing process. It would be better if she didn't see him until he had a couple more days to heal. Hopefully she would still be around town by the time he felt ready to see her again. It wouldn't hurt to give her a call to see if a little persuasion might induce her to stay around a few more days.

Checking his watch to make sure it wasn't too late Hokee called the Red Lion and asked for Glory's room.

"Hi, this is Glory." Her voice was resonant and soft, throaty yet crystal clear.

"This is Hokee, Glory, hope I'm not interrupting anything important?" God, that sounded so lame.

"Oh, hi Hokee. I was starting to wonder what happened to you. I tried calling your office today and no one seemed to know where you were."

"Yeah, well I found myself in a tight squeeze that took me a while to work out." Hokee was aware of the double meaning but knew Glory wouldn't get it and he was not about to tell her of his narrow brush with death. He would have to find some explanation for the damage to his body if it couldn't be hidden.

"I've got an idea about how to proceed with our investigation," he said including Glory as part of the team. He wanted her to participate primarily for the company but didn't want her to think that was his motivation. He needn't have bothered because the girl from New York didn't just get off Ellis Island yesterday and was way ahead of the Wolf man. On the other hand, she was delighted that he had called and equally anxious to see the handsome detective.

Hokee had paused after making his announcement about proceeding, waiting to see if she had any comment.

"Well, what is this idea or am I supposed to guess?" she said with a smile in her voice.

"Well, I can't go into it at the moment and it's going to take me a little time to sort everything out. I was calling to make sure you would still be available in a couple of days to do some sleuthing?"

"Sleuthing? Oh good heavens, you mean like real detectives and stuff?" she said laughing outright.

"Well yeah, sort of, yeah," he responded. "I really want to find this busboy and thought you might like to see how we fellas in the sticks do real investigating."

"How can I turn down such an exciting opportunity? A chance to watch the famous Pocatello P.I. do his sleuthing in person. When are we going to be able to meet?"

"How about I call you tomorrow with a definite schedule? By then I should have my life organized."

"I can't imagine your life ever being disorganized," she responded.

"Perhaps one day I'll tell you about a cougar and her cub living by an underground river," he said as a major tease. He knew this would spark her curiosity and how this all related to his disorganized life would drive her crazy.

"Hey, you can't leave it at that," she responded speaking faster and louder than normal. "What has a cougar got to…"

"Look, I have to go now" Hokee interrupted cutting her off. I'll call you tomorrow, I promise, and maybe we can do dinner or something."

Reading a lot into the word "something", Glory relented knowing it wouldn't do her any good to push harder. "Okay, I'll just have to wait, but then I get the whole dump Hokee." She wanted him to remember that she was a journalist looking for a story even if she was personally interested.

She heard "Good night, Glory," in the receiver as her phone went dead.

Replacing the handset in the cradle she wondered what to make of Hokee's call. She was pretty sure he didn't need her help tracking down the busboy, but on the other hand it was a little difficult to believe he was actually interested in her personally, even with the dinner. While she had felt some definite interest in her from the big man, everything she knew about him suggested that he was a lone wolf, (oh God, another wolf connection), without a desire for female companionship. Still, he had invited her to his home for dinner, and admitted that she was the first person to ever step into his house. Maybe there was more than a spark of interest on his part. She would have to be careful and not be too aggressive as was her normal style. This was a man she was definitely interested in getting to know much more intimately, and not just to advance her career.

CHAPTER NINETEEN

Sleuthing

Satisfied that the reporter from New York was going to be hanging around for a few more days Hokee decided to relax and reward himself for still being alive with a double shot of St. Magdalene. As the smoky amber-colored liquid began warming him inside out Hokee began visualizing his actions for the next few days. While contemplating various activities involving both his friends at the sheriff's office and numerous funeral homes around the area, images of Glory and what she might be like in more intimate situations continued to intrude on his thoughts. Knowing that additional thinking about his problems would not be productive with the woman on his mind, he elected to take an easy stroll through the lava fields with Shilah. After getting properly outfitted Hokee stepped outside to find his faithful wolf waiting with a wagging tail as though he had anticipated his master's intentions. Knowing his companion, Hokee would not have been surprised if the animal had not indeed sensed his plans as soon as the thought entered his head.

Before starting his walk Hokee built a fire in the pit next to the sweat lodge and after all of the logs were burning and the flames were hot he used tongs to lay five medium sized lava rocks on top of the fire. He would return in an hour when the rocks would be glowing red, ready to be put in the rock pit inside of the lodge. With these preparations made he signaled Shilah and together they walked up the gentle southern slope to begin their stroll by following the road to town for the first couple of miles.

A cool breeze was blowing in from the west lending a sharp chill to the late September evening. The desert was always cool in the evening at this elevation and by the beginning of fall it was not unusual for there to be frost on the ground in the early morning. The wind carried a hint of sage and Hokee breathed in the crisp air reveling in the scent and open sky. In this bleak landscape with black lava rock spreading as far as the eye could see Hokee imagined he could still smell a hint of the hot rocks as they cooled over a thousand years earlier. A half moon cast eerie shadows from the growth of small bushes alongside the road and in the distance a coyote howled at something, perhaps just trying to attract a mate or declaring his territory. Hokee's road looked like a silver ribbon in the moonlight but everything else appeared gray or black. Shilah stayed by his side, probably remembering their forced separation from the last walk. On the road it was easy to stay together whereas when they walked in the lava plains togetherness was impossible. Tonight Hokee was wearing his lava boots but left the heavy canvas clothing at home as he didn't plan on venturing anyplace unfamiliar. This was simply an outing to refresh his mind and soul; to become reattached to mother earth. The sweat lodge afterwards would be used to heal the spirit and body.

After a couple of miles Hokee left the road and after wandering along a familiar trail through the lava plains for a few minutes Hokee decided to let Glory hunt down the coffin dispenser by herself while he made a few calls of his own. The assignment would let the reporter feel more involved with the case and would buy Hokee another day alone to heal while he followed up with a few additional hunches. The fact that his adversary was using fake names and addresses added a new dimension to the case indicating that the man was much smarter than originally assumed. So far, they had been playing catch up and Hokee realized that in order to nab this thief they were going to have to begin thinking like their quarry, only faster.

Hokee didn't need much sleep after his refreshing sweat lodge and rising early drank a pot of coffee while planning his day and waiting until eight o'clock to call Glory.

"Good morning, this is Glory." She picked up after the first ring sounding wide awake and in a good mood.

"Based on how quickly you answered the phone my famous detecting skills tell me I didn't wake you up."

"Wow! I knew you were good, but I didn't know you were that good," she teased him right back.

"Yeah, I think it's the mixed blood thing I have going for me. Gives me an edge over you simple white eyes."

"White eyes? Where in the hell did that come from?" she asked. "And I'll have you know there are at least six different nationalities flowing in my veins."

"Whoa, hold up girl. Geez, I was just kidding. Didn't you ever see any old Gene Autry movies? White men were often called white eyes, but forget it. I called to see if you wanted to help with the investigation?"

This got her attention and focused on the reason for his call.

"Absolutely, I'm ready," she said. "What are we going to do?" Hokee could feel her excitement and anticipation over the telephone.

"You remember that coffin we found where the thief left the bread truck?" he asked. Hokee didn't want her to know at this point that she would be doing this investigation by herself. After she was committed he would tell her that he had other plans for the day.

She never even hesitated. "Sure, I remember. Your discovery of that grave was absolutely brilliant." It didn't hurt to stroke his ego, she thought, just don't get too pushy.

"The thief must have obtained that coffin from a local mortuary here in Pocatello. I need you to run that down and see if you can come up with a name. It was probably obtained during the past year and more than likely within the past six months."

There was silence at the other end of the line and Hokee knew she understood that this was a solo assignment. "What do you mean you want me to run down the name? What are you doing?" The disappointment was evident in her voice.

"I've been busy working on another angle and believe we have to change our strategy in order to catch this guy," he offered. "While you're chasing down the coffin I'll be working on our next move. Hopefully by the end of the day I'll have it all put together. What do you say about breakfast tomorrow? I'll pick you up at eight and take you out for the best eggs Benedict on the planet." Hopefully by then his body would not look like it had been squeezed through a sausage machine. The offer of breakfast and his explanation had the desired effect.

"Okay," she said. "I'll get a name even if I have to make it up, but those eggs better be damn good." Hokee could hear the smile in her voice.

"Great, I'll see you tomorrow morning at eight," he said laying the phone back on its cradle without saying goodbye. Greetings and farewells were not in the world of Wolf.

Hokee was not specific when he told Glory he would be working on their next move. It was simply a matter of explanation. Trying to explain his methods and procedures would require too much time and even then, the chances of Glory grasping what he was describing were unlikely. Not many people would understand the shaman view of life or the methods they used to delve into the mysteries of the universe. The sweat lodge last night was only the first step in a ceremony nearly as old as mankind. Last night's lodge was only an initiation to begin the spiritual cleansing. Today's lodge would be much more intense lasting nearly twice as long. Hokee would have to replace the stones used in his first hour as the first round of heated stones will have cooled down. The fire coals will keep a second pile of stones hot which is necessary to complete the ceremony.

When the lodge was hot and ready, Hokee took a brief shower of cold water, then used a fresh pine branch to sweep his aura before finishing with a smoking sage bundle for a final cleanse. Finished with the preparation, he climbed inside of the lodge with his pipe already prepared with a mixture of special herbs plus a pail of water and additional herbs used for transportation, carefully closing the flap to hold in the heat. Seated near the hot rocks, Hokee threw a few sage leaves, some cedar chips and special grass seeds onto the glowing coals. With the aroma of smoldering incense filling his senses, Hokee lit his pipe, taking in a lungful of the old Indian peace pipe special smoke. Letting out the smoke slowly through his nostrils he poured a cup of cold water onto the red-hot rocks. The intense hot steam combined with the incense and peace pipe smoke instantly transported him out of his body someplace into the realm of space and time known only to shamans who have been trained how to program their destination. The uninitiated would simply wander around in outer space overwhelmed by the journey and being completely unaware of where they were or what they were doing.

At first it seems as though you are cast into outer darkness beyond the edge of our known universe. At this point many people panic and become lost; some never seem to return. If you relax and let your spirit be the guide, a faint light is noticed in the distance, seemingly somewhere in another universe far away. Deep breathing and more relaxation brings the light closer until its brightness becomes blinding. It is only when letting yourself go that you enter into this light becoming one with all that is. All of mankind's thoughts, acts and energies create this light and it is up to the explorer to sift through the immense information available to find that which is relevant to his quest. The energy body that surrounds each object in the universe extends outward to infinity.

These vibrations obviously become very subtle at an extreme distance. The trick is to allow your consciousness the freedom to follow the energy vibrations surrounding your body towards the outer limits of existence.

Hokee had only one quest; to understand the mind and program of their thief. Clearly, they had underestimated this man and needed a new direction if they were ever going to catch this pock-faced nemesis. The only contact Hokee had with the man was the pick ax handle he had recovered from the grave. He held onto this chunk of wood as he journeyed into this distant land that countless shamans had mapped throughout time for the minds of those who would follow.

As each succeeding shaman delved into this region of light he is met with fleeting images of ancient fierce looking men briefly indicating the boundaries of safe pursuit. Beyond these planes a shaman's life or mental stability could not be assured. If what was being sought was beyond these known limits of exploration the shaman was literally entering into uncharted territory. He could proceed to seek outside of these charted mental landscapes, but the risks were many and not to be taken lightly. Should the shaman proceed beyond these boundaries and succeed in returning safely his knowledge would be added to the general mapping. However, it was all too easy to become lost and entangled in the unlimited uncharted regions of the mind. Many men had gone into these boundless unknown mindscapes never to return. If a shaman failed to return, one of his acolytes would eventually discover the body and arrange for its burial. Fortunately, on this journey Hokee had no reason to venture beyond the already explored regions of mind and space.

"Who was this thief? What did he want? Where was he going? How and where did he get his power?"

Hokee believed he knew the why; why the man had stolen the money. Officer Brent Morden's withered arm was all he needed to see in order to understand the rage the pock-faced man must feel about life in general and Pocatello in particular. Getting even was just as natural for human beings as breathing. It was just as natural as a wolf pack running down an old elk for food. Turning the other cheek is not something most individuals practice. Knowing why the thief had targeted the bread truck would not help Hokee find him. Knowing what he was planning for the future and where he was going would be more helpful.

Every thought sends vibrations out into the universe. This is the reason mental telepathy is possible and how some people actually can "read the minds" of others. When sitting in a room or near another person such mental mind reading is quite easy for those who have practiced this capability. Getting into the thoughts of a specific unknown person in an unknown location is considerably more difficult. This is one aspect of shaman training and one that Hokee employed whenever the occasion demanded. Finding the bread truck thief had become one such occasion. The difference between Hokee's sweat lodge journey and the thief's doppelganger experience is a matter of conscience. In Hokee's case he was dealing with expanded conscience. He allowed his consciousness to expand bringing into his conscience those specific vibrations in the universe that would help him find the answers to his quest. The thief actually gave his consciousness to the doppelganger retaining the faintest connection with his own body. The thief's focus was on projection while the Wolf's intention was to absorb.

Today's journey into "Shaman Land" had been powerful. Hokee saw the visage of an ancient withered Chinese man surrounded by darkness kneeling by a bloody young man on the sidewalk and knew now that the thief had acquired his training right here in Pocatello. By the time he returned Hokee knew his next step. He was now confident in his ability to find the thief; the question was what he should do once he had found the man because in his journey he also got answers to the rest of his questions. That was always the risk in getting into the mind of another. There is the chance you become empathetic and too understanding. Sure, the man is a thief and what he did was wrong, but in the grand scheme of life the man himself had been wronged. Is there no justice? Does the man not deserve some compassion? On the other hand, he had exacted severe punishment on Officer Morden. Should that not be sufficient retribution? Causing injury to the bank and Yellowstone merchants for an injustice they had no part in creating seemed wrong to Hokee, yet what should be the punishment? Thankfully Hokee's job was not that of judge and jury. Or was it?

Time enough to answer that question in the future once the thief had been located.

CHAPTER TWENTY

Working with Glory

On my way. Damn, Vicky charged a lot for the fake ID but the work was immaculate, just like advertised. Riding the train to Ogden from Pocatello seems like a better way to travel than taking the bus. On this train they served a great lunch. The only thing I needed to take with me was a small suitcase with one change of clothing and a bigger one with all the cash. I'll buy new stuff in the islands. The rest of the stuff is trash and I couldn't wait to dump it on that old cow of a land lady. What a trash heap for a home. Glad that is behind me.

The train is comfortable but I can't wait to get on the road in my own car. I shouldn't have too much trouble finding a ride in a town like Ogden. There must be a dozen car dealers within a few blocks of Union Station on Two-Bit Street. It seems like I remember walking by a few when I came back from India. I'm supposed to get in Ogden about four. I ought to be on the road by six at the latest. Goodbye Idaho. Goodbye Utah. Goodbye USA.

*****

Kendall's Funeral Home on Fourth Avenue was the fifth stop on Glory's trip down Mortuary Road, a wandering, jogging drive covering every neighborhood in the greater urban area. Today she was letting the cameraman Donald Cutler drive her around in their rented limo. It was time to let him earn some of the big bucks he was being paid to carry a forty-pound camera around town.

Kendall's was a large white two-story stucco building reminiscent of Mount Vernon with round pillars instead of the square poles used by George

Washington. The middle portion of the house with the Colonial look was flanked by straight faced wings without columns. It was a stately looking building that looked like a funeral home to everyone who had ever dealt with the grieving process and had to make the final arrangement. Glory had been spared this process in her life but after visiting four previous funeral homes in the Pocatello area she had become sensitive to the feel of mortuaries. They all had that "pearly gate" feel like Saint Peter was just inside waiting to welcome you into heaven.

Actually, it was Herbert Munson, funeral director, who was waiting inside and his mousy comb-over look did little to inspire feelings of heaven. Dressed in a tailored black suit with a white carnation in the lapel, his short stature and buggy eyes reminded her of an old Peter Lorie movie. He did not have Peter's breathy voice but after hearing his squeaky high pitched attempt to sound respectfully sympathetic one could only wish for the real thing. As it turned out he was able to provide Glory with all of the information she was seeking.

The next morning, she was waiting in the Red Lion's lobby and saw Hokee drive under the hotel's large portico. She immediately got up and went out to his truck jumping into the passenger seat.

"It's about time red man. And this better be a damn good breakfast," she began.

"Good morning to you too Glory. Great day for having breakfast with your favorite detective."

Glory impulsively slid over the seat and planted a kiss on Hokee's face as he was maneuvering back into traffic. The unexpected display of affection coupled with Hokee's already racing hormones nearly caused an accident.

"That's the kind of good morning that counts in New York terms," she said with a grin noticing Hokee's reaction.

Hokee could feel his heart beating a little faster and the heat building up in places best left undisturbed. "I'll try and remember that next time," he said trying to control the lump in his throat. He couldn't help but notice the sheer blouse covering something lacy underneath that barely concealed ripe breasts and protruding nipples. Trying to distract his own thoughts Hokee continued,

"We're going to The Dutchman's for breakfast. As advertised they have the best eggs Benedict in the world or one of my favorites, their German apple pancakes. You have to wait thirty minutes for the pancakes to bake but they're worth the wait." For Hokee this amounted to a speech but it succeeded in momentarily taking his mind off the sexy girl still leaning close to his side.

"I don't know if I can wait thirty minutes. I've been starving myself in order to really appreciate this fabulous breakfast you promised. And I want you to know that I've earned every bite. You'll be amazed at what I discovered."

Leaning against Hokee in a manner to suggest close camaraderie Glory continued, "And I want to know what you've been doing these past few days. A girl doesn't like to be kept waiting."

Hokee was already breathing carefully in order to preserve his dignity and Glory's body leaning against his made this even more difficult. He was pretty sure that what Glory had discovered, while undoubtedly accurate, would no longer be of any help but he refrained from telling her. He wanted to keep the relationship moving along and it was not the right time to let her know that what he had learned made her information obsolete.

"Great," he responded, while breathing heavy in spite of his efforts to do otherwise. "I can't wait until we order so I can hear all about your wonderful news."

U.S. Highway 91 through the center of Pocatello runs northeast through the Blackfoot Reservation all the way to West Yellowstone where the bread truck robbery occurred. Near a sharp 90 degree turn in the highway next to the Rail Crossing shopping center is an old brick building which has housed The Dutchman's for over one hundred years. The fifth generation of Gunther's run the place using most of the same menu items created by their forebears. They only serve breakfast items although they are open from 4:30 a.m. until 2:30 p.m. Their schedule was originally intended to accommodate railroad switching gangs who changed shifts at 4:30 a.m. but since customers continued to crowd the restaurant even when the railroad changed schedules and operating procedures, the restaurant never changed its hours of operation.

The worn dark hardwood counter and booths appeared to be the same ones installed by the original owners. Countless butts had polished the hard-wooden seats to a high gloss and grooves had been worn into the tabletops by unnumbered coffee cups and hot plates. The floor was covered with new linoleum, probably also a fifth generational thing although Hokee had never asked if this was true. Although old, the kitchen and dining areas were spotlessly clean, no doubt a legacy from the old German immigrants who had founded the restaurant. There was always a wait for a seat, but Hokee had been a longtime customer and Ingrid, the hostess, who was another woman with a long-time crush on the handsome detective, acted like he had a standing reservation and whisked him to an open booth next to the front window.

The waitress brought two coffee mugs without asking and inquired after Glory's drink order while pouring into Hokee's mug. Glory also opted for coffee although she also requested cream and sugar. Must be a New York thing, Hokee figured. Real cowboys and cowgirls took it black. Glory stuck with the eggs Benedict but Hokee wanted the apple pancakes which meant a thirty-minute wait. This gave them plenty of time to compare notes while waiting for their breakfast.

Glory went first, anxious to show Hokee how much she had learned. The thief's name was Leonard Foote and he did have a friend, Junior Hill, who worked for a mortuary. They sometimes met at a bar someplace downtown and had a few beers together. It was on one of these occasions that Junior had told Leonard about a shipment of pauper's caskets they had received, one of which looked like it had blood running down the side. It was a scary creepy sight which made it worthy of storytelling by Junior, but to Leonard it was an answer to his prayers. Herbert Munson, the funeral director, was happy to give the cheap pine box to Leonard just to have him haul the unsightly mess away from his beautiful funeral home.

Glory had naturally gone to visit Junior, who after getting a good look at the sexy New York reporter didn't require much prodding to give up his friend and current address. Feeling like she had earned at least another invitation to one of Hokee's special dinners, Glory sat back with a self-satisfied look on her face and a twinkle in her eyes suggesting something playful besides just a dinner.

Hokee was impressed by her diligent work and the information she had gleaned. Looking at the smile on her face and recognizing the gleam in her eyes it was painful for Hokee to contemplate spoiling her pleasure. Because unfortunately almost everything she had learned about the thief was wrong.

CHAPTER TWENTY-ONE

Breakfast

Feeling unsure how to tell Glory what he now knew about the thief, Hokee began by congratulating her on a great investigative effort and thanking her for all that she had accomplished.

"Why do I get the feeling that you are patronizing me Hokee?" Sensing that he was holding back, Glory asked the question with a little trepidation, afraid of the answer.

Hokee glanced down at his coffee cup looking for inspiration while trying to find the words to explain the situation without making his companion feel used or manipulated.

"Well," he began then hesitated, "it is true that our thief got his pine box from the mortuary, but I'm afraid that almost everything else you discovered about this guy was based on a deliberately obscure trail sprinkled with misdirection. Leonard Foote was just another fake name in a long list of aliases he's used including Bruce Jacobs, the name he gave his landlady. No one knows his real name, including the thief himself. He was dumped on the steps of the Baptist Church up on Chapel Road while still in diapers and was given several different names over the next fifteen years by different foster parents. He ran away from his last foster home when fifteen and began using different names every few months to avoid getting caught. He likes to think of himself as The World's Greatest Imposter. He saw that 1961 movie about the true life of Ferdinand Waldo Demara, a real imposter more than twenty times."

Glory thought about it a minute looking for some way to respond. "It makes a gal feel better about being wrong - a whole lot better, knowing she was duped by a real professional." Glory said it with a wry smile that hinted at being happy to know the truth but showing a little unhappiness at her wasted effort.

"Yeah," he said with a wry grin of his own, anxious to let Glory know that she wasn't alone in feeling bad about being wrong. "I was really thrown for a loop myself. I thought our thief was only using one or possibly two different names and I totally missed out on seeing his intelligence."

Glory was quick to respond. "You don't have to play dumb in order to make me feel better." She was still smiling while feeling a warm tingling brought on by his effort to ease her pain and embarrassment.

"Nope, just being honest, but happy if my misery helps make you happy."

"So, how did the world's greatest detective learn all this stuff?" she asked with a grin that had turned mischievous.

Hokee felt trapped by his own efforts. In attempting to help ease Glory into seeing the truth he had left himself wide open to her question. How much to say? She was after all a reporter and anything he said could ultimately wind up in the paper or on television. "It's a shamanistic practice using the sweat lodge; a little medicine man magic to you white eyes," he said with a big smile hoping it came across as teasing and just maybe help to change the line of questioning.

Hokee was not about to have such luck. "Come on Wolf man," she growled but with a friendly smile. "Don't give me this old medicine man shit." Feeling instinctively that the "sexy girl in revealing clothes look" alone would not work with Hokee, she went for the sincerity and honest interest approach. "You owe me, and I want the full story. Tell me exactly how you came by your information," she said using her professional look and voice while continuing, "which by the way you have not even bothered to share with me."

"You're right. I'm sorry. Here's what I know," he said. "Right now, our thief is on a train heading out of state to buy a car. From what I can gather he intends on driving south someplace to catch a plane to some other country where he can live on the money he stole."

"Okay detective. Now tell me how you know this stuff and which train going where?"

Shaking his head from side to side as though in pain Hokee said, "Remember, you asked for this." Reluctantly he began, "Maybe you have heard the term collective conscience or collective intelligence? I prefer the term universal mind. The terms all refer to the collective intelligence of all mankind. All information including every thought of each individual is simply a form of energy that is recorded and stored in this gigantic database."

"I've heard of this collective conscience thing but I always thought it was just some woo-woo crap put out by the hippies and new agers," Glory said.

"That's probably the prevailing opinion," Hokee said with a smile. "But a few scientists are slowly starting to think otherwise based on the latest thinking in quantum physics. Scientific experiments have actually been conducted that seems to validate the theory. Anyway, shamans throughout history know this universal mind exists and learned how to access the information."

"So now you're also a shaman besides being the world's greatest detective?" Glory displayed a mischievous grin but it wasn't difficult to see a little skepticism in her eyes. She was after all a New York reporter.

Hokee didn't miss the skeptical look in her eyes. He was after all the world's greatest detective. "Nope, I'm not a real shaman," he said. "I did some apprentice work once and learned a few things. Anyone can learn to access this information. You just have to be very focused on your quest." His stern voice and serious look let Glory know that this was no joking matter with the Wolf man.

Sensing that she was treading on nearly hallowed ground, Glory was careful in how she phrased her next question. "How do you find what you are looking for in this giant collective universal mind thing, or whatever?"

"If I answered that I'd have to kill you," he said with a grin. "Usually it takes a lot of training, learning and practice to focus. You're right. It's a giant land mine and easy to get lost in the vastness of infinite space. Without training and a guide, it would be very easy to get lost. A lot of folks lose themselves trying to navigate in that territory without taking these sensible precautions."

"You really can't tell me how you learned about our thief?" Glory was reluctant to let this drop without getting some sense of how Hokee got his information.

"You know I use the sweat lodge for meditation and medicine work, right?" he asked.

She nodded.

"After the initial preparation and when I'm completely ready I focus my mind on a particular event or time until I feel the vibrations of what I am seeking. It then just becomes a matter of tracing those feelings or vibrations to their source. Once I located the thief I delved into his mind. It isn't perfect, for instance, I could not find out what train he is on or where he was headed," he said grinning, "but I figure with your help that will be easy to track down."

"Could I do this sweat lodge thing?" she said skipping right over the train hunt hint.

"If you really want that experience" he said. "We can do a sweat lodge tomorrow if you're up for it. Although for the first time don't expect too much. It takes some getting used to the heat and different sensations. I'll be there to guide you and keep you from getting lost," he said with a wicked grin. "You are aware of course that you have to do the whole thing naked?"

"Oooh," she purred, "I think I might like that."

Hokee was spared from making a response as their waitress arrived with steaming breakfast plates.

CHAPTER TWENTY-TWO

Glory's Sweat

Looking out of the train car window as the train slowed coming into the Union Pacific Station in Ogden you can't help but notice all of the used car lots lining Wall Avenue. The train track runs parallel to Wall Avenue and just two blocks from the station he saw Honest Al's Used Cars, the kind of place one could expect to arrange a shady deal. As the old rock ballad puts it, "you don't have to shout the truth." Anybody pushing honesty in their name means that only a sucker thinks it's true. Knowing that Honest Al could be depended on to cut corners makes buying one of his cars a priority if one is seeking anonymity. Al couldn't care less the name you use and it would be easy to persuade him to offer an under-the-counter registration for a little extra cash. Cash is king. The car didn't need to be great, just good for a few thousand miles or so. It was going to be dumped anyway so the cheaper the better as long as it had decent rubber and would meet safety regulations. You didn't want to be pulled over for a faulty brake light, turn signal or broken tail light lens.

An old black 1963 Cadillac Eldorado was perfect. It is a respectable car but just old enough to warrant a good deal for cash. The rubber was adequate for a few thousand miles although the spare was bare. Better not get a flat or blow-out. There were rust spots along the door bottoms on both sides and the left rear quarter panel had been replaced with a yellow fender which gave the entire car an old hippie look, but Al threw in a car air freshener. What a guy. Fifteen hundred cash dollars later the thief was on his way south towards Vegas with a full tank of gas. The steep, rugged Wasatch mountain range was riding his left hip on the east with the Great Salt Lake on his right side disappearing behind him on the west. No one was gonna catch him now. Nobody knew his name, where he was or where he was headed. So long Idaho and pretty soon, goodbye Utah.

*****

The U.S. Congress passed the Rail Passenger Act in 1970 creating Amtrak. By 1971 there were 21 routes across and through the country which pretty much eliminated rail passenger service as it had existed. By 1978 Amtrak no longer used the big brick depot monster owned by Union Pacific which now stood abandoned in what used to be the heart of Pocatello. Over the years, urban sprawl had moved the town's center a few miles east and north. It was here that an old weathered frame building with an attached coffee shop serving hot and day-old cold sandwiches for road weary train riders now served as the train depot. The Formica countertop was so worn and scratched the original pattern was no longer visible, but under the metal drugstore tables and chairs it was still possible to see the black and white cross-hatch pattern of the original linoleum. The checkout counter also served as the train station ticket office and it was there that Glory and Hokee went for information about recent passengers. Jennifer, the cashier on duty, was an overweight fifty-something with stringy brown hair and dish-pan hands. Wiping wet hands on a kitchen apron hanging from her neck, she waddled over to the counter and while looking at Glory, asked if she could help the beautiful blond lady, ignoring her side-kick. Jennifer recognized Hokee Wolf, but was one of the few women in the area immune to his good looks and engaging personality. She considered herself much too high class to talk with the half-breed directly, unless absolutely forced. This was a reaction not unusual in small western towns but highly unusual in the eclectic swarm of humanity comprising modern Pocatello. There were thousands of African-Americans and a few hundred Chinese residents in Pocatello as a result of the railroad. The Blackfoot Reservation to the north contained several thousand American Indians where many had left to work and live in Pocatello; but still, small minded people can be found almost anywhere. How a woman like Jennifer could be responsible for being an Amtrak ticket agent was a mystery that Hokee had no desire to solve. Her family probably had the Amtrak franchise rights to Pocatello or she had some other kind of connection. It wasn't like train customers had a big choice.

Recognizing the slight to Hokee, Glory was surprised at the woman's lack of manners, but managed to keep the disdain from her voice and kept a smile on her face while addressing the clerk. She had learned long ago in the reporting business that at times you had to ignore your dislike for others if you wanted to get the story. "We're seeking information about a possible customer who left Pocatello by train sometime during the past 24 hours. Would you be able to help us with that?"

"I can try if you tell me who the passenger was," Jennifer responded smiling back at Glory. Apparently she didn't hold it against Glory that she was running around with an Indian.

"The man we're looking for is about middle-aged and wears his brownish-gray hair in a ponytail. He's about five ten or so tall and built slight with a badly acne-scarred face. He's the kind of man you would remember. He has piercing black eyes."

"Now him I remember," the clerk frowned recalling the memory. "Unpleasant little man. Wanted a ticket to Ogden." With this statement, Jennifer scrubbed her hands on the front of her apron as though rubbing out some unseen stain.

"Can you tell us which train he took?" Glory asked. "I mean when did it leave?"

"There ain't that many passenger trains anymore. Mostly freights. They have the right of way, ya know. Part of the deal those railroad bastards made when they let Amtrak run the passengers. We only got two trains a day now and your man left on the ten o'clock yesterday morning. I sold him the ticket myself. Happy to see the little creep get on the train to tell you the truth," she added sensing a kindred spirit in Glory. "He would get into Ogden sometime in the middle of the afternoon. I can look up the exact time for you if you want."

"No, that's alright," Glory said. "You've told me what we needed to know. Thanks for your help," she added giving Jennifer another dazzling smile purely as a reflexive gesture. You just never know when someone can give you the scoop on a big story and Glory had learned a long time ago that a smile costs very little and can buy a ton of goodwill down the road. With her it had become a habit leading many to consider her shallow and insincere. Glory could not have cared less.

Taking Hokee's arm she led the way back out of the diner. They waited until they were back in Hokee's truck before talking and then it was Glory who asked, "What now chief?"

With a big grin showing plenty of very white teeth while hiding a whole lot of apprehension Hokee said, "It's time for your initiation to the sweat lodge; you ready?"

"What about going to Ogden?" Glory asked.

"That will be a waste of time Glory. Think about it. This is a very smart man we're stalking. He knows he's being hunted. He doesn't want to leave a trail so he didn't buy a car here in Pocatello because he has to pay cash and it would raise too many questions. Ogden is far enough away so that with the robbery happening several weeks ago, it would be pretty much forgotten. He could buy a cheap car and pay cash with no one the wiser, especially if he gets a shady operator selling old wrecks. He won't want to travel by train any further than Ogden or Salt Lake City or take a train or airplane from there because they leave trails. In Ogden, he can buy a car and travel anywhere and by paying cash there would be no way to track his movements. The only way I know how to find him now is to get in his head and the only way I can do that is in a sweat lodge."

*****

For Hokee this long speech was probably the most talking he had done at one time in years, but he wanted Glory to know the score.

She was silent for a few moments digesting the information and shaking her head in understanding asked, "So what do I need to do for this sweaty thing?"

With that devilish grin back on his face Hokee said, "If you need to let anyone know where you are now is the time. Once we get started you won't be able to contact anyone for a few hours."

No contact, she thought. *What in the hell have I got myself into?*

During the drive to his house Hokee told Glory a little about the history of sweat lodges and their various uses over the centuries. She was amazed to learn that their use dated back before the Egyptians and were often used to treat illnesses and simple body cleansing besides their well-documented shamanistic value. She tried listening to Hokee as he was explaining the various types and uses of the sweat lodge but in her mind Glory kept thinking about being naked and seeing Hokee without his clothes. The images in her mind caused her nipples to harden and as they rubbed against her silk blouse she could feel herself getting moist. It was a struggle to sit still and pretend to be interested in sweat lodge history. Thankfully the ride was brief and before she realized it they were driving around the giant fountain in Hokee's front yard. She followed him around the side of his house behind an invisible wall to a courtyard with a small oval hut beside a fire pit and a pile of stones. Using wood from a nearby stack Hokee quickly had a roaring fire going in the fire pit onto which he piled a half dozen medium sized lava rocks.

"Okay Glory," he said looking very serious. "From now on every act we perform must be deliberate, precise and with a focus on our upcoming journey. We seek to be present with every thought and act. While the rocks are heating up we'll take a little meditating walk to concentrate our thoughts on exactly what we wish to achieve with our sweat lodge experience. Since you don't have good walking shoes we'll stick to the road."

The seriousness, concentration and precision with which Hokee had prepared the fire brought Glory back to the present and the reason for their upcoming sweat. "What do we do on this walk Hokee?" she asked.

"From this moment on we focus and meditate on our quest; the questions we wish answers for. Our only thoughts are to be related to the journey we are about to take into what my shaman friend calls the great unknown."

Glory could not help herself wondering how she was ever going to concentrate on the great unknown after getting naked in a small enclosure with Hokee. Hoping not to betray herself she couldn't help but ask, "You mentioned journey. What is this journey all about anyway?"

"Every subconscious journey is a trip into the unknown realm of our minds and must be programmed. Those stories you hear about bad mushrooms or LSD trips are the result of poor or inadequate mental planning, inattention to the amount of the drug they are using and poor choices for their environment. Our mind connects to the great universal consciousness which expands out to the edge of infinity. The vastness of this space makes it easy to become lost which is why these trips are usually taken with a guide familiar with the territory. Everyone is connected to this consciousness and every thought is recorded. Our job is to locate one particular thinker and tune into his or her thoughts. During the walk, we concentrate our thinking on the person we wish to locate. All of our thoughts and energy goes towards locating this person and tuning into their thoughts. The more focused we can make our thoughts, the greater our success will be in locating the target."

As they walked up the slope of Hokee's driveway onto the long access road back towards town Glory developed a greater appreciation for the immense lava fields and their forbidding nature. The giant jagged black rocks falling into deep pits seemed foreboding. It was a stark, bleak landscape. How could anyone live in the middle of such desolation? Suppressing a shiver Glory asked, "So all I do is think about this horrible little man with the piercing eyes and ugly face?"

"No," he said. "Besides visualizing the man, you formulate the questions you want answered. Where is he? Where is he heading? What is he going to do next? In other words, think of all the questions you would ask him or what kind of information you wish to know?"

Hokee grew silent and glancing over at him Glory could see that he was not with her anymore. She marveled at his ability to concentrate and focus his intention. Feeling chagrined at her own wandering mind she decided to give it a chance. Amazingly, as soon as she started thinking about the scary little man with the pockmarked face she was no longer distracted. Without even trying her thoughts focused on the man and where he was. She wanted to know what he was doing, where he was going and what he was thinking. It came as a surprise when Hokee touched an arm bringing her back to the present. To her amazement, they were back at the sweat lodge and her moment of truth was about to unfold.

CHAPTER TWENTY-THREE

Out of Mind

Hokee was busy with metal tongs lifting hot rocks from the burning coals for the pit dug in the center of his sweat lodge. His focus and concentration was complete. After the rocks were all placed Hokee started undressing, hanging his clothes on wooden pegs he had placed in the lava rock wall behind the lodge. Glory found herself admiring his physique in spite of his admonition to focus her thoughts on their quest. Noticing the extra clothes hooks, Glory started undressing and was dismayed that Hokee didn't show the slightest interest in her nude body. She had never known anyone so completely focused.

"First we take a shower to wash away whatever residual stuff is clinging to our bodies. Everything we touch and every person we pass leaves a little of their energy in our own energy field." This was said with the cadence and voice of a shaman leaving Glory to wonder about her forthcoming experience.

After their shower from a convenient shower head installed in the rock wall Hokee continued. Picking up a fresh cut pine bough from a nearby rocky ledge, Hokee said in that voice Glory recognized and now thought of as the shaman's voice, "I will brush your energy field removing those unwanted particles of energy stuck to yours. Watch what I am doing then you can do the same thing for me."

Glory stood still as Hokee swept the brush all around her body about six inches from her skin. The strokes were all from the top to the bottom. Glory couldn't help but notice the concentrated look in Hokee's eyes. He was not seeing the glorious body she had worked so hard to sculpture but was focused instead on his actions. As Hokee was working he commented, "The brush strokes are from the top to the bottom sweeping the dirty energy into the ground. Mother Earth knows exactly what to do with this negative energy. As you sweep your hands over my energy body, see in your mind's eye the negative energy being swept down into Mother Earth."

When finished with brushing Glory he asked her how she was feeling. She was amazed to discover that she actually felt much lighter. Hokee then handed her the pine broom so she could do the same for him. As she began brushing Hokee's aura the fact that he was standing before her completely naked was almost lost in her dedication to the task at hand; the key word being almost. There was this little part of her consciousness that could not help but notice what a splendid body this good-looking man possessed.

After the aura cleanse Hokee picked up a sage bundle from the same rocky shelf that had held the pine bough. Stooping to the fire he started one end of the sage bundle burning which produced a thick white cloud of pungent, almost stringent odor that had a pleasant earthy quality. He proceeded to sweep the burning sage all around Glory's aura from head to toe. As he was using the sage Hokee explained, "The shower and aura sweeping were to rid our energy fields of the toxic energy we picked up on our daily activities. The sage smoke is to purify our energy field and seal in our own positive energy. When we undertake a serious journey into the unknown we do not want to carry along any unwanted travelers in our energy field."

Glory didn't pretend to understand exactly what was going on but she had complete trust in Hokee and relied on his training and experience to guide her. Taking the burning smudge from Hokee she did the same thing for his energy field. She went around his body several times sweeping the smoking sage up and down filling his aura with the white sage smoke.

Satisfied with the status of his rock pit Hokee reached into a small cavity in the wall retrieving a few small leather bags. Without a word, he pointed to the lodge opening in a gesture to usher Glory inside. She had to crawl on hands and knees in order to enter the lodge but once inside found there was plenty of room to sit comfortably. Hot. Oh, my God was it hot. Glory broke out into a whole body sweat with saltwater gushing out of every pore in her body. Hokee crawled in after her, pulling down a thin, white leather flap covering the opening. The thin leather covering was adequate to keep the heat inside while letting in just enough light so she could make out Hokee sitting across the red-hot lava rocks. Their red glow painted the Indian's face in dramatic bold lines enhancing the fierce look in his eyes. There was no mistaking the seriousness with which he viewed this exercise. Without a word, he handed her a large bottle of cool water.

Hokee pulled an odd-looking pipe from one of the leather bags he had brought into the sweat lodge. A leather wrapped stem was inserted into a bowl made from some kind of bone or horn. Glory couldn't tell which. Zodiac symbols plus other designs she couldn't identify decorated the stem and bowl.

Taking some leaves from another bag he packed the pipe before putting the bag away. He next held a slender long cedar stick against the hot fiery rocks until it began to burn. Using the burning stick, he lit the pipe taking in a lungful of smoke. To Glory the smoke reminded her of an ancient pagan relic she had once seen in a New York museum. It seemed odd that the smell and sight evoked the same feelings of nostalgia for something old and lost. The smell was not unpleasant yet the feelings were very disconcerting. She seemed to be lost in another time and place. Before being able to assimilate these feelings Hokee handed her the burning pipe indicating that she should also take a puff. Wary, but determined to please Hokee and follow this adventure wherever it led she reluctantly took the pipe inhaling a lungful of smoke. Without expression Hokee took the pipe and put it on the ground next to his body. He then closed his eyes and began chanting.

She found it difficult to breathe the hot air and was afraid she was going to pass out. The discomfort made it difficult to focus her thoughts. Just when she thought it couldn't get any worse, Hokee threw a few pinches of sage, cedar and other herbs onto the hot rocks. The aroma assaulted her senses like a runaway Mac truck knocking her thoughts into an uncontrollable array of disjointed associations; her feelings sent her emotions spinning while flickering images from some unknown origin made her dizzy, producing an urge to vomit. Trying to decide whether or not to give into her urges she was unprepared for the next moment. Just then Hokee threw a cup of scented water onto the rocks. Scorching steam immediately filled the small lodge. The shock sent Glory out of her body far out into space. She never knew what hit her.

She no longer was conscious of her hot sweaty body. She was definitely no longer in a sweat lodge. Instead she felt as though whatever part of her existed was drifting in a sea of darkness seemingly nowhere. The experience was frightening and disconcerting. It seemed as though she was a tiny speck of nothingness, yet at the same time she filled the universe. How could that be? And, where was she?

At first the light was faint, barely visible in the near total darkness. The one dim light became two, then a dozen and finally it was like the nighttime sky full of little dots of light. The light continued to grow until it was a blinding, uniform field of white that was almost painful, consuming her entire being.

Glory was totally lost, confused and frightened. She had no eyes to shut out the painful light, and had no idea where she was or how to find her way home. Feeling lost and abandoned it was a complete surprise when she heard a faint voice coming from a great distance. While straining to hear the voice, it became apparent that Hokee was speaking to her. "Listen to my voice Glory and you will be fine. I'm sure you are a little frightened. That's normal. Just listen to my voice and follow it wherever you go. First though, take a few deep breaths. You have probably forgotten about breathing and we must take care of our bodies." To her surprise, Glory discovered that she had completely forgotten that she even had a body or that it was sitting in a hot, steamy room oozing sweat by the gallon.

"Take a drink of water Glory. Your body needs it," Hokee commanded.

Keeping her eyes closed Glory found the bottle lying next to her knees and greedily sucked in several swallows of cool clean water. My God, but that tasted good. She had never tasted water with such a delicious flavor.

"Now Glory," Hokee continued, "keep your eyes shut and look into the distance; you will see millions of tiny bright lights."

"Oh yes," she said excitedly with the discovery. No longer was she immersed in a brilliant field of uniform whiteness. "I can see them."

"Those little bright spots are energy containing the thoughts of every person. Now let yourself drift towards these thoughts but keep listening to my voice. Never let yourself stop listening to my voice. I will be your guide and keep you from getting lost but you must never stop listening to my voice."

As he was speaking Glory found herself getting closer and closer to the little white lights until she was surrounded by the lights and finally totally immersed in blinding white light.

"You are probably in the light now," Hokee said. "The task at hand is to find our target's thoughts in this field of white. Keep listening to my voice and concentrate on the questions we formulated during our walk. Where is our thief? Where is he going? What are his plans?"

Glory now found herself floating in this sea of white light. At first it burned her eyes. How could this be since her eyes were shut? She opened her eyes just to check and sure enough in the dim light there was Hokee sitting across the fire pit looking every bit the Indian medicine man she had pictured such men looking in her imagination. The small enclosure started spinning so she immediately closed her eyes again. With her eyes closed she was instantly back in the burning white light feeling almost completely lost.

"Concentrate your thoughts on the questions Glory." Hokee's voice seemed to remonstrate with her as though he knew that she had opened her eyes and lost concentration. When she did finally focus on the questions it was with a great surprise that she actually saw the frightening little man sitting in an airport. With just a little more questioning she discovered that he was in San Diego. Thrilled with her discovery she couldn't wait to tell Hokee but this brought her back to the present and Hokee's voice.

"You are probably experiencing some answers to your questions at this time but be aware that you are in mind space and a long way from home. In order to return safely you must listen to my voice. This is one of those places novices get lost. They get so excited about all the thought they are finding that they lose track of their own mind. You have to remain Glory while employing your energy in the discovery of mind space."

She felt a little reprimanded but on the other hand what he said had been the truth. She was so fascinated by what she had discovered that she wanted to play in this field forever. It was with real reluctance that she let herself be guided home.

"Just keep listening to my voice Glory. I'm going to retrieve you now and bring you back to your body. We have done everything we can for this trip."

Glory was disappointed to hear that she had to leave this beautiful white scape and it was a shock to find herself back in her body. Looking up she saw the grinning Wolf man. "Come on Glory, let's go take a shower and get rid of this sweat," he said almost laughing. "Don't forget to bring your water bottle."

Crawling out of the sweat lodge Glory was astounded to discover that it was nearly dark. She had been in the lodge for nearly two hours and it had seemed like only a few moments. My God, how had that happened?

Hokee took her hand helping her stand and she was amazed at her weakness. Her legs felt like jelly and she was a little bit dizzy.

Leading her gently to the cold shower Hokee explained, "Your weakness and dizziness are because you lost so much water and partly the incense and drugs used in our ceremony. Keep drinking your water and the cold shower will help revive your body in no time."

Glory had never felt anything as wonderful as the ice-cold shower. With the sweat being washed from her body she became increasingly aware of the still naked man at her side and was unable to keep her nipples from going rock hard. The emotional release from the intense sweat lodge experience was more than she could handle. Throwing her body at Hokee in a full-frontal hug she threw her arms around him and exploded with a verbal command. "Hokee Wolf, you are going to take me to bed right now or I am going to make your life miserable." With this said, she began kissing him with all of the passion she had stored from several days of harbored lust.

CHAPTER TWENTY-FOUR

The Morning After

Wow! This was his thought when late the next morning Hokee finally rolled out of bed and headed for the shower. His bedroom of black lava rock precluded anyone inside from knowing the time of day or night without a watch much like a Las Vegas casino. As he turned on the water faucet a big grin threatened to split his lips. Glory lounged naked on top of the sheets reviewing her fantastic night. She was certainly no virgin. You didn't get to have her status in the man's world of prime-time television reporting by being Snow White. For a few minutes, she tried counting orgasms, not for the night, just hour by hour. Never had she had such a tender, giving, lover coupled with gigantic power and feeling. It was like he was inside of her body giving it exactly what it needed in order to become satiated. On one hand, she was totally exhausted and another part of her had never been so alive. While lying on the bed ruminating she wondered if she could ever be Mrs. Gloria Wolf. Somehow that just didn't work, but maybe she could keep her maiden name. Women were doing that more and more. What in the hell was she thinking? One night of fantastic sex and she was ready to marry the guy. Well, hell yes. She hadn't missed the big grin on Hokee's face and it didn't take a reporter's instinct to know why.

Wearing only a towel Hokee went into the kitchen to prepare breakfast, or brunch, or whatever you wanted to call it. They had skipped dinner although at one point in the night he raided the refrigerator for some cheese, summer sausage and corn bread snacks. This was going to be a kind of hit and miss sort of affair as he had not planned on having company. A three-cheese omelet with mushrooms and smoked bacon would have to do. Naturally this would be accompanied with gourmet coffee and a juice drink of combined fresh squeezed orange, pineapple and banana run through a blender. He was back to the naked vision of Glory in no time. Setting the tray down at the foot of the bed Hokee picked up the colored pillows from the floor and arranged them so they formed a back rest against the beautifully patterned headboard. Picking up the tray he set it on the bed between them and adjusted the pillows for maximum comfort to sit against the headboard. The tray contained a couple of throw towels for their laps so they could eat from the hot plates without getting burned. Glory followed his example setting up to eat as she leaned back against the headboard. With her magnificent breasts sticking out over the tray it was all Hokee could do to keep from attacking her once again. With iron will he conquered his lust and took a swig of juice.

"Maybe we should take a few minutes to talk about our case," Hokee said reluctantly. Although sore from their night of heavy sex he couldn't help but be aroused by the beautiful naked woman sitting on his bed. He could easily spend the rest of his life in bed making love to this fantastic woman.

"Oh Hokee!" she exclaimed with excitement. "I saw him. I saw the thief at the airport in San Diego." Glory was so proud and excited with her discovery and revelation that for a moment she forgot all about sex.

"Hey, that's great," he replied. "Did you happen to get where he was going?" Hokee was pretty sure that if she had gathered that information it would have spilled out with her data dump but he wanted to get her thinking about all aspects you want to consider when traveling in the cosmic mind.

Glory thought for a minute. "No. I was so surprised and excited at actually seeing him in San Diego that I didn't even think about where he was going. But we can get that information from the airport, right? It's like they have a list of passengers and stuff."

"Well, yes we could do that if we had his name," he said. "Did you happen to catch that during your séance?"

Hokee knew she did not have the name and was not trying to be mean; but to Glory it felt like he was berating her for messing up.

Seeing the hurt in her beautiful eyes he knew that he had gone one step too far and tried softening the moment. "Hey Glory. Be happy. You did a hell of a lot for your first trip. You hung in there like a real trooper and I have to tell you, only one in a hundred ever have a vision on their first journey."

"Really?" she said. "You aren't just saying that to make me feel good, are you?" Part of her already knew the answer but she wanted his verbal confirmation.

"No, in all honesty I think you did very well. I haven't had anyone share a sweat with me besides my shaman for many years but old Silver Fox used to talk to me about some of the people he worked with and from what I gathered having a vision on your first sweat is very rare."

Satisfied that her performance in the sweat lodge was satisfactory if not really good Glory asked, "Did you get his name and destination?" She assumed that the master detective/shaman had that information and was just using his previous questions as a teaching moment.

To Hokee's credit he picked up on Glory's question and understood the reasoning for her query. Her intelligence and quick mind were always a delight.

"I got lucky," Hokee said by way of easing the pain for his pupil. "Our master thief went to the cemetery for names he could use as an alias, probably for a fake passport. There are folks here in Pocatello quite proficient at turning out bogus paper."

"Lucky how?" she said.

"Donald McKenzie was killed five years ago in a drive-by shooting. The police were unable to find the shooter so the family hired me to help find justice so they could get closure. Turned out to be a case of mistaken identity but unfortunately too late for Donald. The shooter is doing life up in Boise. Anyway, Donald McKenzie is probably only one of about ten names I would recognize from the tombstones in Pocatello. Since I was familiar with his name it popped up in my scan during the sweat."

Glory knew that Hokee would have probably gotten the name regardless and was just using luck as a way to make her feel better, but his thoughtfulness still melted her heart and the handsome naked man lounging next to her started the heat to build up again in all the right places. Before she attacked him in another round of lustful sex she continued with a question. After all, she was a trained investigative reporter. "So where was Mr. McKenzie going?"

"St. John in the Caribbean. I suspect that our thief will continue using the McKenzie name in the islands. He has to assume by now that he has safely escaped detection and the chance of bumping into anyone from Pocatello, Idaho in St. John who knew the real Donald McKenzie is very unlikely. He shouldn't be too hard to locate once we get to the island."

"Whoa, big fellow," Glory nearly jumped out of bed with that statement. Watching her breasts bounce gave Hokee an immediate erection which Glory noticed but with fierce self-control was not a sufficient enough distraction to

CLARK VIEHWEG

keep her from asking the next question. "I appreciate the 'we' business but in case you have forgotten I am a journalist on temporary assignment to Pocatello. How in the hell do I get my editor and the station management to okay a trip to St. John?"

"Hey," he said quickly. "I thought you were supposed to investigate the robbery. Surely, telling your boss how cleverly you discovered that the thief went to St. John should be enough to continue following the case. If he refuses, I'll buy you a first-class round-trip ticket myself."

Glory thought about it for a minute before responding. "Well, that might work, but I doubt it. They really only sent me here to get me out of New York for a few days. The story was only bait and if I really did come up with something reportable so much the better. I'll call the news director, but I'm pretty sure he'll say no."

"What do you think about the story as it now stands?" Hokee asked. "We've got a mysterious thief with a number of aliases; he uses paranormal power to create doppelgangers for the actual robbery while he lies in the ground in a real coffin and then skips town with the money. Isn't that enough to create an interesting report for New Yorkers, or are they too jaded for this kind of Hicksville activity?" Hokee was too worked up to care about the sarcasm and for a moment even forgot about sex with the fantastic reporter still lying naked in his bed.

Hokee didn't like making long speeches which Glory already knew and she wasn't miffed at the slight about her home town. "It isn't too late to call New York. Give me your telephone and I'll call Levi, he's my news director. You're right. It actually is a hell of a story and they should let me follow it up. The doppelganger part is going to take some explanation but that is what really makes the story. Well, that and the brilliant detective work by Idaho's most famous detective," she said reaching over with her hand to ruffle his hair just to let him know she was kidding.

"The only telephone I have is in the living room by my chair," Hokee said.

"Well damn. I'll just have to leave your magnificent body for a few and go make my call," she replied with a grin. "But stay there, I'm coming right back for round two. Or is it round fifteen?

I've kinda lost track."

She flounced out of bed and walked out of the bedroom without any kind of inhibition. Strolling around naked in front of her lover didn't faze her in the least. The same can't be said for Hokee who watched her leave while he was still stiff as an old corn stalk. He couldn't take his eyes away from the splendid body being displayed. The fine sculptured and well-toned legs, her tiny waist and firm butt and voluptuous breasts, the beautiful long neck supporting an angel's face with long flowing blond hair. Every man's dream woman.

While she was gone Hokee took the time to change sheets on his bed. He used only 1000 thread red cotton sheets which contrasted nicely with the black lava wall background and white feather comforter presently wadded up on the floor. The black polished stone floor was partially covered with beautiful woven Navajo rugs which Hokee had especially commissioned by squaws in his old reservation. The design used in the rugs featured the same kind of spiral Hokee utilized in his kitchen floor and dining room table. By the time Glory returned from making her call Hokee had the bed remade and was somewhat composed although the sight of the gorgeous naked woman entering his bedroom caused his heart to once again begin racing.

She couldn't help noticing the look in Hokee's eyes and was delighted to have such an effect on the otherwise stoic man. Finding herself feeling the same way it was difficult to keep her composure long enough to complete their business. "Good news Redman," she joked in an effort to help maintain dignity long enough to give a report. "They're going to fly me to St. John. Although they won't spring for my cameraman, especially since I told them that you would be going along and could run the camera when necessary."

"Well then," he responded. Clutching her hand when she came near the bed he dragged her onto the new clean sheets murmuring, "Let's celebrate our forthcoming trip."

And celebrate they did, for the rest of the day and well into the night.

CHAPTER TWENTY-FIVE

Going to St. John

Although they had little rest, on the following day they were both more alive and energized than ever. When finally emerging into the light Hokee fixed another breakfast masterpiece. The main course was smoked sage hen with Idaho potato and sweet onion hash browns topped by melted cheddar and perfect poached eggs barely firm complemented by homemade cornbread biscuits to swipe yolk off the plates. Neither lover could keep a silly grin from their face nor did they even try. They had no interest in keeping their affair secret. For her part, Glory was from New York and far away from anybody who might be interested for whatever reason, good or bad. And Hokee, well he just didn't give a damn what anybody thought. They started making plans for visiting St. John which fortunately didn't require a passport since they were both U.S. citizens. Otherwise an out of the way visit to New York would have been required since Glory had left her passport at home in her Greenwich Village loft.

Hokee dropped Glory off at her hotel so she could collect her luggage and make preparations for their trip. She had to tell Donald Cutter her cameraman that he would be going back to New York alone. They hadn't spent much time together on this trip but Glory didn't feel the need to apprise him of her plans even though he was her favorite shooter. After hooking up she told Donald about Hokee's sweat lodge and what they had discovered about the thief. She produced the map she had drawn for directions to Hokee's house and asked Donald to drop by there before leaving town and shoot a few shots of the house, his sweat lodge and the surrounding lava fields. It didn't hurt to keep on the cameraman's good side. You never knew when you might need a friend and in her business, they were hard to come by. The jealousy, backstabbing and grind the news business generated in order to produce entertaining television made for unstable and delicate relationships. She was unsure about just where the story was headed but wanted to be prepared, just in case. There was a little guilt associated in shooting pictures of Hokee's house without his permission, especially now that they were sharing a great deal of intimacy, but in Glory's business sex was a tool she had used so often it was almost second nature. She was after all a reporter and over the years she had pursued stories relentlessly regardless of the consequences. True, she was violating a kind of trust she had built up with Hokee, but he was a big part of the story she was investigating and his shamanistic work was part of that story. There would be time enough, and hopefully the right time would present itself when she could justify her actions to the handsome detective if it ever came to that.

*****

Hokee dropped by the office to check in with the lovely Hilda Worthmyer for any important messages. The look in Hokee's eyes was all she needed to see for her world to collapse with great stabs of pain and disappointment. Using that feminine intuition common to all women Hilda knew immediately that her boss was involved with another woman. True he had never encouraged a romantic relationship by anything he had ever said or done, but that didn't stop her from wishing and wanting and fantasizing. If Hokee noticed the hurt in his secretary's eyes he gave no notice. There were no missing students from Idaho State needing saving and nothing else really mattered. He told Hilda about his trip to St. John leaving his return date open. There was no one else he needed to inform of his plans and after telling Hilda to take a few days off while he was away, Hokee left to return home. Their flight from Pocatello to Boise didn't leave for several hours and Hokee wanted to have one last sweat before leaving Idaho. He wanted to be mentally and spiritually prepared to meet the thief who possessed such amazing paranormal skills. He also wanted to have a little talk with Shilah. His wolf knew something was up having experienced Hokee's absences before. And as before when Hokee explained that he was leaving and Shilah must stay behind and guard their home; the wolf seemed to understand. A drooping tail always indicated his unhappy acknowledgement.

As he was about to make preparations for his sweat, Hokee looked up and was surprised to see a big black Lincoln limousine parked at the top of his driveway. He saw Donald Cutter huddled over the steering wheel with Shilah standing guard down at the bottom of the drive. Glory failed to mention the wolf and Donald didn't know what to do about the big animal blocking his way. It would have been difficult if not impossible for him to back up the limo for four or five miles without driving off into the treacherous lava field and going forward didn't seem like such a good idea either. True the wolf could probably not get at him inside of the car but Donald was reluctant to proceed and possibly run over the animal. It was with real relief when he saw Hokee's Explorer come up behind his Lincoln.

Hokee walked up to the driver's window by Donald. Signaling Shilah to stand down he pantomimed rolling down the window so he could talk to the cameraman without yelling. As the window came down Hokee could see the crudely drawn map on the seat beside the driver. Looking up at the tall frowning Indian with blazing eyes Donald didn't know who frightened him the most; the wolf or Wolf.

"Donald. What are you doing here?" he demanded. There was no friendliness in the question or the face of the man doing the asking.

"Oh, uh, um, I'm just here to take some pictures." He really didn't want to confess the reason for visiting this remote home site but Hokee's countenance left no alternative. It was inconceivable that any lie would work in this situation.

"What in the hell were you thinking? Why did you want pictures of my place?" It was all Hokee could do to keep his mounting anger in check.

Seeing no alternative, the cameraman meekly said, "Glory asked me to take some pictures of your house and sweat lodge for her story." He was really frightened and hated sounding like he was blaming someone else for his transgressions, but Hokee's stern glaring face would brook no fallacious argument.

Hokee shook his head in both anger and disappointment. Angry that someone uninvited had driven onto his property and disappointed that Glory had not seen fit to mention this little invasion of privacy. Striving to remain civil he still came across as mordant when ordering Donald to leave.

"Turn around in my yard and leave," he commanded pointing to the fountain and circular drive down below. "You are not to take pictures or return to this property ever again. If you do Shilah will tear you apart. I'll follow you down to the fountain so you can take the road back to Pocatello."

Without another word Hokee turned around going back to his vehicle. For his part, Donald was happy to just get out of the situation in one piece. He knew going onto private property taking pictures without permission was wrong, but hell, they violated the rights of people all the time in the news business. One thing he was sure of, he never wanted to see that big Indian get angry with him again. As it was he had leaked a little piss in his pants. This was also another experience he never wanted to repeat.

Hokee was so angry it took all of his willpower to refrain from calling Glory uninviting her on the trip to St. John. He concentrated on building the fire for a sweat slowly releasing the tension in his muscles and mind. Before the rocks were ready for their pit inside of his lodge Hokee had regained his equilibrium and composure. Clearing his mind of everything but the business at hand Hokee finished preparation for his sweat and entered the mind space looking for ways to defeat the thief's power.

When Hokee picked Glory up from her hotel later in the day he was focused on his forthcoming battle with the thief and paid little attention to the sexy New York reporter. Glory could tell that Hokee was preoccupied but also suspected that he was purposefully shutting her out of his mind. She didn't know that he had discovered Donald at his house and was unaware that he knew of her underhanded invasion of his privacy. In her mindset, the actions she had undertaken were not anything that any other hardworking investigative reporter wouldn't do, and although uneasy, she was yet to really feel guilty about an attempt to betray Hokee. Still, she knew something was not the same between them and she could only hope it was not something that Donald had done on Hokee's property.

The Pocatello airport consisted of a single cinderblock building with a picture of a twin-engine airplane in flight in blue skies painted on the building's front over gray paint. There was a single check-in counter with a pretty black haired Indian girl wearing a tan leather dress behind the counter who issued their tickets and then carried their luggage out to a single propeller plane not much bigger than a piper cub.

"I know it doesn't look like much," Hokee said without expression, "but it gets us to Boise in time to catch our flight to Chicago. I don't like leaving a vehicle in Boise," he explained in a stilted voice. "Their airport security leaves a little to be desired."

"Hey, this beats a lot of the rides I've taken over the years following stories," Glory said grabbing ahold of his arm just happy that the big guy was talking to her again, even if it was in a monotone.

"I can't imagine a pretty little thing like you ever traveling anything but first class." Hokee's comment was meant to be a little humorous but there was no smile on his face and it ended up sounding sarcastic.

Glory noticed that Hokee wasn't smiling but didn't want to push her luck. Hokee wasn't sure how, or even if he wanted to confront Glory with what he knew of her plans to take pictures of his property. For now, he just wanted to let things proceed and see what she had in mind for her story. Clearly, she intended on resuming her career in New York relegating their love making to just another roll in the hay. While it had been very pleasant, Hokee had wanted it to be more and felt used by the beautiful reporter, who it seemed was out for just another story. Well damn, he was a big boy and should have known better. It wasn't like it was the first time he had been disappointed in love, although it had been a long time since he had let himself feel that way towards a woman. With just a little luck it would be the last time.

Trying for something to loosen up her companion Glory asked, "How much layover time do we have in Chicago? I didn't check my ticket."

"About four hours in Chicago. And another six hours in Miami." Hokee was back to his short, terse unemotional statements. Knowing that they were probably going to be spending a lot of time together, he decided to at least try and get along. In an attempt to be civil he continued, "Altogether this little trip is going to take just over eighteen hours. We'll be a couple of tired Indians by the time we reach St. John. Well, one tired Indian and one tired white girl," he amended, this time with a brief tight smile.

Glory was happy to see at least a glimmer of the old Hokee again and hoped that sometime during the next eighteen hours she would discover what had put a strain on their relationship. She just hoped it wasn't her act of betrayal.

During the next few hours Hokee slipped back into his reticent self regardless of his recent attempt at civility. He became a man of few words. Glory tried several gambits to get him speaking but most of his answers were single worlds. "Yep." "Nope." "Sometimes." "Maybe." "Probably." He seemed to be drifting away. Finally, in response to her continual probing Hokee decided to give in a little. "Look Glory. We are going to be meeting our thief pretty soon and I have to be prepared. You do not understand the kind of power this man possesses. What happens when we meet him will probably not be something that you understand and will not be useful for your New Yorker's entertainment. It will just be too unbelievable. There are powers in this universe about which our brilliant, educated, highly regarded leaders and university savants don't have a clue. Everything they witness for which there is not a rationale, that is to say sensible logical explanation is ignored as though it doesn't exist. We will not have that luxury. Unless I am prepared to fight the thief's power with my own we could both lose our lives. Until this is over I am afraid that I will not be very good company."

Everything Hokee said was true but he was ignoring the real reason for his reticence with Glory and he knew it. Still, it just didn't seem the time to bring up such a sensitive matter.

Having made one of the longest speeches of his life Hokee leaned back in his seat and adjusted the turquoise sweatband relieving some of the pressure on his forehead. He often used the headband to hold his hair in place when not wearing a hat. Leaning back against the headrest he closed his eyes closing off any further conversation.

To say that Glory was shocked would be an understatement. True, she had experienced a trip into the great universal mind, but these powers Hokee mentioned seemed to be beyond her depth of understanding. Doppelgangers were not something she could relate to and the withered arm of officer Morden seemed like just another bad disease of some kind. Hokee's speech left no doubt in her mind how much contempt he felt for the wisdom of our brightest intellectual stars and her New York citizens. There was also no doubt in her mind that there was something right about Hokee's statement regarding powers beyond our understanding.

For the first time she felt a bit frightened. Would Hokee be able to protect them? Would he have the power to match and overcome the thief? She worried over these and similar questions.

The small fear she had felt initially continued to grow as she contemplated these questions during the remainder of their trip. She may have been a bit hasty in agreeing to make this trip with Hokee. As her fears grew, so did a feeling of regret for ordering Donald to take pictures of Hokee's property. Just now she was beginning to understand the need this man had for his privacy and why he lived alone far away from everyone else. In order to get centered and control the shaman's power used in his everyday private detective life he needed space and solitude. Just as scientists located their giant telescopes far away from city lights to avoid luminescent interference Hokee lived in an inhospitable landscape far away from the thoughts, feelings and energy of others in order to focus his own power.

CHAPTER TWENTY-SIX

The Shaman Way

St. John in the U.S. Virgin Islands is a tropical paradise. Once a slave trading hub owned by the Danes it was purchased by the U.S. for twenty-five million dollars to serve as a forward military base during WWI. When Hokee and Glory finally reached the island, a blue painted Quonset hut leftover from the war days served as the main airport terminal to welcome weary travelers. The structure's faded peeling paint didn't inspire any travelers but most were too tired to care. Neither Hokee nor Glory had bothered making a hotel reservation assuming that there would be plenty of rooms available. The ancient Douglas C47 Skytrain they flew on from Miami was a real rust bucket that shook and rattled as though it would fall apart at any second. Fortunately, there were only fourteen passengers simplifying their luggage retrieval and rapid exit from the stifling building. Glory wondered how anyone could work in this hot building without air conditioning. Hokee was inside of himself going through the outward motions of normal body movement on remote control. Part of him was aware of their surroundings and what they needed to do next but the biggest share of his attention was focused inward on his forthcoming battle.

A dented, faded lime green 1958 four-door Chevrolet with one red rear panel stood outside of the terminal. A cheerful fat man wearing a red Tam-o'-shanter on his head stood by the car waving at the couple as they were leaving the airport terminal while yelling "taxi". After stowing their luggage and confirming that his passengers wanted to travel to the area's best hotel, he began a running travel monologue about the island's unusual and beautiful highlights. While his Scottish brogue was so thick as to be almost incomprehensible, Glory was too tired to ask for clarification and Hokee just tuned him out the entire ride.

They arrived at Hotel Ambassador twenty-five minutes later. The hotel was a stucco, three-story building painted flamingo pink looking like an aging Hollywood dowager. Glory thought the taxi driver was probably paid a commission for every fare he delivered, but it looked presentable and otherwise she was too tired to care. Hokee still in his robot mode overpaid the talkative taxi driver probably because he liked the guy's hat. Without even asking for Glory's input Hokee asked for one room with a king bed. Glory didn't know whether to be happy or angry. Too tired for anything romantic and yet happy that Hokee didn't shuffle her off to a private room she still felt like she should have been consulted about their sleeping arrangements. After arriving at the room and stowing their luggage Glory discovered that maybe a little romance might be okay. That was after seeing Hokee's fantastic body as he got undressed for bed. Hokee was not similarly aroused by the sight of Glory in all of her glory. Unable to put aside his anger and disappointment he ignored the beautiful undressed body as he flopped in bed closing his eyes. He focused his attention on the forthcoming battle with the thief as sleep descended on his troubled soul.

Breakfast in their room was chosen in order to save time. That way they could shower and get dressed while waiting for the food. Traditional American fare was selected over the local favorite, honey-mooners stew featuring pig tails. Not that pig tails were really a bad breakfast food. Glory had discovered the dish in a travel brochure on the coffee table and couldn't help but wonder how that dish tasted, but maybe some other time.

After breakfast Hokee took Glory out to a very private sandy white beach. Seeking shade, they found a secluded nook where a mild trade wind quietly ruffled fronds of the giant palm trees overhead. The breeze carried whiffs of salt water, perfumed flowers and hot sand. Sitting down and leaning against the tree trunks Hokee explained they were about to encounter strange powers and he wanted her to be prepared. He told her that belief in what he was about to tell her was not required; however, she needed to keep an open mind and be prepared for their eventual meeting with the thief who now called himself Donald McKenzie.

Making sure that Glory was comfortable and in a place she could concentrate on his voice, Hokee began.

"The prevalent belief system is that supernatural power doesn't exist.

University professors, scientists of all stripes, religious leaders and our mass media all maintain that all supernatural power is some version of a fortune teller's reading or simply a hoax. Outside of real shaman, medicine men and women from some native tribes scattered around the world, very few people have an experience enabling them to know that supernatural power is real. It just doesn't fit into the western culture or religious thinking."

"But," Glory interrupted, "I thought religious teachers believed in faith healing and stuff like that. Isn't that like supernatural power?"

Kicking off his moccasins in order to better feel the sand Hokee explained, "Matters of faith are related to the supernatural, but religious teachers put faith in an outside power for their miracles while shamanism is the science of acquiring and using energy emanating from yourself. Using 'science' and 'shamanism' in the same sentence probably sounds incredibly weird, but that is one of its most powerful secrets."

"You're telling me that shamans use science?"

"Probably in a different way than you're thinking about, but yes, shamanism is based on ancient scientific principles."

With the two investigators sitting quietly having this conversation two white herons started wading in the shore close by while grebes dived for a little ocean snack. Glory pushed breeze blown hair from her face allowing Hokee to see the skepticism in her expression.

"You've got to be kidding me," she jibbed. "Remember I'm a trained investigative journalist so I have to be skeptical."

"No," he insisted. "Shamanism is soundly rooted on scientific principles."

"Okay. But you have to convince me of that."

"Einstein and his buddies like Heisenberg, Schrodinger and Niels Bohr pretty much proved that everything in our material universe is simply energy. Our human body is condensed energy surrounded by a field of energy created by our thoughts. Remember when we brushed off our auras before taking a sweat lodge? We were actually cleaning the energy field that surrounds our body."

After saying this Hokee checked out Glory to see if she was following his thinking as a grebe came up from the ocean with a small fish in its mouth.

Seeing that she was paying attention he continued, "We know that everything is energy including words whether written or spoken. Whether they know it or not those priests muttering incantations and prayers are actually projecting energy. In fact, this has been measured but that will have to wait for another time. This is another way in which the supernatural and religion overlap. Shamans and priests both use words, phrases, diagrams and objects in their invocation of power."

Plainly Glory was not convinced but at least she was listening. "You're telling me that the words I'm speaking are actually energy?"

"Yes," he replied quickly. "What you say and write are all forms of energy. Think of the power simple words like 'I love you' can have on another person. And as for either written or spoken words, you should be the last one to question their power since you use them so effectively in your profession."

This last thought really hit Glory hard and Hokee could see that his arguments were having an effect. He was happy that the skeptic was starting to understand the kind of power they would be facing.

"Now," Hokee continued, "when two people pass each other on the street it is inevitable that their energy fields will collide. In fact, your energy field impinges on everything around you and the opposite is also true. There are people who feast on other people's energy which is why some people leave you feeling tired and worn out. We call those people energy vampires. There are also people who are sources of fantastic energy that can leave you feeling enlivened and refreshed. Concerts with professional musicians or great theatre are examples of group energy transmitters."

Glory sat stunned as she thought about what Hokee was telling her. "Damn," she exploded. "That explains Hanna, the bitch in our news room. She leaves me feeling drained every time she is in my cube. I always thought it was because of her snide remarks, but maybe it is more than that."

Knowing that he was getting through to the skeptic Hokee said, "Many energy vampires are unaware that they are sucking the life out of other people. They just know that dumping on others makes them feel better. Unless you are trained to protect yourself the best thing you can do is avoid contact with anyone who robs your energy."

Contemplating about what Hokee had just explained, Glory let her eyes play, scanning over the dark blue ocean with little white caps while listening to the gentle breaking waves on the sandy shore. It was an ideal Caribbean day and with the soft breeze she thought that maybe she could really get used to a life like this. Especially with a man like Hokee around who had a habit of building her up rather than tearing her down.

"So, what does this have to do with our thief?" she asked getting back to the topic at hand.

Hokee had been giving her the time to digest everything he had said before continuing.

"Our thief has learned how to build up tremendous amounts of energy which he projects outwardly. He can project this energy into a focused laser beam like he did to Officer Brent Morden back in Pocatello withering his arm; or he can project the energy into his doppelganger using this entity to further project energy into the minds of others affecting what they see and hear."

"Oh!" Glory said finally understanding the whole coffin thing. "By projecting all of this energy the thief had to leave his real body on extremely low energy hence the need to protect it by hiding it away from others."

As before, Hokee was pleased to see how quick Glory's mind worked. For just a second he wondered about a life with this woman, but immediately focused his mind back to their conversation. Some small part of his mind was still aware of her deceitful attempt to invade his privacy and he knew that was an issue that had to be discussed before going much further together in this melding of their powers and minds.

"The difference between my shamanic training and the thief's black magic power is that he projects energy outwardly while I assimilate the energy around me taking in small doses at a time. Hopefully no more than I can process to understand and then dissolve back to its original state. I also can and do project energy at times, but only for a benevolent effect to change a situation. To do otherwise would be against all shamanistic creeds."

"Okay," she said, "How do we apply this to our investigation?"

Smiling, Hokee replied, "We will have to be totally present in the moment as it unfolds to feel and know what actions to take. That is where faith in our own abilities comes into play. But you have enough to think about for now. Further lessons will have to wait until later."

Hokee took Glory by the hand and looking deeply into her eyes said, "It's time to go have lunch and then start finding our boy. But first we have to clear up one more little item."

Glory had been expecting something like this for several hours and was more than ready to get this weight off her mind and soul. "I believe I know what has been troubling you," she said with a troubled face and sorrowful appeal in her eyes.

Squeezing Hokee's hand she continued, "I know you are disappointed that I had Donald go out to photograph your home and I'm truly sorry for that invasion of your property. Please understand that my first instincts are as an investigative journalist. This bakery truck robbery has become an incredible story and you are the central figure in this story, whether you like it or not."

"Think about it," she said pleading with her eyes and quiet submissive voice. "A robbery committed with paranormal powers baffling the local police and sheriff's department; a detective from Pocatello using shamanistic powers solves the crime and locates the thief on a Caribbean island. This dear one," she said with moist eyes, "is one hell of a story. Being the central figure in this amazing narrative, my journalistic impulse was to get all of the photographs I could to enhance the viewer's pleasures. This is how I made my reputation."

"Unfortunately," she continued, still pleading for his understanding with the look in her eyes, "I didn't take the time to think about the invasion of your property. I remembered too late your telling me that I was not only the first person to visit your home but the one and only person besides yourself to ever set foot in your incredible house. I know now how significant privacy is for the type of work you do and I humbly apologize for my transgression. Please, please forgive me. I promise, and this is not a reporter's promise, but my very own personal promise, to never do such a stupid thing again."

With a smile Hokee stood slipping the moccasins back on his feet and then offered a hand to help Glory stand. Wrapping his arms around the humbled figure he gave her a big hug then a gentle kiss on the lips.

"Thanks for explaining your actions. I know you are one hell of a reporter and I really can understand your thought process. Consider yourself forgiven," he said with a twinkle in his eyes and another kiss; this one a little longer and with a lot more feeling. "But don't let it happen again," he concluded faking a scowl which Glory understood perfectly.

Their actions startled the birds hunting in the ocean causing them to take flight. Watching the two graceful birds soaring into the sky he couldn't help commenting as he waved towards the disappearing white specks, "That could be our Ka bodies returning back to their elemental nature if we don't act with impeccability in dealing with the black powers of this thief."

Not sure she even wanted to understand what that meant Glory let herself feel the big man's strength and wonderful positive energy. What could go wrong when she was with this unusually gifted, strong man?

She was soon to find out.

CHAPTER TWENTY-SEVEN

Glory Learns Shamanism

Walking back on the sandy white beach Hokee couldn't help commenting, "Man, but that white beach is hard on the eyes in this sunlight."

"Yes, but this is a really beautiful beach. I love that it isn't crowded. Almost like our own private chunk of paradise."

Walking back to the hotel they passed by a bed of Frangipani with its brilliant white petals and yellow center surrounded by palm trees and ferns. "I just love the smell of those flowers," Glory said. "Mixed with the salt air and this cooling tropical breeze it seems like it really is paradise."

"This is really a picture worth remembering," Hokee replied. "Freeze this image in your mind because it may come in handy later on."

"You're starting to scare me."

"There is some reason to have a little fear." Hokee was serious while trying to sound reassuring. "Fear can be our friend if we don't let it paralyze our minds and bodies."

Glory was beginning to feel like this trip was becoming some kind of personal initiation. Her maternal grandmother with a fair amount of Cherokee blood running through her veins came into her thoughts. As a little girl, this grandmother had insisted that Glorious Gloria (the only way her grandma ever referred to her) was destined to experience magical and mystical events in her life. This trip was turning into some kind of prophetic truth and it was a little scary. She felt a little unease in spite of her faith in the great Idaho detective.

"So, what's next shaman man?" she said.

"Let's grab some lunch while I explain a little about how shamanism works.

I hear their lemon grass steamed mussels are really good; maybe followed by a plank baked salmon served with a Thai mint-truffle sauce."

"Oh, I love to try different dishes," Glory said with excitement, forgetting for the moment her fear. "I'll bet the food here is fantastic."

They were strolling along the beach among the sun worshipers lathered in suntan oil. Mixed in with the obese visiting mainland vacationers baking in the direct sun were a few colored beach umbrellas shading the sleek jet setters being served Painkillers by dark-skinned natives. Painkillers are a delicious orange-colored drink that features orange and pineapple juice with coconut milk and rum with a dash of nutmeg. The name is derived from the copious amount of rum in each drink that is virtually undetectable in the juice and milk mixture. After a couple of these you don't feel any pain. And this includes the mental pain of a jilted lover or a business deal gone badly.

Finding an open-air restaurant near their hotel, Hokee and Glory found seats facing the ocean with an occasional breeze to ruffle their hair, while watching the waves break on the beautiful white beach. After ordering their lunch Hokee began explaining. "Shamanism is a serious undertaking requiring many years of preparation and practice. The learning process involves the study and assimilation of the four elements; earth, air, fire and water. By assimilation I mean the shaman actually becomes each of the elements. Study begins by learning the nature of each element and how it affects life."

Hokee paused to sip his coffee while giving Glory a chance to digest this information. His lecture was interrupted by their waiter bringing a steaming bowl of mussels. The mussels and lemon grass mixture was too tempting for Hokee to continue the lesson. Glory seemed to be relieved at having a break. All of this information was challenging her belief system which is never easy for anyone to be comfortable with instantly. She was happy to scoop out a mussel and sip the savory juice right from the shell. Chewing happily, she grinned at Hokee to let him know she was hanging in there, but the going was a bit rough.

A small flock of seagulls were scavenging outside of their open window squabbling over food thrown out of the windows by other patrons in spite of a little white placard on each table advising against the practice. They often shrieked at each other making a nuisance of themselves disturbing those who wished to eat in peace. Hokee just shook his head at the racket and gave Glory a winsome smile that said "*what ya gonna do?*"

"Shamans spend several years learning protection rituals that enable them to ward off negative energy," Hokee said continuing his lecture between bites of succulent mussel. "Much of their training includes learning numerous rites and rituals including how to access the astral plane. They use amulets and talismans. A talisman is used to draw things to you. An amulet keeps things away."

"Are you talking about things like a witch's black cat?" Glory asked.

"No. They are called a 'Familiar' which is an animal-shaped spirit, or some believe a minor demon that serves a witch or magician as a domestic servant. They can act as a spy and companion. A talented witch or magician can use their Familiar to bewitch enemies and obtain astral information."

"Oh yeah. I kind of remember that stuff, but I thought it was all fairy tales and make believe."

"It sort of is in a way," Hokee said. "This is a view portrayed by Hollywood and suspense writers; often by those who really know. It is kind of like hiding the truth in plain sight."

"That witch stuff is really interesting," Glory said. "Are there black witches as well as white ones?"

"Oh, absolutely," Hokee said with force. "In fact, our little thief is a practitioner of black magic which is why we're doing this little lesson in energy and power. The thief's doppelganger is actually one grotesque form of a Familiar. Remember this all relates to energy and how it can be used. A shaman becomes adept at channeling energy for their particular purposes much like our thief has done. Whether the energy is used in a positive or negative manner depends on the practitioner. A shaman spends several minutes each morning performing protection rituals to ward off any negative energy thrusts that might be encountered during the day."

With her head spinning, Glory was happy to see their server reappear with several plates containing their salmon and side dishes of Thai mint-truffle sauce. There was also a loaf of fresh baked local bread made with island spices and whipped butter. The restaurant specialized in beautiful presentations of fantastic cuisine. Hokee and Glory were not disappointed. Each plate of salmon was decorated with spears of lemon grass and mint leaves with a beautiful green sauce dribbled around the plate in an exotic island pattern. Diving into their meal it was several minutes before Hokee continued. Neither party could prevent moans of satisfaction from escaping their lips as they devoured the salmon.

Finishing his meal Hokee asked, "Would you like to end with a cordial? This might be our last chance to relax for a while. I would actually like to have a Grand Marnier."

"That sounds great although I prefer a Frangelico. I think that Hazelnut flavor would go better with the salmon," Glory answered.

Signaling their server Hokee ordered drinks to suit each appetite.

"After we finish our lunch I think it is time to start working," Hokee said after sipping on his Grand Marnier. "I suggest checking out the hotels to find out if Donald McKenzie is registered."

"Are we all through with the shaman lessons?" Glory asked.

"I think you have heard enough to understand what we're dealing with," Hokee answered. "There is not enough time to teach you any protection rituals so you will be fair game when we meet our thief. You must stay very close to me in order to be covered by my shield. That is the primary reason I have told you so much about shamanism. I wanted you to understand that this is no game. The powers are real as you must know by what you have learned about the actual theft."

"I believe," she said. "I don't pretend to understand everything you have been telling me, but I believe. I'll stay close." She was secretly delighted to be included in the hunt and was smiling inwardly at the thought of sticking close to the big mystical detective doubling as a shaman.

CHAPTER TWENTY-EIGHT

Finding the Thief

Returning to the Ambassador to use the telephone in their room they discovered only one instrument in their entire suite. Hokee agreed to let Glory use the telephone in their room while he would return to the front desk to book another room. Using the telephone guide in their room they discovered 120 hotels that would be appropriate for someone like their thief. They divided up the hotels alphabetically with approximately half of the hotels listed before the H's with the remainder between I and Z. Glory took the first half leaving I to Z for Hokee. Giving Glory a light kiss and hug he left the room leaving her to begin phoning the hotels on her list. Unfortunately, their division gave Glory the first part of the alphabet with the Ambassador right near the top of the list.

Playing a hunch Glory called the front desk and asked if a Mr. Donald McKenzie was checked in as a guest? It was really no surprise to discover that he was registered with a room on the first floor right beside the large kidney shaped swimming pool. Ignoring the warning bells going off in her head regarding Hokee's description of McKenzie's power Glory decided to take a quick peek at his room to see where he was staying. What could be the harm in that? She was just a little ashamed to go running off on her own while Hokee was still calling hotels looking for the thief but she was after all an investigative reporter. Besides, wouldn't Hokee be surprised when she told him that the thief was registered in their very own hotel. She couldn't wait to see the look in his eyes when she would tell him that she had actually seen his room and knew exactly where he was staying. She might also get lucky and see the thief out by the pool catching some sun or flirting with one of the guests.

*****

She was not to be so lucky.

The Ambassador hall floors were golden yellow tile squares interspersed with colorful stones in a mosaic pattern of flowers and leaves. Glory was wearing a pair of island flip-flops that squeaked on the floor as she walked. Since nearly everybody else was wearing the same kind of footwear she didn't give the noise a second thought. Unfortunately, she was the only person walking down the hall at that moment and the noise from her feet caused the man in a straw hat and Hawaiian shirt standing by the door with a room key in his hand to turn and see who was making the noise. Too late she recognized the busboy from the restaurant. Before she could think of some way to react the man calling himself Donald McKenzie reached out to stroke her head with his right hand, then quickly walked into his room and closed the door. There was no one else within sight that could associate him with the girl. Glory was left standing in the hallway with no memory. She had total amnesia. Not only did she not know where she was, she did not know her name or what she was doing in the hallway let alone the hotel. The man in a straw hat and colorful shirt carrying two bags leaving his room in a hurry a couple of minutes later and walking down the hallway towards the front desk never registered on her brain.

Hokee had spent two hours calling hotels and inns all over the island without success before taking a break. He was a little disappointed that Glory had not checked in but thought she was probably just as busy as he was and didn't give the matter much thought. Getting up and stretching out his back he decided to go check out Glory and see if she was having any better luck. Knocking on the door to give her a little warning that he was coming he used his key opening the door to their room. To his surprise there was no Glory.

Her purse was on the bed and a chair was placed over by the table with the telephone. A pad of paper and a pencil was by the phone where she had been working but there was absolutely nothing to suggest where she might have gone. Thinking she might have just gone out for a little walk to stretch her legs he decided to take a stroll to see if he could spot her maybe down by the pool or even in the bar having a cocktail. Before leaving he wrote a short note on the pad of paper she had left by the telephone telling her what he was doing just in case he missed her and she returned and then tried to get in touch with him.

He checked the pool area, the bar and restaurant before walking down to the beach. There was no sign of Glory and Hokee was starting to get a bad feeling. Knowing Glory's competitive nature and her reporter's penchant for being first he started thinking that perhaps she might be in some serious trouble. He checked with the doorman out front to see if she had taken a cab but the doorman had no recollection of seeing her come by his station. He swore that if she had come out of the front door looking for a cab he would have noticed and remembered.

Hokee checked with the front desk to see if Glory had checked in for messages or information but the girl in a bright green sarong behind the counter had no information. He returned to their room hoping he might have missed her and she was back at work calling hotels. In his gut, he knew the room was empty before he even opened the door. Everything was exactly as he had left it thirty minutes earlier. The question now became what to do next?

Before embarking on a hunt that could involve movement in many different areas Hokee's rule was to take time and give the situation some thought. What could possibly have happened? Why would Glory leave the room without letting Hokee know where she was going? What would entice her to leave the room without her purse, her money and identification? The answer to every question seemed to be somehow related to Donald McKenzie. And if he was the reason she had left that meant she had found him. And if she had left the room leaving behind everything but her room key that meant that McKenzie was probably staying right here in their hotel. Glory was tasked with calling all of the hotels beginning with A and Ambassador certainly began with an A. Picking up the phone Hokee called the front desk and asked if Donald McKenzie was registered as a guest. It came as no surprise to discover that McKenzie had been registered but had checkout out nearly two hours earlier. Room 107 had not been serviced since his departure and was not scheduled for maid service until tomorrow morning. Thanking the desk for their help Hokee hung up the telephone and headed downstairs to find room 107.

Hokee stopped by the front desk on his way to room 107 inquiring after Mr. McKenzie. He was informed that McKenzie had checked out rather abruptly a few hours earlier. He had been alone and seemed to be in a hurry. Checking with the doorman Hokee learned that yes, McKenzie had caught a cab earlier in the day and had been alone at the time. With mounting concern twisting a knot in his guts, Hokee went back to the front desk and asked to see the manager.

Hector Rutherford was a small, thin, mousy man with a bald head and a long handle-bar mustache wearing bifocals. Introducing himself, Hokee explained about his missing partner and their search for a dangerous thief. It didn't seem wise to elaborate on exactly what kind of danger the thief represented. Hokee asked for immediate access to room 107 hoping that Glory was simply tied up inside but knowing that was very unlikely. Remembering Brent Morden's withered arm he could only surmise the kind of damage McKenzie might have done to Glory. The fact that the thief had checked out so abruptly and alone suggested that Glory had encountered him and been recognized. She did mention previously that he had been her busboy back in Pocatello. Glory was not a person you would be likely to forget.

To his credit the manager did not stall and ask a bunch of needless questions but simply grabbed a master key and took off for the thief's room leaving Hokee to trail along behind. Opening the door, Rutherford entered with Hokee right behind. The room had evidence of a very hasty departure. Bedding and towels were strewn about the room and heaped in piles. Clothes hangers were scattered around the room. Dirty socks and soiled underwear were left on the floor. The room was a mess indicating that the occupant had left in a hurry. What was not in the room was any sign of Glory. Hokee was almost positive that the thief had left the hotel in a hurry without Glory and she was not being held in the vacated room. What had happened to the beautiful, intrepid, investigative reporter from New York? What did McKenzie do to her and where was she now?

Hokee enlisted the manager's help to begin a thorough search of the entire hotel. Within five minutes the manager organized a search of the hotel and surrounding grounds utilizing every available hotel employee. Every closet, cubbyhole, and storage area was searched. The grounds and pool area were thoroughly combed with someone looking under every bush, behind every hedge and tree. With great reluctance after thirty minutes of searching every available place a body might be stored with no sign of the missing woman, Rutherford called off the search releasing his staff to resume their normal duties. He was obviously distraught showing signs of fatigue. Drooping shoulders and hound dog face streaked with worry lines were evidence of a man under considerable strain. A missing influential guest with suggestions of foul play would not enhance the reputation of his hotel. Hokee had Rutherford contact the local police to see if they would begin searching the island for any sign of his missing partner. He gave the manager a copy of Glory's driver's license photo to give to the police, keeping the license for his own use. Using the old Wolf technique of thinking before action Hokee returned to their room for a brief period of meditation and thoughtful planning.

CHAPTER TWENTY-NINE

Glory's Nightmare

Losing one's memory is a very frightening experience. Imagine a magnetic computer disk holding all your life's precious information; pictures, sounds, names, dates, friend's names, family information and every event in your life suddenly being wiped clean by a strong magnet. This was what Glory was experiencing standing in the Ambassador hallway outside of the thief's room. She not only didn't have any idea where she was or what she was doing there, but she didn't even know her name. She had no identity. No knowledge of who she was. When the thief wiped Glory's memory banks, the operating systems had not been included. Her brain still retained the programs to walk, speak, and control her bodily functions. She had just lost everything she had ever learned since birth that did not include internal programming. While standing in the hallway with a totally blank mind the only assets she had were her keen intellect and her imagination.

Unfortunately, there was nothing in her mind with which to compare anything. How can you imagine anything if you don't know anything? Walking towards the glass door leading outside to the pool and beach she noticed this person walking towards her. It was only when she was about to bump into the door that she realized that the person she saw was herself. She didn't know she was looking at one of the most beautiful people on the planet as she had no concept of beauty. She just saw someone in the glass and realized that this person was her. Standing there in front of the door she was studying her image when three girls from the pool came in and saw this beautiful creature looking at herself. They immediately assumed that the woman was full of vanity standing there admiring herself. Whispering snide comments to each other just loud enough to be sure they were overheard as they passed her, Glory felt their disapproval, but had no idea what the feelings meant. She only knew that the women passing by made her feel sad and lonely, although those labels could not be affixed to her feelings as she had no idea of sadness or loneliness. She just felt the women's hostility and knew it to be unpleasant.

Wandering outside she saw women and men, boys and girls playing around and in the pool, reading or just catching some sun. They were all expressing feelings of pleasure which made Glory smile, although the sun was ungodly bright. The brilliant sun was hurting her eyes and she noticed that almost everyone was wearing something covering their eyes. Since the bright sunlight was hurting her eyes she could imagine that the eye coverings people were using must somehow help ease the pain. She could also feel the sun's heat on her skin which she could imagine was the same thing that was hurting her eyes. Naturally she wanted something to cover her eyes but had no idea where she might get some for herself. Glory was on her way to ask someone where she could find an eye covering for herself when she realized that she had no idea what they were called or how to ask that simple question. Even with no memory, she still had her incredible brain and could figure out that approaching someone without knowing what you were doing could cause a problem. She remembered all too painfully how awful she felt when the three girls passed her in the hallway making unfriendly remarks about how some people just couldn't get enough of themselves.

Without stopping to talk with anyone, Glory kept walking, going out to the beach. Plenty of people noticed the stunningly attractive blond with a killer body walking around the pool, but St. John's was full of beautiful people and once passed by she was almost immediately forgotten. She found walking in her flip-flops on the sand very difficult as the sand kept getting between the soles of her feet and footwear. Kicking them off she started walking on the sand in bare feet carrying her foot wear, but the hot sand burned so fiercely she immediately slipped them back on. Glory didn't know she was on sand or that the entire big expanse of blue was the ocean. She didn't even know it was water but she knew sand was different than water and seeing the people play in the blue stuff she imagined that it must feel good. She wandered into the water feeling the coolness on her skin marveling at how great it felt. She kept wading out in the ocean until the waves were nearly up to her armpits rendering her typically thin dress transparent. There was no glass door to show her what she looked like but the attention she was attracting from both men and women made her realize that she must be doing something wrong. Glory didn't know that exposing yourself on a public beach was forbidden nor did she even know that she was exposing herself. She only knew that whenever the water dropped below her neck everybody kept looking at her. The men's looks were accompanied by feelings that were very uncomfortable and the women's looks caused her uncomfortable feelings of a different nature. Neither feeling made Glory feel good about herself but she had no idea what she was doing wrong or what to do to make everyone stop staring at her.

The only way to prevent the looks everybody was giving her that caused such discomfort was to stay deep in the water exposing only her head. Seeing that the show was over, everyone went back to minding their own business except for an occasional glance to see if maybe the pretty woman would show them her body once more. As the day drug on Glory bounced around in the ocean with the sun beating down on her head and reflecting onto her face from the water; without even being aware she was slowly being roasted alive.

Hokee enlisted as much of the hotel staff as possible to assist in locating Glory. By now he was convinced that she was alive although had somehow been damaged by the thief. Knowing how the thief had caused Officer Morden's arm to wither Hokee was sure that Glory had likewise been damaged, although trying to guess the nature of the damage this time seemed impossible. It was clear that the thief had left the Ambassador alone and it was equally clear that Glory's body was not stuffed in a closet or hidden under a bush. This could only mean that Glory was alive and not all that far away. Starting by the pool just outside of the hallway from the thief's hotel room Hokee started questioning everyone he could find showing them the driver's license photo of Glory. Several people admitted seeing the beautiful woman wander by but no one could tell where she had gone.

Leaving the pool Hokee went onto the beach repeating his questions to everyone he could find. Before long someone pointed to this head bobbing in the water fifty feet from the shore. Her face was so badly burned that without her long blond hair Hokee would have had trouble recognizing Glory as the missing woman. Wading out into the ocean Hokee started calling her name softly. He could see the glazed look in her eyes and knew that she had to be disoriented. She needed help soon or her face could become permanently scarred.

Glory saw the big tall man with the long black hair and brown skin wading towards her in the water but for some reason his smiling friendly face put her at ease. She could feel that the man meant her no ill will. When Hokee finally reached Glory, he took her hand attempting to lead her back towards the shore but she resisted. The uncomfortable looks she had been receiving made her reluctant to leave the water. Not understanding her problem, but knowing she needed help, Hokee placed his thumb on her neck at a precise spot just below her right ear and applied pressure. Glory slumped into his arms unconscious. Picking her up Hokee carried her to shore and up to their room.

Hokee packed her face in crushed ice wrapped in a hotel towel to begin drawing out the heat. Knowing she would be unconscious for a while longer, he returned to the hotel grounds to look for some aloe. There were several big plants scattered around the buildings and along the walkways as ornamental shrubbery. After picking a few big leaves he quickly stopped by the hotel's kitchen for some comfrey. Returning to their room he squeezed aloe juice mixed with comfrey and crushed ice onto a new wash cloth. This new poultice of ice, comfrey and aloe was placed over her face leaving only her eyes uncovered. As Glory struggled to regain consciousness, Hokee had to restrain her from pulling the cloth from her face. It was only after looking at his friendly smiling eyes and feeling the wonderful coolness from the ice pack on her face that she relented and left the poultice in place.

Using sign language, Hokee conveyed to Glory that he had to leave for a few minutes but that she was to remain lying down with the wrap on her face. Once he was certain that she understood his instructions and would obey, he left to obtain additional supplies. He wanted some vitamin E cream, honey and lavender oil. Returning to the hotel with his purchases he made a paste of crushed and powdered comfrey leaves, lavender oil, vitamin E cream, and aloe juice. A little honey was stirred into the mixture to add some antibacterial properties. Satisfied that the ice pack had pulled most of the heat out of her face, Hokee smeared a thick layer of the poultice paste over her burns, instructing Glory to remain lying down. He held her hands until ultimately, she fell asleep. During the next several hours Hokee alternately used an ice poultice followed by another layer of paste. By the following morning, Glory's face was pitted by small white blisters but there was no swelling and the underlying color was healthy. She wouldn't win any immediate beauty contests but there would be no permanent damage and within a few days her complexion would be normal.

Getting back her looks was one thing. Getting back her memory was a whole different matter.

Chapter Thirty

Finding Glory

Hokee had them stay in their hotel room for the next two days away from the sun and crowds. By the third day, Glory's face was almost normal and meanwhile, Hokee had determined that the thief had erased her memory. He had never tried restoring anyone's memory before and to his knowledge it had never been accomplished. Throughout his years as a shaman in training, Hokee had seen his master perform many miracles, but restoring someone's mind was not among them. However, just because he had never seen it done was not sufficient reason to believe that it was impossible.

If they had been back at his home in Pocatello, Hokee would have at least been able to formulate some kind of plan. Here at St. John in the middle of the Caribbean what was he to do?

First, he needed some herbs, and not just any herbs, some special herbs. His shamanistic training had taught him that throughout time on every land there were certain herbs with hallucinogenic and healing properties. Medicine men, holy men, healers and shamans throughout history have known about these plants and used them in a variety of ceremonies, particularly those ceremonies that helped them obtain and hold onto their power. While he was training under Why-ay'-looh, Hokee had learned how to identify which plants possessed these powers and how to prepare them for ceremonial use.

He had found Glory a large broad-brimmed hat to keep the sun from her damaged skin. After coating her face with a heavy layer of his special paste he helped her get dressed. While she had been resting and recovering in their hotel room, Hokee had purchased her a pair of chic H.I.S. designer jeans and some decent white Famolare walking shoes. This was complemented by a long sleeve red silk shirt that was tight enough to show off her body but loose enough to be comfortable. With a new pair of extra dark sun glasses for her eyes and wearing the floppy large brimmed hat they set out for the hills above Cruz Bay.

Hokee had rented an old American WW II Jeep that had been painted bright red. The paint had faded to a dull orange but with body dents on every surface the paint was chipped showing the underlying Army green in several places. Although it was your basic rust bucket, the old Jeep still had a rugged engine and good tires. Driving as far as possible into the hills they parked the Jeep and began hiking. Hokee had read about a waterfall located almost at the center of the island at the end of a very steep trail. Taking their time, the couple climbed an overgrown trail covered by a thick canopy of lush green trees. Scattered palms were interspersed with Manchineel, calabash and mahogany. There were occasional flamboyant trees with their bright yellow and red blossoms. Along the creek bottom the bay tree grew with its distinctive aromatic leaves. Along every step of the climb they could hear song birds singing a warning about interlopers into their domain, while occasionally catching a glimpse of a warbler, blue bunting or tanager. Nearing the waterfall its noise drowned out the sound of birds and other forest dwellers. Water mist in the air made the ground and dark rocks slippery. They had to be careful to avoid slipping on the steep trail. Glory was unused to such physical activity and she was almost out of breath when they finally arrived at the waterfall's base. This waterfall was not spectacular but its mist was cooling and the pool at its base made for a beautiful refreshing dip.

After they cooled off in the pool Hokee began sampling vegetation in the surrounding area. He knew that vestiges of ancient religions exist in every part of the world. Hokee remembered visiting Tahiti where the indigenous people had worshiped the God Oro before the Christian missionaries arrived. Long, long ago, Oro had been a fun-loving God presiding over festivals and celebrations. Over time he became a cruel, demanding God, who could only be satisfied by the sacrifice of a virgin girl with large pointed breasts. Special raised temples were constructed which still exist. On the highest platform, the priest would cut the throat of the virgin allowing her blood to soak into the lava rock and cinders from which the temple platform had been constructed. Visitors today can buy carved statues of island girls with large pointed breasts, although none of the buyers have any idea why these statues are significant or prevalent in the islands. During Hokee's visit he had met the descendent of one of the old priests who had performed the sacrifices. The descendant, named Malachi, was now a Christian minister. He showed Hokee some temples preserved in the thick forest and described the sacrificial ceremony. It wasn't any wonder why the people were so easily converted to Christianity. The ceremony included feeding the girl certain hallucinating drugs to make her pliable and easy to control. No doubt the priests enjoyed a few other liberties before sacrificing the virgin. Plants from which the drugs were obtained grew in abundance if you knew which plants to select. Malachi showed Hokee the plants chosen for the old sacrificial ceremony and described how they were prepared for the virgin.

Hokee had selected this particular spot hoping that it would provide him with the hallucinogenic herbs he was seeking. With both the water plants and those on the nearby hillside there was an abundant source of vegetation from which to choose. Taking a leaf from each of the likely candidates Hokee would take a very small bite. He would smash the small sample between his teeth and roll the remains around his gums and under his tongue. After observing its effects on his body, he would spit out the residual and wash out his mouth before repeating the process with another leaf.

After a few minutes, he had collected several handfuls of leaves that seemed to offer promise.

Satisfied with his leaf collection Hokee began looking for island fungus. He knew that the most likely place to find the particular mushroom he desired was somewhere up here on the mountain where it was a little cooler and near the waterfall. He searched for several minutes before finding a mahogany tree with a split trunk. The split was facing the north side of the island away from the blistering Caribbean sun. Surrounding forest canopy had kept the tree trunk in deep shade promoting the growth of forest fungus, or what Hokee called magic mushrooms. Without this particular mushroom and its psilocybin Hokee was not confident in his ability to help Glory retrieve her memory and even with this plant he was not certain of his success. He just knew that the space you can acquire by ingesting psilocybin was conducive to tremendous out of body experiences. There are many hallucinogenic drugs but they all induce different kinds of experiences. Hokee knew that LSD had more time distortion while peyote buttons created more of an alternate reality. Psilocybin on the other hand put the user into a multidimensional space where the user's awareness of the universe expands allowing perception of the infinitely small to the macro. Peyote and mushrooms were both used by Hokee's shaman to help someone on a vision quest but Hokee had always found it easier to navigate using the mushrooms. In any event, he was delighted with his find. Now all he had to do was provide a safe place for the next few hours. The mountain they were on was an attractive tourist spot for the adventurous and Hokee didn't want to take a chance on someone coming to the waterfall and discover them out of their bodies.

The couple carefully made their way back down the trail with Hokee's leaf and mushroom collection stowed in a small backpack. Reaching the jeep safely, they drove back down to the marina where Hokee had already made plans to rent a boat. During Glory's recovery from the sunburn Hokee had asked the hotel employees and several of the natives where he could find a private beach without being disturbed. Everyone almost unanimously said Europa Bay. It had a small ugly grey and black sandy beach which extended into a short ten-foot high bluff. The best part was that it could only be accessed by boat and since it offered no bright beautiful sandy beach or coral reefs for snorkeling no one ever went there.

*****

An old 25-foot aluminum fishing boat complete with dented sides and a warped bottom was the only boat available for rent. While ugly it was also slow with a 15 horsepower Evinrude motor, but that was all the boat they needed to make the short journey around the coast to Europa Bay. Hokee made sure that Glory kept her hat on and a coating of paste over her face. The scared, vacant look in her eyes was heartbreaking, but Hokee knew that somewhere in the vast universe her mind still existed. The question was, could the apprentice shaman find her mind and get it back into the woman?

The bluff above the gray sand on Europa Bay was composed primarily of limestone from untold centuries of decaying sea shells. Wind and wave action over the years had carved out large overhangs and a couple of small caves with flat sandy floors. Choosing the cave with the deepest penetration which offered the most privacy from any boat that might pass by Hokee began unloading the boat. He had brought plenty of fresh water, his pack including the herbs and mushrooms, and a small picnic basket for later. The most important item was his handmade leather shaman's bag with the pipe they would use for part of their journey.

Making sure that Glory was seated comfortably with her back against the

174

rear of the cave Hokee gathered driftwood for a small fire. Once he had the fire going he started tearing some of the plants he had collected into little pieces about the size of his small fingernail. By the time he had a good pile of torn up leaves the fire had burned down so there were a few hot coals. Pulling a pot from his pack Hokee poured in a couple bottles of fresh water before stirring in the herbs. He set the pot on the hot coals to heat up the water and make an herb tea. Selecting four of the mushrooms he had picked from the old split mahogany tree was a difficult decision. He could guess that Glory probably weighed around 110 pounds and he wasn't about to ask. His weight was a little more than twice that so he would obviously consume twice as much of the mushroom concoction he was about to make. The problem was the mushrooms were all of different sizes and he was unsure of their potency. Knowing he was probably only going to get one shot at recovering Glory's mind he opted to go big. He just said an old shaman prayer to keep him and Glory safe. He wasn't too worried about getting lost himself, but with Glory and especially given her state of mind he was concerned that she would get lost before he had a chance to make an astral connection.

Using his pocket knife Hokee cut four of the biggest mushrooms into small pieces. Taking an orange, some raw coconut and an apple from his pack he also cut them into small pieces and mixed it all together with the mushrooms making a mushroom salad. By the time his salad was finished so was his tea which now had to cool down before it could be drunk. Hokee's final preparation was selecting another group of leaves he had picked up on the mountain. These leaves had been picked from the plant's bottom so they were dry and crumbly. These he crumbled up into fine little bits which could be packed into his antelope horn shaman pipe. All of the preparations for their journey had been made. It was now up to Hokee to see if he could find Glory's mind.

He began with an old shaman's chant. A chant that has been handed down for so many generations no memory can recall the beginning. While continuing the chant, he undressed and took a quick swim in the ocean to begin preparing his body. Using some of the native grass growing along the top of the bluff he brushed his aura several times making sure he had completely removed any unwanted travelers from his energy field. Lighting his pipe, he breathed in a big lungful of smoke which he blew out quickly into a cloud that surrounded his body helping to seal and protect him from any unwanted negative energy bursts. With the pipe burning he went into the cave where Glory was sitting handing her the pipe. She had been watching Hokee throughout his preparations and had seen him smoke the pipe so she knew this was what he wanted her to do. She took in a long lungful of smoke and Hokee had to hold up his hand to stop her from expelling the smoke too soon. After a few seconds, he indicated that she could exhale and taking the pipe he repeated her actions. From his shaman training Hokee knew that the smoke would calm their nerves, relax the muscles in their bodies and make the transition into an altered state of consciousness much smoother.

Resuming his chant Hokee brought in the pot with the tea and a couple of hotel coffee mugs. He then brought in the salad with a couple of bowls and two hotel forks. The mushrooms would take a little longer to have an effect so Hokee had them each eat a bowl of salad with Hokee's salad twice the size of Glory's. Hokee hoped that the mushrooms he had found were like those he had used in Idaho. They were intended to promote a shift in consciousness allowing that aspect of our conscious being to expand beyond the reaches of our normally limited perspective.

Pouring their tea, they sat side by side while they drank it washing down the remainder of their salad. Hokee used the tea to heighten their senses. While traveling in the void one needs every possible help in order to survive and return. By the time they had finished their tea Hokee was beginning to feel the hallucinogenic effects of the drugs so he put one arm around Glory's back and took both of her hands with his other hand. Their journey was about to begin. There was one final chant Hokee performed before falling silent. This chant invoked the spirits of all shaman masters throughout history to help keep them safe and render whatever assistance was possible.

Their journey together into the vast reaches of the unknown was beginning. Only by using everything he had ever learned about the shaman's way could he succeed. He could only pray that it would be enough.

CHAPTER THIRTY-ONE

The Search Began

In the Infinite, there are no atoms, no molecules, no matter. Everything is pure energy. Physical eyes are useless. Energy pulsates, vibrates and swirls in spirals like water flowing in a creek. The colors and shapes are everywhere but only visible with the eyes shut. In fact, you don't really have any eyes. You don't even have a body. There is no distance in space and no measurement of time. In this hallucinogenic state time and space do not exist. Initially you feel lost in the infinite realm of nothingness, called the "Void".

After the transition of separating from his body, Hokee began the process of searching for the physical entity of Glory sitting beside him in the cave. First, he had to locate his own body. In the earthly 3D reality, his body was still sitting in the cave, but Hokee was now in another dimension. His first task was to utilize his mental concentration to create an arm for his body in this nonphysical reality where he needed to function.

After ultimately forming an arm, Hokee had to find Glory's body and get her to recognize his presence. After groping around with his newly formed arm he was able to locate Glory's body and her hand. Grasping her hand and squeezing it gently, he tried to establish communication.

"Glory," he said aloud as he squeezed her hand. "Glory, it's important that you listen to me. I know you can hear me, but I may sound far away. Glory, answer me." He continued to put pressure on her hand.

"Glory, remember our sweat lodge experience back in Idaho? You probably don't remember that experience right now but this is almost the same thing. No matter how far away I sound listen to my voice and come to me."

Hokee kept speaking her name and gently squeezing her hand until he felt a slight response in her fingers. After a couple more tries she finally answered, "Yes, I can hear you."

Hokee had never before experienced such overwhelming relief. He knew that if he could experience the rest of his body right now, his heart would be hammering against its cage. Now that Glory could hear his voice, if she could concentrate her mind on his instructions, it might be possible to actually succeed in locating her memory. Since he had established contact they could begin searching for Glory.

Knowing from his shamanistic training that every thought exists in the collective consciousness, he also knew that the collection of distributed thoughts was accessible all the time by anyone who could tune into this dimension. It is much like tuning your radio to a specific frequency. The space surrounding each individual on earth is saturated by a variety of signals from their experienced realities throughout the universe, creating a unique signature. It was now Hokee's job to locate that stream of consciousness that was Glory, intact as her astral body, also known as the Ka, that could not be damaged or have its memory stolen. The thief may have been able to wipe the memory from her brain functioning on earth, but he could not destroy the infinite thoughts and memory that made up the Glory consciousness that existed in the collective mind. Hokee would not only have to find her Ka, but would then need to help Glory realize that this memory body of thoughts belonged to her. How could he tune into the thoughts of Glory in this vast universe of collective energy?

Initially he tried thinking about Glory and how she looked; how she sounded and remembering her mannerisms. It took a few minutes before he realized that these were his thoughts, not Glory's. Man, this was harder than he had imagined.

He had to continually speak her name and squeeze her hand in order to keep her with him and meanwhile try to figure out how to find her thoughts. It's kind of like trying to find one particular drop of water in the ocean. Somewhere in this vast ocean of thoughts there were those that had once emanated from Glory.

Entrainment is a scientific process that mentally produces the bonding of thoughts by aligning their vibrations. Thoughts are vibrations seeking harmony, which means that every wavelength wants to join with like wavelengths and thoughts manifest as energy wavelengths. If Hokee could get Glory to start thinking about something she had thought about before, maybe it would attract the previous thoughts she had cast outward into the collective consciousness where she always exists.

"Glory," he called. "Are you listening to me?"

After a long hesitation, "Yes, I am listening."

"We put a beautiful dress on you yesterday. Do you remember that beautiful dress?"

This time the hesitation was shorter. "Yes, I remember that dress."

"Did you like how you looked in that dress?"

Without hesitation, "Oh yes. I loved that dress"

"You have a lot of beautiful dresses and you look great in every one of them. I want you to think about wearing your dresses and how much you would enjoy looking beautiful in those dresses.

Will you do that for me?"

"Okay, I can do that." She sounded weak and far away so Hokee gave her hand a slight squeeze. "Glory, try really hard to think about how you look in your dresses; this is important."

"Glory you worked as an investigative reporter for television. Remember the television set in our room at the hotel?"

In a weak voice glory responded, "I remember the television in our room."

"At one time, you used to be one of the people talking on the television set. Can you imagine yourself being on the television and talking to the people watching?"

"Okay, I can try." Glory sounded weak and far away. Hokee was afraid that he was losing her.

"Glory," he yelled squeezing her hand. "Come back to my voice and don't leave me. I need you here."

"I hear you Hokee." She sounded better and he could feel her presence way out there in that sea of consciousness.

"Okay Glory. Good. Now see yourself wearing that beautiful dress you were wearing yesterday and see yourself on television talking to people watching you and telling them about staying at the hotel."

He could feel Glory's presence growing stronger and felt that he was on the right track. "Okay Glory, keep thinking about being on television and talking to people. See yourself on television in front of cameras. Keep on having those thoughts while seeing yourself. This is very important."

The more he talked to her about her previous life and linking it to events of the past few days, the stronger he could feel her presence was becoming

179

identified. Even so, it came as a complete surprise when Glory suddenly announced, "Hokee, I can remember, I remember everything. Oh, I'm so sorry I tried to see the thief alone. You must have been out of your mind these past few days."

Hokee was so happy and relieved it seemed like the entire universe was suddenly filled with light as he busted out laughing in a body he couldn't feel. "Glory, you're the one who's been out of your mind, but yes, I have been more than a little concerned. Welcome back."

*****

They kept talking, with Glory recounting her experiences while being locked in a vacuum inside of her own head. Hokee needed her voice to connect within this astral world, as the physical body just wasn't strong enough at this point to travel without getting lost in this infinite space of consciousness. Although Hokee had no idea how strong the drugs were that he had given himself and Glory, his previous experience led him to know that if you just kept your thoughts consistent throughout the procedure, eventually the energy within the drugs runs its course and you will return home to your earth-body.

Gradually the effects of the strong drugs began wearing off and their bodies become more solidified. When he could see Glory's body he knew their trip was nearly over. Hokee led Glory out of the cave and into the beautiful blue ocean for a cleansing dip. Hearing her laugh made the big man feel strong and whole once again. It was with a heart full of gratitude that he silently gave the Silver Fox a gigantic thanks. He knew that somehow the old shaman was aware of his recent journey and would not have been surprised if the old Fox had not actually been out there with them in the sea of consciousness.

After fully regaining earthly consciousness, Hokee pulled a picnic basket out of the old aluminum boat. He didn't know when he packed the boat for their trip how everything would turn out, but from previous experience he knew that a powerful cosmic trip required some recovery time. So, he had packed a basket with yellowfin tuna sandwiches and a couple bottles of cold Red Stripe beer packed in a bag of hotel ice. This was one of the situations when a cold beer is the only solution to a deep thirst.

With her body cleansed by the ocean, Glory was lying naked on the beach with a cold beer, "My God Hokee, I don't know how to thank you for giving me my life back."

Looking at the fantastic naked body lying at his side, Hokee responded with a face-splitting grin, "Oh beautiful woman, I think this clever Indian will figure out some way you can thank me."

"How did you know how to help me get my memory back?" Glory had a puzzled look on her face as she remembered how it felt being so lost and couldn't imagine anyone ever finding her memory let alone getting it back into her mind.

With a straight face and serious tone to his voice Hokee responded, "Heap big shaman secret, pale face," and then he busted out laughing. Not so much at what he thought was a clever response, but mostly a release from the tension and fear he had been harboring and the relief he was feeling at having been successful. "It's really great having you back Glory. Words will never be adequate to express how much you were missed."

Hokee made sure that Glory kept her face lathered in sun block and wore her big floppy hat as they ate their fish sandwiches, drank the beer and talked about the past few days. After exhausting that topic and having regained most of their body strength it was time to get back to work. After making sure the site looked pristine and clean again Hokee put the packs and picnic refuse into the aluminum boat and headed back to the marina and their hotel. It was time to make a new plan for finding and dealing with the elusive thief.

CHAPTER THIRTY-TWO

Making Plans

How did that bitch find me? Probably that big Indian freak. God I hate those snoopy do gooders. I could really like living here. The women here don't seem to be too put off by my looks and I love all that sun. My headaches do seem a lot better as well. If only they would leave me alone and let me live here in peace and enjoy my money. And hell yes, it is my money. I earned that shit. And besides, they owed that to me for all the pain they caused.

What am I going to do with that big Indian? He'll keep nosing around until eventually we'll run into each other. He knows a little bit now about what I can do but I doubt he fully understands my powers. What do I know about his power? Not much. But what kind of power does it take to find a bunch of missing kids?

Okay. He found me. But what kind of big deal is that? We know he's smart and probably just figured out that I was using fake names to skip town. I never heard of him performing any miracles or anything. Yeah, yeah! He lived with some old Indian medicine man or something for a while when he was just a kid but what the hell do they know? They just beat on old drums and shake bone rattles to chase away the evil spirits. It probably doesn't do any good but even blind rats can find the cheese.

No, I know he ain't no damn blind rat, but still; just because he can find people don't make him God or something. Don't wanna underestimate the bastard and it doesn't hurt to be careful, but what can he do against the power I got? Not too much I'm thinking. I just have to keep watch and make sure that I see him first. If I can just touch him before he sees me the ball game is over. I win. He loses.

I'm gonna make that big Indian sorry he ever thought about coming after my ass. Hell, when I get through with him, he'll wish he never heard of me, but then again, he won't be doin any more wishing, again-ever.

CHAPTER THIRTY-THREE

Preparation

A storm brewing out east across the Atlantic brought a tequila sunrise to Hokee's hotel window. The red orange and gold light played across the man's troubled features as he stood looking out across the ocean. Glory was still sleeping after their reunion celebration which lasted most of the night, so she missed seeing what looked like firelight dancing on his dark skin. It was just as well since it was a scene that portended trouble. Hokee was under no illusion about the thief's unbelievable power. While he basically understood that kind of power and how it could be generated, he had never personally experienced that kind of power in the physical form. He knew a certain amount of magic and protection rituals. The question was, did he know enough? Was all of his protection and shaman knowledge strong enough to withstand the thief's powers?

There was no question in Hokee's mind that sooner or later they would come across the thief. He also was under no illusion that the thief was just sitting around waiting to be found. The thief was intelligent and elusive. He had proven that time and again. Had it been Hokee whose mind had been erased there was no doubt that the search would have ended right then because Glory would not have had a clue about where to look for the disappearing thief.

That wasn't Hokee's problem. The old Wolf knew exactly where his quarry was hiding. He hadn't wasted the opportunity with the excellent hallucinating drugs. While helping Glory he used the power to locate the thief and determine his mindset. The location had been easy; the mindset not so much. There was no question of the thief ever returning to Pocatello. It was equally improbable that they would be able to haul the thief back without extreme difficulty. He would die first and undoubtedly take others with him if at all possible. It was kind of like catching a badger in his hole. There is no more wicked or dangerous animal than a threatened badger when backed into a tight corner. Badgers have been known to kill three and even four large dogs that had been attacking it as a pack. Hokee saw the thief as a frightened badger. Any confrontation must be handled with great care.

These were his troubled thoughts reflected by a gorgeous sunrise. While Hokee saw the beautiful sky and a few floating gulls playing in the ocean breeze they barely registered on his consciousness. So preoccupied was he with his thoughts that when Glory walked up behind him and threw her arms around his waist in a big good morning hug, he nearly jumped out of the window.

"Wow! I hardly expected that reaction to a simple hug," she said.

Turning around Hokee had a sheepish grin on his face reflecting his surprise and chagrin at being caught so unexpectedly. "Wow back at ya, and good morning to you, beautiful," he responded trying to regain his composure.

"I must really have startled you," she said as he turned around facing her. "Where were you just now?"

"Yeah, you really caught me." The surprised face had turned into a sheepish grin. "It isn't often that I let myself get surprised like that."

"Oh, I get that. But you didn't answer my question," she teased.

"There will be time enough for that later," Hokee responded, avoiding the subject of his concerns. "Let's order room service, or we can go downstairs if you prefer. I've been waiting for the sleepyhead, that's you, to rise and shine so we can get fed. Speaking strictly for myself I worked up quite an appetite last night."

Glory knew he was avoiding the subject of his thoughts and had a pretty good idea of what they might have been, but she was willing to wait until later to discuss the issue. "I could eat," was her response followed by, "you weren't the only one who worked up a hunger. If you don't mind, I'd rather order room service. I still don't feel comfortable showing my face."

"The peeling will stop in a couple more days," Hokee quickly responded. "You actually look fantastic. Just keep that moisturizing lotion slathered on and you'll soon have beautiful new skin. How about an old fashioned three egg ham and cheese omelet with a side of bacon, a couple of English muffins with fresh jam and two pots of coffee?"

"Sounds good," she responded. "How about you order while I take a shower and make myself look as good as possible."

"No problem," he said, "but first, take a quick look at this fantastic sunrise before it slips away. You've missed the brightest colors but I was too lost in my head to really appreciate it as well." Hokee spun her around so she could see out of the window while he looked over her shoulder. "Looks like a storm way out over the horizon," he said. "That's what gives us these great colors. With any luck, we should be long gone before it gets here, if this is even where it's headed."

"It really is quite fantastic," Glory said as she peeled away and headed towards the bathroom. Looking back over her shoulder as she walked away she gave Hokee the full Gloria Bingham 100-watt smile while she twitched her ass. "You just make sure we have some breakfast after I get beautiful."

"Yes ma'am." And then she was gone.

With breakfast over they relaxed outside on their balcony drinking coffee watching the day come alive. Hotel gardeners were going around picking up dead leaves and blossoms that had fallen during the night and maintenance workers were hosing down the sidewalks washing off the sand left by the nighttime beach partying crowds. A slight breeze ruffled palm fronds sending a quiet clattering across the courtyard. Gulls were riding the wind searching for something to scavenge and a song bird was singing up a storm, but Hokee couldn't identify the species. The air carried a hint of perfume from a variety of scented blossoms and sitting there in the shade on their balcony it really did feel like paradise. At least it would be paradise if Hokee could relax his mind. He was not afraid for himself. He had faced many kinds of danger and was not afraid of confronting the thief. His concern was for Glory. He knew she would not let herself be left behind and she had earned the right to see this affair to its conclusion. Besides, she had insisted on having her employer pay their expenses predicated on getting a fantastic story. Unless she was there at the end she could not honestly complete a full report.

Glory was finally through waiting. "Okay, big guy, it's time to come clean. What in the hell is going on in the fantastic detective brain of yours?"

Hokee couldn't tell her that his concerns were for her safety. That sounded too paternalistic and too much like macho male bullshit even if it happened to be the truth. Instead he opted to tell her the real danger. "Our Mr. Donald McKenzie has some awesome powers as you now know firsthand. I don't know how well my protection rituals will work against his power. I'm pretty sure that I can protect myself, at least from serious harm, but I'm not really sure how to protect you. I can teach you some basic aspects of the Kabala and ritual Magick which will give you a frame of reference for the 'Banishing Ritual'. You will have to learn this basic ritual today before we proceed. Unless you understand the meaning of the ritual it will not be powerful enough to provide adequate protection. True practicing magicians and shamans spend years practicing and perfecting their craft. I spend a few minutes each morning doing my own protection rituals, but that just keeps me from making any serious blunders."

"Whew. That's quite a speech Hokee. In other words, you're afraid for my safety."

Once again Hokee was taken by her quick mind. "Well yeah, I am not even sure I can protect myself since I do not know exactly what power he commands. I would not think of leaving you behind, but how to best protect you is my main concern."

"What's this Kabala thing?" she asked. "I've heard of it but never paid much attention. Isn't it some kind of religious thing?"

"No," he answered. "The Kabala is a millennial old monotheistic tradition that teaches us that the ultimate divine source is beyond our human comprehension. Having just experienced the collective consciousness of our universe you have a glimpse of just one aspect of the Divine. We need to cultivate an aspect of divine protection now to establish our power for when we encounter Mr. McKenzie."

"Okay," she said showing wrinkles in her forehead and at the corners of her eyes. "I'm seriously committed." Glory wasn't about to back down but proceeding with caution certainly made sense. Remembering how lost she had recently been was also fresh on her mind. "Teach me this protection ritual."

Hokee stood up arching his back in a luxurious stretch. "We need to go inside and shut the balcony doors so the whole world won't hear us shouting and call for the police. In order to really get into the protection ritual every cell of your body has to be activated. You must move and speak loudly and forcefully so that your body resonates with the sound and your intention. Are you ready to begin?"

Glancing ruefully at the peaceful scene below their balcony, Glory reluctantly stood up and grabbed Hokee's hand. "Okay lover, teach me what I need to know."

*****

187

Walking her inside and sliding the door shut Hokee began, "First you need to understand 'The Tree of Life'. The Tree of Life is the foundation for all Kabalistic teachings and the basis for all true magic. It shows us the relationship between all of the significant life forces."

With a focused look at Hokee showing that she was really ready to undertake this training seriously Glory said, "Wow! How come I've never heard of this powerful teaching before?"

CHAPTER THIRTY-FOUR

Protection

Hokee spent the entire day working with Glory, teaching her as much magic and shamanism as he could in the time they had available. He had her drawing a pentagram with the proper orientation on their bedroom floor marking the points with shoes. The four cardinal directions were emphasized with the correct colors using clothes from both of their suitcases. He had her construct an alter using a lamp table draped with a folded white sheet from their bed. A wine glass made her challis and Hokee gave her a knife for the dagger. Fortunately, Hokee's shaman survival kit, which he never went on long trips without, had a candle for her fire and a simple water glass full of bottled water that completed the alter preparation.

They worked straight through the day skipping lunch. Towards sunset Hokee felt that they had accomplished as much as possible without having a significantly longer period of time. Pulling Glory into his arms he dropped the serious teacher persona and as his face broke into that wide grin that showed off his pearly whites, he said, "Hey beautiful, let's straighten up the room and go out for a magnificent plate of shrimp and a cold martini."

Glory was so exhausted she could barely focus, "Hey yourself lover," she croaked. "let's screw the room and go eat now. We can straighten out the room later."

"Look," he said smiling. "You go use the facilities and get ready to go. I'll fix the room. It won't take but a minute. I don't want the maid coming in while we're gone and seeing what we've been doing. It's a private matter, kind of sacred."

True to his word, when she returned to the bedroom you would never know it had been a site used for Magick.

Francine's Seafood Restaurant featured some of the best shrimp on the island. It was housed in a squat, wooden building with faded red paint built out over the water so that sitting at the tables by the railing you could look straight down into the ocean. The inside had been well maintained with heavy-oiled, wooden plank floors gleaming in the candle light. There were dozens of candles in white chimney glasses arranged around the room on wall sconces and on each table. A heavy, polished brass rail highlighted the bar along the wall on one side of the room. The waiters were all men dressed in pleated black pants and bleached white shirts. It took Hokee a couple of seconds to realize that the bright white shirts were augmented by discreetly placed black lights.

Seated at a corner table with the ocean on two sides Hokee and Glory could both look down at white seagulls riding the gentle waves waiting for scraps of food thrown over the railing. Sipping a really cold Bombay gin martini, Glory had recovered enough to ask, "How are we going to find the thief, Hokee?"

"This seems like a good time to tell you that I know where the thief is," Hokee said, trying to refrain from showing off but happy to share what he knew.

"You son of a Bitch-Wolf," she screeched trying to sound angry but with her tired voice it came out sounding more like petulance. "I've been worried about that for days and you haven't told me." Now the look in her eyes showed hurt.

"No I didn't tell you Glory." Hokee did not sound or look apologetic. With a very serious look in his eyes that made one pay attention he continued, "You had enough to deal with just getting your memory back. After we found your memories while doing our recovery ceremony, I had some time before we came out of it so I used it to locate McKenzie. He isn't going anywhere. He knows running is futile so he's waiting. I wanted you to focus on you and then your protection. We're going to face him tomorrow."

Glory took a few moments to think about what she had just heard as she watched a sparrow dart into the open dining room looking for food that had spilled onto the floor. The sparrow perched on the back of a vacant chair a couple of tables down the railing. It was a pretty little bird with dark brown feathers tinged with black tips. As Glory took another sip of her drink she watched the sparrow tilt its head towards one side like asking a question, "Are you ready?"

"Is that why you pushed me so hard today? Because you already knew we were going tomorrow?"

"Yes. There isn't any point in postponing our encounter and you are as ready as you can be without extensive training."

"Does he know we are coming?"

"Oh yes. He obviously doesn't know when, but the fact that he encountered you proves he knows we're here. Since we found him he also knows that it's only a matter of time before we find him again. He doesn't know how we found him the first time and I hope that he believes it will take us a few more days to locate him again. The only chance we have at some kind of surprise is to go before he is really expecting us. That means tomorrow."

Glory sat in silence watching the gulls riding waves letting her mind come to terms with the future. She was truly frightened. This was a new experience in her life. Sure, she had moments of high anxiety and worry and there were times when facing the camera, she had been scared. But those scares were not life threatening. She had been afraid of blowing an assignment or making a fool of herself in front of the camera where the whole world might think she was a phony, but that was not real fright.

She now knew real fright and was not sure how to process this new emotion.

Bringing her attention back to the table she asked, "Hokee, have you ever been truly frightened?"

Hokee had watched Glory's face as she studied the seagulls and felt that he could understand the play of emotions she was undergoing. "Yeah, maybe when I was little. When nobody wanted me and I didn't have a home. I was probably really frightened then. But that was a long time ago and I really cannot recall those feelings. I've worked very hard to erase that part of my past. I have never been frightened since living with my shaman. Fear is paralyzing. Whenever faced with a challenging life threatening situation, and I was very recently, the only thing you can do is keep on living and doing until you cannot live or do anymore. As long as you can take one more breath, as long as there is still life in your body you keep on doing."

"Okay, but how do you get rid of the fear?" Glory was deadly serious and Hokee could see the fear in her eyes.

"Oh, Glory sweetheart," he said with a twinkle in his eyes. "You don't get rid of fear. You use it."

CHAPTER THIRTY-FIVE

Meeting Heather

The man calling himself Donald McKenzie sat in a wicker wingback chair staring out the window of his luxurious hotel suite at the distant sailboats on the blue Atlantic Ocean. The boats were heading home racing the coming storm as darkness was only a couple of hours away. His mind was not on the vision outside of his window but focused inward on the problem of defeating the Indian shaman. Gloria, the reporter was not a problem. She might be smart and good looking but powerless against him; he had already proven that. And besides, she was probably so terrified of him that in any future meeting she would literally shit in her panties. But, that damn Indian was a problem.

He had cut off the ponytail and shaved his head. It wasn't so much a disguise as simply a change in persona. He was no longer a long-haired hippie child of the sixties but a mature man with money and a chance to live a normal life. The policeman who caused his injury had been justifiably dealt with and the community at large had provided for his future welfare. Maybe they didn't provide the money voluntarily, but he felt not the slightest bit of guilt about collecting what he felt was owed.

They were getting close. Energy vibrations in the structure of his universe were twitching much like a fly landing in a spider's web sent tremors along the filament to the spider's lair. Undoubtedly that Indian had access to some formidable power in order to locate him so quickly. It wouldn't pay to underestimate the man. The thief had no idea how powerful his adversary was or for that matter the nature of the man's power. Over the years, he had read stories in the newspaper about the amazing successes of Detective Wolf with suggestions that he was using some kind of sixth sense. After being discovered so quickly he no longer considered the detective's powers some super sixth sense. No, it wouldn't pay to fool around with this guy. Maybe it was time to resurrect a friend.

Digging a grave somewhere on the island to hide his body didn't seem like a good idea. First it would take too much time to locate a spot he considered safe and even then he would worry about someone seeing him dig a hole in the ground and investigate the reason. On the other hand, if he did this correctly, he wouldn't need to construct his helper for a long period of time. He was pretty sure that the reporter and her Indian lover boy were holed up in the same hotel he had abandoned a few days previously. All he had to do was find their room and shoot them dead. Dead. Dead. Dead. That had a real final sound.

The old short barrel 32-caliber revolvers he had brought with him from Pocatello only held six shells, but how many bullets did it take to kill a brain-dead woman and an overrated detective. He had bought the gun at a pawn shop shortly after getting his brains scrambled just in case. Well, maybe it was time to make that purchase mean something.

Okay, he could just stay in his room. Hang a "Do Not Disturb" sign over the outside doorknob. It wouldn't take much time to create his new friend. Maybe a couple of hours to get all the details figured out and construct a believable persona. During that time, he could be busy preparing his body for a few hours of deep sleep. Yeah. This could work. The more he thought about it the better it sounded.

Make it a woman. Less threatening. A woman in a sexy bathing suit would cause no alarm. She could walk right up to the two of them and bam, bam, bam. Goodbye detective, goodbye reporter. Hello freedom. Oh yeah. He was liking this more and more. Her name would be Heather and a package would be waiting for her at the front desk. Couldn't have her come to his room. Oh no. Ole Heather just might decide she liked being alive and seeing his helpless body lying there on the bed would be just too much temptation. Better she didn't know where he was and just collect the damn package at the front desk.

Having decided on a plan of action the thief decided there was no reason to wait. Standing up he closed the drapes to his room closing out as much light as possible. He needed a box for the gun and some wrapping paper, so he left his room and walked down the hall to the gift shop in the lobby. After returning to his room and packaging the gun, he wrapped it in plain white wrapping paper and then he addressed it to Miss Heather Dopper. He thought the name rather appropriate. Leaving the package at the front desk for pickup by Miss Dopper, the guest named McKenzie returned to his room.

The preparations were simple. He needed to hydrate his body and evacuate whatever possible before beginning his deep breathing. It normally took thirty minutes of deep heavy breathing to saturate his body with enough oxygen to keep his cells healthy. After going into the hibernation mode, he would breathe once every two or three minutes. His heart would beat twice every minute just to keep his blood circulating. The room air was already around eighty degrees but the thief still wrapped himself in a couple layers of blankets to maintain body heat. After completing all of his preparations, the thief took one final drink of water before lying on the bed. He immediately began a slow deep breathing pattern with a full in and out breath lasting thirty seconds. Heather was about to come alive on the beach.

Several people were lingering in the late afternoon sun, lying on hotel beach towels slathered in lotion. After spending the whole day sunning on this beach, they knew who their fellow beach mates were, and were therefore quite surprised to discover a beautiful girl with long, dark hair lying in their midst. No one could remember seeing her arrive which was shocking, given her fabulous golden-tanned body and revealing white bathing suit. All eyes followed her as she languidly got up and strolled towards the hotel.

The beautiful girl approached the front desk and was immediately attended to by a very willing male desk clerk. "May I help you miss?"

"Are you holding a package for me? Miss Heather Dopper."

"Oh yes," stammered the clerk. "It was left here just a little while ago. It's right here," he said reaching under the counter and handing her the package.

The beautiful girl didn't say anything. She just took the package and walked out the front door looking for a taxi. The agent watched her leave the hotel with mixed emotions. On one hand, she was very attractive and alluring, but those black holes for eyes made him feel very uncomfortable. Maybe even a little frightening. But that was silly, to be frightened of a beautiful long-haired goddess.

CHAPTER THIRTY-SIX

Surprise

Holding hands Hokee and Glory strolled along the beach towards their hotel. Glory's nerves had prevented her from eating much but a couple of stiff drinks were helping her relax. The setting sun was not nearly as spectacular as their brilliant golden Tequila sunrise but every sunset on an island in the Caribbean is fantastic. Hokee was thinking the same thing as they walked along together although he chose not to share the thoughts running through his mind with Glory.

"Do we have a timeframe for tomorrow?" Glory asked as the sun dipped below the horizon.

Jerked back to real time Hokee had to think for a minute. "I haven't picked a time but early is probably better than later."

"I just want to get it over with Hokee. Now that I know what you have planned the waiting is grating on my nerves. I'm so antsy I can hardly stand it."

"That's unfortunately part of the game we're playing. We could go tonight with a few minutes' preparation; however, I believe a good night's rest would do us both some good. You had a pretty intense day."

Groaning in response Glory said, "I doubt I'll be doing much resting, let alone getting any sleep."

Giving her hand a gentle squeeze as they entered the hotel lobby, Hokee predicted, "I know how to make you sleep tonight. Don't worry about resting."

Misunderstanding what he said and maybe unconsciously revealing something of her own mindset she responded, "I don't think I'm up for any of that, and besides fantastic as you are, that isn't the answer."

"I wasn't talking about making love Glory, appealing as that thought might be at the moment," he quickly answered. "I just know a few other tricks that can put you down for a few hours' rest."

"If you're talking about giving me some more of your magic drink shit, no thanks," she said pulling away to push the elevator button. "I'm still half sick from that last batch of drugs you made me swallow."

Laughing Hokee replied as he followed her into the elevator, "No, this is a kind of deep massage therapy where I poke at a few spots on your body that not only relaxes but actually puts you into a deep sleep. It's really quite restful."

*****

Catching his mood Glory had to laugh as well. "It seems to me you've already been poking around in my body."

"See," he said laughing. "You're already starting to relax and I haven't even touched you yet."

They were both still laughing and grinning like happy fools remembering their last love making session when they got off the elevator. Heading down the hall towards their room they noticed a beautiful dark haired girl standing just outside of their door. There was something in her hand mostly concealed down by the side of her legs. The sheer sun cover-up was just gathered enough to make identifying the object difficult.

Hokee knew instinctively that no one should be bothering them at this hour. No one had any business being outside of their door. Instantly on the alert he felt the energy vibrations. They were somehow familiar yet hard to place. It took him a couple of beats before it all clicked into place. That was almost a beat and a half too late.

The highway by Lake Henry.

Those strange feelings he had at the robbery site.

The doppelganger.

The woman turned when she heard their laughter and was also momentarily taken by surprise. She had expected to find them in the hotel room. The blond reporter girl was not supposed to have any mind left and she shouldn't have been out walking around. The slight delay was all Hokee needed to grab Glory and dive into the intersecting hallway. The gun shot was a deafening explosion in the enclosed hall. The first bullet nicked Hokee just above his hip. While diving out of the way he just happened to notice the woman's eyes as she turned and looked at them. They weren't eyes but black holes in her face. There was nobody home.

Hokee and Glory found themselves in a long hallway with a number of doors, all closed. It was a good hundred feet to the other end of the hall to an exit door and the shooter was only about thirty feet away around the corner. There was no way they could make it to the exit before the doppelganger came around the corner. They would be trapped in an enclosed space where it would be almost impossible to avoid being shot down like shooting cattle in a slaughter house.

Knowing their time was limited, Hokee quickly stood jerking Glory up beside him at the same time. Pointing towards the exit door at the far end of the hall he whispered in his most commanding voice, "RUN," while giving her a big shove in the proper direction. He flattened himself on the wall by the corner waiting for the shooter. He knew that the doppelganger would keep on coming no matter what. It was a machine with only one objective. Kill.

This was an old fashioned executive beach hotel with polished hardwood floors in the hallway. Glory made a racket as she ran stumbling in her leather flats towards the exit and Hokee hoped that the shooter would assume they were both fleeing. Their only chance was if that creature with the gun came hurrying around the corner to shoot them before they could make an escape.

It almost worked.

Instead of a beautiful brunette turning the corner with a gun it was a big tall giant with muscles like Mister America. With the element of surprise gone, the thief had changed the doppelganger to an entity more adept at fighting. When the giant came bursting around the corner holding the gun out in front, Hokee was able to chop the gun out of its hands, sending the revolver skittering across the floor, but he now had a different kind of fight.

The brute had a large shaggy head with the same black holes for eyes sitting on top of a thick neck that was bigger around than Hokee's waist. His hands looked like a fielder's baseball mitt and his arms seemed longer than most people's legs. Massive muscled shoulders topped rippling biceps and forearms. What seemed destined to strike fear into any man's heart was the sneering wide open mouth with long vampire-like blood soaked teeth. To make matters even worse this frightening apparition moved with a quickness and grace that belied its exaggerated bulk and size.

Hokee was initially shocked at the beast's size and appearance but not completely surprised. He quickly spun away from the long reaching arms that had attempted to put him in a life ending embrace. How could he defeat this monster?

The gun was out of reach and besides, he wasn't entirely sure that a bullet would end this apparition. He knew only one thing for sure. This doppelganger's entire strength and appearance was strictly due to and limited by the host's willpower. While Hokee knew that the thief obviously was strong-willed there had to be some limit to his power. Unfortunately, there was no way to know what that limit was. In the meantime, the giant began stalking Hokee down the hall as he backed away trying to figure out some kind of strategy to stay alive.

The maniacal grin never left the monster's face as it pursued Hokee down the hall. It was as if this entity considered the investigator's death inevitable. Hokee was desperately trying to figure out some way to avoid this nasty conclusion. His protection rituals had prepared him for a different kind of fight, not a physical confrontation. With Glory somewhere down the hall behind him Hokee knew that if he failed in defeating this being Glory's death was also inevitable. His only option was to fight this giant death machine and somehow win.

With its black eye holes focused on Hokee the giant continued stalking him down the hall. The wicked grimace on its face indicated that there was only one outcome to this slow death march, death to the pursued. While backing down the hall, Hokee slowly bent his knees flexing his thigh and calf muscles up and down getting ready to spring. He let the doppelganger get just beyond its reach before springing. Using all of the strength in his legs, Hokee leaped towards the giant thrusting out his fingers at the last moment directly into its eye holes. With his own muscled hands and arms he jerked downward tearing open the giant's ugly face. And just like that, with that move, the fight ended. The doppelganger disappeared.

The lunging Wolf man nearly fell down on his face stumbling in an effort to regain his balance.

Turning around Hokee saw Glory now halfway down the hall peeking out of the exit doorway with a frightened look on her face. "Hurry Glory," he called. "We have to move quickly."

Running towards the exit doorway where Glory had been hiding Hokee grabbed her hand hustling her down the stairway.

"We have to move quickly Glory," he said as they raced down the stairs. "The thief will be very weak right now from the effort he put into creating his doppelgangers. If we can get to him before he regains his strength, we can end this right now."

Glory didn't understand exactly what had happened but she trusted Hokee and hurried with him towards the front doors of the hotel hoping to find a taxi. They were in luck as one the few taxis on the island was just letting off some new arrivals. Jumping into the backseat before the door could close behind the departing riders Hokee gave the driver the thief's hotel name and address with the admonition to hurry. "It really is a matter of life and death."

CHAPTER THIRTY-SEVEN

Meeting at Last

The taxi driver took one look at Hokee's face and tore out of their hotel parking lot squealing rubber. Whatever demons this man possessed was more than he wanted to deal with. The taxi hurtled down the road swerving around other cars and screeching around corners. It was only a couple of miles to the thief's new hotel which they covered in near record time. Throwing a few bills over the seat for their frightened driver, Hokee and Glory flew out of the cab and up the front stairs of the hotel.

"Do you know the room number?" she asked as they hurried across the hotel's splendid flower decorated lobby before realizing this was a stupid question. Of course he knew the room number. She barely noticed the colorful floral arrangements the hotel manager proudly provided fresh each day.

For some reason known only by the thief, he always took a room on the first or main floor. Hokee and Glory hustled down a short hallway carpeted in a brilliant rose pattern to room 48. Without knocking Hokee kicked the thick wooden door in, tearing its frame from the wall, sending the whole mess bouncing on the floor with a loud crash. He tore into the room followed closely by Glory. The thief was acting drugged and slow, getting up from his bed still wrapped in the green cotton hotel blankets. Ignoring the putrid room odor and without giving the thief a chance to recover, Hokee flipped him over on his face then dug his fingers into the back of the thief's head just behind his ears. Feeling for and finding the right spot, Hokee put him into a deep sleep.

With the thief safely tied up and unable to escape, Hokee had Glory help him fit the door still in its frame back in the wall. No one had come to investigate the commotion and Hokee didn't want to be bothered by anyone during the next hour or so. With the door returned to its rightful position a person needed to be extra vigilant in order to see that there was some kind of problem with the way it looked. They were both satisfied that any hotel guest walking by would be too preoccupied to notice the door to any room but their own. He then had Glory help him move the thief's body into the bathroom.

"What is that horrible smell and what are we doing Hokee? Why the bathroom?"

"That stink is the evil shit coming out of this man's pores," he said nodding towards the thief, "and I want a steam room. After our man is fully awake I need him to drink some special tea I am going to make. We cannot take the chance of transporting him someplace for a sweat lodge so the shower stall will have to suffice. He should stay asleep while I'm gone, but you will need to stay here and watch him while I return to our hotel for my kit. Can you do that?"

"He looks safe enough," she said although you could hear the doubt in her voice. "You won't be gone long will you?"

"No. It won't take me long and you should be perfectly fine. I'm sure he'll stay asleep until I return. I just want to make sure he's still here when I return." Seeing the hesitation in Glory's beautiful eyes combined with some residual fear from her recent ordeal Hokee continued, "On second thought, there is no need for me to go. You can go back to the hotel and get my kit instead and I'll stay here."

Glory didn't want to show the relief she felt but couldn't keep the smile from her face. "Oh Hokee, thank you. I know I shouldn't be afraid but this man really terrifies me. I'll be happy to go fetch your magic potions."

Hokee gave her a full body hug and a long meaningful kiss. He then provided her with the exact location of his medicine bag. The one he never traveled without. Glory was delighted to be given this chore instead of watching over the thief. Tied up as he was and fully asleep she was still afraid of the man. The loss of her mind had left a lasting impression. She didn't think she would ever feel completely safe around that man ever again.

*****

While she was gone Hokee turned the shower on full hot starting to fill the bathroom with steam. Heat combined with hot moist air enhanced the hallucinating effect of the tea Hokee planned on giving the thief upon his awakening. This was going to be hot sweaty work so Hokee stripped down to his briefs. His clothes were neatly stretched out on the bed to prevent additional wrinkling. Now nearly naked, the bullet crease across the top of his hip bone was revealed. It was more of a burn than a cut with very little blood which he ignored while completing his preparations.

He wanted the thief to be sitting on the toilet lid where it would be slightly warmer than the floor where he intended to sit on folded towels. Positive that the room had been arranged to his satisfaction, Hokee started alternately slapping the thief's face then rocking his body, trying to get him awake. He was just showing signs of awakening when Glory returned with the medicine kit.

Glory looked at Hokee with surprise. "Where are your clothes? And what's with the shower and hot water?"

Taking his medicine kit from Glory Hokee explained, "I could just try the old shaman ritual I used to help find your memory, but I think in this case a sweat lodge experience is called for. I can exercise more control and monitor my own reactions to the drugs better in the heat and moisture environment. I don't want to completely destroy the thief's mind, just incapacitate him to a certain degree."

Glory didn't look convinced but was too preoccupied with the rapidly changing events to question Hokee's judgement.

It was time for her to get revenge.

CHAPTER THIRTY-EIGHT

Losing Your Mind

Years ago, after first claiming the lava flats as his home, Hokee had discovered an antelope with its foreleg caught in a sink hole. The leg was broken and there was no way to fix it; besides the animal went nearly crazy whenever Hokee tried to approach it in order to help secure its release. Unwilling to let the animal continue suffering and eventually starve to death, Hokee could see no alternative than to take its life. He shot it in the head giving it a quick merciful death then carried the body back to his house where it was skinned. The meat was carefully cut up and prepared in packages for Shilah. The skin was treated and stretched to dry. Afterwards when it had been properly tanned Hokee cut the hide into pieces for moccasins saving the choice underbelly skin for a new medicine bag. He figured that the antelope had given up its life in order to present him with a powerful totem to hold his special plants and spirit holders. The antlers were fashioned into the ceremonial pipe he used for smoking.

Hokee thanked Glory for fetching his bag and began opening the drawstring on top. Originally the bag had been nearly white with flecks of sandy tinted hair around the edges but years of use had given it a shiny dark brown coloring. He removed some of the leaves saved from their recent excursions to the island's mountains. These were some of the same leaves Hokee had used for the shaman's ceremony where he helped Glory recover her mind. This time they would be used for something strikingly different.

Each hotel room was furnished with a coffee pot for the guests that Hokee plugged in to make a pot of hot water. As the water was heating he crumbled a few leaves into one of the room's coffee mugs. As the water was heating he began searching the thief's room.

"What on earth are you looking for Hokee?" Glory said. The look on her face said she couldn't believe her partner was ransacking the thief's room.

"Come on honey and help me," he responded. "The money is here someplace. Let's find it."

The coffee pot buzzed signaling that the water was ready so Hokee quit his search to pour hot water over his "tea" leaves. Meanwhile Glory caught on and continued the search as Hokee used one of the hotel spoons to stir plant leaves around in the hot water. As he was stirring the leaves Hokee noticed steam creeping out from under the bathroom door. With the drink nearly ready it was time to see if the next phase of his plan would work. "Glory," he said catching her attention. Then very quietly so he couldn't be heard in the bathroom by the now fully awake thief. "I'm going to go have our bathroom guest drink this cup of special tea. Then we are going to have a little chat. It's going to be hot and steamy in there but you are welcome to join in, clothing optional," he said with a wicked grin.

"I think I'll pass on that part. I'd rather find the money then leave you here in this rotten odor with each other." She said it with a smile but Hokee thought she might just be ready to get away from a place that felt and smelled almost evil and he wouldn't blame her.

"Okay, but don't forget to write," he teased taking his tea into the hot steaming bathroom then quickly shutting the door. He then put a folded towel along the bottom door crack to help contain the steam.

The thief was tied up in hotel towels Hokee had shredded in order to get long strips he could use like ropes. The man's thighs were tied against the bottom of the toilet so he couldn't stand up and his hands were tied together behind his back then laced to the ties holding his legs down to basically immobilize him from making any serious movement. The bottom of his legs were likewise tied together and bound to the back of the toilet. The only movement left to the thief was to move his head and shoulders. He gave Hokee a sullen look full of hatred and you could feel his power and see the desire in his eyes to give his captor one little touch with his hands.

Hokee placed the hot tea down on the floor while he talked with the thief. "Hey Donald, I guess you want me to call you Donald unless you want to give me your real name?" The thief just shrugged saying nothing.

"This is how it's going to be Donald." Hokee slid down the wall opposite the thief with his back against the blue patterned tile next to the tea cup. "You are going to drink this special tea I made just for you. We can do this the easy way or the hard way. The choice is yours."

"What is it?" Donald asked, his eyes blazing daggers he hoped would kill this offensive bastard.

Seeing no reason to lie about what was going to happen, Hokee answered with a slight whimsical smile. "It's a hallucinogenic concoction made from local plants. You should probably be somewhat familiar with its effects. I'm sure that at some time during your Tibetan training you experienced something similar."

The thief showed surprise that this ignorant back country detective knew so much about who he was and what he had learned. "What do you want from me? And what do you mean the easy way or the hard way?"

Still smiling Hokee said, "The easy way is I hold this cup up to your lips and you drink it down. The hard way is I put you in a head lock and pour it down your throat. I'm just being honest with you here. It will be a lot easier for me if you just drink it down without a big fuss; and a lot quicker. On the other hand, I cannot tell you how much pleasure it would give me to take that ugly pockmarked face of yours and force you to swallow this tea one gulp at a time. Like I said the choice is yours. Just so you know, I am not on any sort of time schedule so saving time isn't a big deal for me. What do you say, Donald?"

For the first time the thief was showing just a hint of fear in his eyes. The way they twitched side to side without looking directly at his tormentor. There was the beginning of a crease in the skin between his eyes as the muscles in his forehead began contracting. "What will this do to me? What do you hope to accomplish?"

"Well, I'll tell you slick. You stole my partner's mind. I want yours in return. My plan is to leave you with enough brainpower to function. You'll be able to get food and take care of yourself; but you'll be like a person with an IQ of maybe 65 or 70. You can function, just not at a very high level. On the other hand Donald," he said Donald with a sneer and disgust in his voice like his mouth was full of excrement, "if I have to force this liquid down your throat, I'll leave your brain empty, just like you left Glory." At this point Hokee was no longer smiling. His own eyes were blazing and you could see the determination reflected in his whole body. "What you did to Glory was cruel and potentially a death warrant. I kind of understand why you reacted that way which is why I'm being so generous by offering you a chance to live a somewhat normal, if restricted life. Just don't piss me off. I remember the way you left Glory all too well to be overly generous."

205

The room was quiet except for the shower water as the thief considered all that Hokee had said. Both men were now drenched in sweat. Steam from the hot shower was making visibility difficult. The thief continually flipped his head from side to side in order to shake sweat away from his eyes. Hokee was sitting stoically against the wall seemingly untouched by the steam. A veteran of literally hundreds of sweat lodges, the hot steam was like an old friend.

Taking stock of the look in Hokee's eyes the thief knew there was really no choice. He couldn't get out of this situation with his magnificent powers. This detective/shaman could not be dissuaded by any argument he might make. With his hands bound behind his back he was unable to transmit any damage. "Okay, I'll drink your tea. You promise me that I'll still be able to function, right?" he asked almost like a child begging its parents for one more chance.

"I'm good for my word Donald. I will tell you that I have only had one experience with this particular batch of leaves. They're pretty powerful. I'll do my best to make sure you have enough mental capacity left to operate with; however, there is a chance I might underestimate the drug's power on your mind. I want you to drink about three-fourths of this tea. I'll drink about one quarter of the cup first for myself so I can get into the same space. That way I can be somewhat of a guide to make sure we recover part of your mind."

Giving up any hope of a last-minute reprieve the thief said, "Okay, I'm ready."

Grabbing the cup which was still pretty hot although the tea was drinkable Hokee stood and took a couple of quick swallows before approaching the thief. Holding the cup to his lips Hokee poured a little bit at a time into his throat allowing him to swallow before giving him another sip. After the thief had finished his portion Hokee resumed his sitting posture on the floor.

"This won't take too long before we start feeling the drugs," Hokee said. "However, it will last several hours. When you are mostly back from your trip I'll remove your bindings setting you free. If all goes well, we'll leave you a little present in your bedroom."

"Present?" he replied. "What sort of present?"

"You are going to need money in order to survive. I plan on leaving you some of the money you stole from the bread truck. If you don't go crazy it should do for you. Just stay away from Pocatello."

"No problem. I sure as hell didn't leave anything there that would make me want to return. Why the generosity? I haven't done anything but cause you and the pretty blond lady problems."

*****

Hokee was starting to feel the drugs in his body and knew it wouldn't be long before they were both tripping. Although he had taken only a small drink compared to what he had given the thief he would still get into the same space. Knowing this was probably going to be their last cogent conversation he answered the thief.

"I know what Officer Morden did to your head. You didn't deserve that and your life has been difficult. While I can't undo the past, your actions must also be taken into account. I cannot leave you with your doppelganger powers. You have shown a proclivity to use them against others. On the other hand, once stripped of your harmful power and with only partial use of your mind you will need survival money. I just feel generous and I'll give you most of my share of the recovered money. I don't need it and you will. Just remember to show a little kindness to others."

There was no way to tell how much if anything the thief really understood of this message. By now Hokee was feeling himself going into the void outside of his body. After waiting a couple more minutes he began calling, "Donald. Hey Donald. Can you hear me?"

The detective tracked the thief's mind into the void dispatching into the infinite all of the unwanted memories, information and mind power that could be used in a harmful manner. Hokee sent it to the far reaches of space and time beyond where he had ever gone personally and would undoubtedly never experience. That part of the thief's mind he now identified as Donald McKenzie he brought back with him to the body still sitting on the toilet. Jabbing Donald in his ribs, probably a little harder than necessary, and slapping his face, Hokee started bringing Donald McKenzie to life. Feeling the body begin to respond, Hokee undid all of the bindings leaving the man sitting on the toilet seat bathed in sweat. It would take the new Donald McKenzie a couple of hours to fully regain consciousness.

Hokee and Gloria would be long gone.

CHAPTER THIRTY-NINE

Going Home

Hokee had turned off the hot water and steam as soon as he felt himself coming fully back into his body. After freeing McKenzie from his bonds Hokee took a quick cold shower to wash off the sweat and cool down. Using some of the hotel towels he dried off and leaving his wet shorts in the bathroom waste basket he left the bathroom shutting the door behind him.

Glory was sitting on the bed surrounded by stacks of beautiful green money. Seeing the naked Hokee she couldn't help but quip, "Did you boys have fun in there?"

With a fake growl and grunt Hokee responded, "Yeah, it was wonderful, you should have been there."

A grinning Glory's response even made the tired Hokee smile. "I was just waiting with all of this money so we could make love on piles of real dough."

"I couldn't think of one thing I would rather do more but I'm afraid that will have to wait. Do you know how much money you have found?" Hokee looked around for his clothes and began getting dressed.

Knowing that Hokee had probably really exhausted himself, Glory quit teasing and responded, "Yeah, a little over three million dollars. It's something over three point one and then I kind of quit counting. There's a few thousand more than that but not much."

"Hey, that's great," Hokee said. Now pack up one and a half million in a suitcase. We're taking that back to the bank."

Glory was confused, "How come we're only taking one and half million? What about the rest?"

An exasperated and tired Hokee replied, "My agreement with the bank was to return half of what I recovered. In my book one and a half million is close enough. We're leaving the thief, I mean the new Donald McKenzie one and a half million. We're taking the rest for expenses."

An angry frustrated Glory nearly yelled, "Why are you giving that bastard your share of the reward money? Don't you realize what he did to me?"

Helping Glory pack up the money she had separated Hokee replied, "Yeah honey, I know what he did to you and I'm really sorry you had to go through that experience. You should know that I left him with only half of his mind. He's going to need some money in order to survive. I don't need the money and after what that deputy sheriff did to him when he was just a kid I kind of feel sorry for the man. I plan on leaving him here with about half of the stolen money so he can stay alive. I also programmed him to use the money for benevolent purposes besides his own survival."

Glory thought about it for a minute before responding. With a frown and furrowed eyebrows, she said, "Okay, it's really your money anyway so if that's what you want to do I guess I can't do anything about it."

Grinning in spite of his fatigue Hokee said, "Yeah, you can carry the bank's money to the car. I need to write a quick note to our bathroom host in case he needs a little help figuring out his own future. Think about it Glory. Do you really want to haul his ass all the way back to Pocatello? Leaving him here with living money and no power to inflict his evil on anyone else seems the most humane thing we can do. Are you on board with this?"

"I guess that's why I find you so terribly fascinating and loveable," she said. "You have this big macho persona yet inside you're just a little pussy cat."

"Meow," he responded as he sat down at the room's desk and began composing a note for the still recovering thief.

Glory finished packing the bank's money then separated the thief's money while Hokee was writing. By the time Hokee stood up ready to go Glory was ready with the final tally. "It looks like we have almost two hundred thousand dollars for our expenses. Still not a bad pay day," she said finally smiling.

"Your half should buy you a couple of pretty frilly smocks," he replied with a big grin.

"Hey, you're the detective," she said. "The reward money is all yours plus you paid all the expenses. Well, what the station didn't cover."

"We've been partners on this venture Glory. I know this is a big story for you and I hope your employer is happy and gives you a big bonus, but you earned half of this money. Besides it will make me happy."

"Well, now that you put it that way," she purred, "maybe I can find some way to reward you." The sexy lascivious grin on her face left no doubt about what kind of reward she had in mind.

The money they were leaving for the thief was left stacked next to the note Hokee had written. Pocketing the money they intended on splitting Hokee picked up the suitcase with the bank's money in it and opened the outside door. The sun was just about to come over the horizon illuminating the day with a brilliant display of streaking reds and golds. "Take a look at that Glory. Looks like we're leaving just in time. The storm that's coming is a lot closer. Let's hit the hotel for our things and head for the airport. We'll take the first flight out regardless of where it's going. What do you say?"

"Oh, that sky is beautiful and this island is really spectacular," she said, but you didn't have to look very hard to see the pain that lingered in her eyes. "I can't wait to put this all behind me. I must say Hokee, you sure do know how to entertain a girl."

Seeing the pain and knowing the hell she had experienced having linked into her mind during their sweat lodge, Hokee responded with a wry grin, "It isn't every woman that I take on these exotic excursions you know; only sexy New York reporter type women."

A taxi was waiting for departing guests right outside the hotel's veranda. After collecting their belongings from the other hotel, they arrived at the airport in time to make an early morning departure for Miami. About the same time, he was buckled in his seat Hokee closed his weary eyes and dropped off into a deep sleep. Glory stashed the suitcase full of money overhead and was soon fast asleep as well. Neither one woke up until the plane's tires bumped onto the tarmac and skidded on the landing.

The weary couple deplaned and entered the Miami terminal only to find out they had just missed a flight to New York. There was a two-hour wait until the next flight.

It was decision time for the pair. What did the future hold? They had two hours in which to decide their fate.

CHAPTER FORTY

A Long Flight Home

Hokee and Glory had a big breakfast with a large pot of coffee at the airport diner. Hokee ate a double portion of blueberry pancakes, three sausage patties, half of a plateful of hash browns and four scrambled eggs plus four slices of whole wheat toast. Glory only had one stack of pancakes and two scrambled eggs but otherwise she pretty much matched Hokee's meal. In fairness, she probably only drank about half as much coffee. Their breakfast consumed most of the two hours they had between flights and they avoided "the big topic". It wasn't until they were finally on the plane to New York that they broached the future.

The flight from Miami to New York is about two hours which could seem like forever at times and yet when you needed the time it only seemed like seconds. They both knew that the decision time had arrived yet neither one could find the right words. Feelings and mixed emotions do not make for clarity of expression.

Both wanted their freedom. Both wanted their careers. And they wanted each other. She was a New York City girl. Hokee was a country boy. She was a classy, sexy, intelligent reporter with a great future in the investigating and broadcasting business.

He was a uniquely gifted detective with a desire to help others but knew that he would be lost in New York. There was no way on earth he could leave his cave and Shilah. But, what could Glory ever do in Pocatello that would measure up to her life in the big city?

They were both intelligent intuitive beings who could read the tea leaves with the best Chinese sorcerers around. Yet, neither wanted to be the one to express those thoughts out loud. They both wanted their adventure to never end, but they knew that every story had an ending.

It was Hokee who finally broke the ice. "Do you think you could ever be happy in Pocatello?" Hope and desperation played across his handsome face. His eyes were shining with hope and the desperation wrinkled his forehead. In his heart, he also understood the inevitability of life's thrust on each individual. Glory was relieved to finally have the conversation she had been avoiding for hours. "I really don't know Hokee. You know I have to get back to New York in any case. I have to wrap up this story, and believe me, it's a real killer. My producer is going to go crazy."

A smile played across her face as she thought about how this crazy story would come across. Hopefully Donald, her cameraman, had some decent shots to go along with the story. He was going to be really pissed off at missing the trip to St. John. She was going to have to find some way to make it up to him. But, she also knew that when he was told about how she lost her mind he would be glad that he had been dumped in Pocatello.

Taking his hand just before landing she leaned over and kissed his cheek. "Tell you what big guy. Give me a few weeks to finalize the story and make some arrangements in New York and I'll see about dropping by your cave for a visit. We'll just see what develops."

"Okay Glory. I'll have Shilah keep an eye out for you." Hokee gave her hand a gentle squeeze to let her know that he understood. She might make it to Pocatello, or maybe he would visit her in New York to explore the big city. Only in the future now would they both know.

CHAPTER FORTY-ONE

New York

On Glory's first day back to the office she was almost greeted like a hero returning from the war. That is to say Levi Morgenstern grunted as she walked into his office and her colleagues kept peeking around the corner of their cubes trying to see what the clothes hound was up to now.

Without giving Levi a chance to even say welcome back or how was your trip Glory launched into her elevator pitch. Within two minutes Levi had called for Donald's pictures and summoned several assistants to help put the finishing touches on an incredible story. "This may not get you a Pulitzer, Glory," he said, "but it is one hell of a story. To be honest, we weren't expecting much of anything to come out of this trip and boy you really delivered a surprise. Congratulations."

The Mysterious Bakery Truck Robbery ran as a three-part series during prime time earning Glory every broadcasting award available at the time. Donald's Idaho pictures augmented with stock photos of sweat lodges and native American lodges provided a dramatic framework for the series. The viewer's groans could almost be heard back over the air waves when Glory reported that they had left the thief with one and a half million dollars. There was no mention of the Caribbean, or of any island for that matter. Viewers could only speculate as to where the thief was living with the stolen money.

A week after completing the series on the truck robbery Glory walked into Levi's office without knocking.

"I'm going to take a few weeks off for person reasons Levi," she said. "I'd like to leave next week but I can hold off another week or two if you have something urgent you want me to handle."

"Let me guess," he smirked lighting up his cigar. "You're gonna go visit your Indian boyfriend."

"Actually," she replied with a smirk of her own, "It isn't any of your business where I'm going or what I'm going to be doing. But yes boss, I'm going to visit Hokee for a couple of weeks and see how Pocatello really feels to this New York girl."

"But you are coming back? Right?" He asked just a little bit panicky at the thought of losing his ace reporter.

Glory had a far-away look in her eyes as she responded. "Probably.... Maybe.... I really don't know. Don't fill my position right away. Okay?"

For the first time in their relationship the famous Levi Morgenstern acted and looked almost human. "Go on Glory. Get out of here. Good luck and we'll always have a job for you here if that's what you want."

*****

St. John's Island

St. John's native island's population before the Europeans brought their shiploads of disease and decadence were simple happy healthy people, if somewhat laidback and easygoing. Their dependents inherited a number of crippling diseases and misshapen limbs caused by poisons brought to the Caribbean. Baptist missionaries established a hospital and clinic in 1889 to help the native population deal with the various health-related issues brought on by the white man's invasion.

The hospital is long gone, but the clinic remains still staffed by new missionaries and descendants of the old missionaries. Like most such charitable organizations, they are forever out of money begging the island's wealthy for a few more dollars to help meet this year's inadequate budget. Chloe Williamson was on duty at the front desk when a bald-headed man with a pockmarked face and sunken chest came into their lobby one afternoon and handed her a stack of hundred dollar bills. He grunted a few unintelligible words which made him sound kind of slow witted before leaving. Chloe hurried out after him to at least say thanks but he had disappeared.

CHAPTER FORTY-TWO

Hokee and Shilah

Shilah heard Hokee's car when it was still a half mile away and within seconds was trotting alongside when Hokee got to the top of the sink where his home site began. There were several minutes of hugging and tongue licking before Hokee was able to retrieve the bag from his vehicle and go inside with Shilah at his heels. Although he had only been gone a few days, the place felt stuffy so Hokee left the front door open to air out the living room and kitchen.

After checking in with Mrs. Hilda Worthmyer for office messages Hokee called the bank to schedule a visit. Although delighted to have nearly half of the stolen money returned Weeb Dillford was not happy that Hokee had not returned with the thief in tow as well. There had been nothing said about apprehending the thief but to the bank manager's mind that was understood. Finally accepting the inevitable Dillford thanked Hokee for his outstanding detective work and success. The Pocatello sheriff's department was less than thrilled to have another one of their failures resolved by Pocatello's leading detective. Officer Brent Morden was delighted and relieved when Hokee told him in private that the thief would never return to Pocatello, although Hokee refused to tell the policeman exactly what happened.

It seems that someone has been stealing bidding information from Olson Construction causing them to lose out on several large international contracts. Olson's internal security had been unable to find the leak and the call had gone out for Hokee Wolf. Hokee didn't really want this job opportunity but Olson had been so generous that he found it impossible to refuse. It would mean spending several days, possibly weeks in northern Idaho and with Shilah that was always a problem. He couldn't leave his brother alone for what might be an extended period of time and it was always difficult finding a good place that would accept a wolf as a guest. This usually meant that Hokee ended up leasing a house that offered some privacy for an extended period of time. He wasn't worried about the expenditure as Olson would certainly cover the costs.

He also wanted to be in Pocatello in case Glory ever did decide to come for a visit. He wasn't expecting a phone call. If she was going to come she would likely just show up one day. He could always leave her a note. After all, she had to expect him to continue doing his work.

With trepidation Hokee set out for Nampa, Idaho. If Glory came she would either follow him or not. As he had learned many years ago; life happens.

AUTHOR'S NOTES

Eddy's Bakery really did haul money from West Yellowstone to Pocatello during the period depicted in the story. This practice was maintained for many years but I am unaware of any robbery. The streets and locations of important landmarks in Pocatello and Henry's Lake are as described although time and progress has changed or destroyed many of Hokee's favorite hangouts.

The farmers in southeastern Idaho and northern Utah did import hundreds of reservation Indians to help with the mundane chores of farming. Farming at that time was hard work seven days a week and many farmers didn't have enough children at home to do the work. More than one Indian maiden was "used" by the farmer. Whether by consent or otherwise, I never knew.

Hokee's lava plains are as described as is the underground river although I confess to never making the trip described. As far as I know there is no house built like Hokee's, although I have seen some pretty interesting and fascinating houses built in the desert.

The Caribou Mountain mines were real and the supposition that the Chinese miners and their families were sealed up inside has been speculated for years, but to my knowledge no one has ever tried to verify the truthfulness of this legend. All of the mine entrances were dynamited and sealed off when the mine was closed and the Chinese disappeared. They may have just left since there was no longer any employment, but who knows? Perhaps another mystery for Hokee to solve? This saga is explored in my novel *The Broken Seal,* which has been a work in progress for several years.

St. John's has the landmarks described in the story although what they really looked like in the story's timeframe is the author's imagination. The meals described and Hokee's own cooking are authentic.

The Silver Fox's lodge is real although that was not the name of the shaman I knew. The doppelganger phenomenon does exist. There are modern day spiritual gurus trying to teach a positive way to utilize your own doppelganger, but the dangerous practice described in this story is unfortunately also true. And finally, the sweat lodge and shaman practices described throughout the story are as experienced and remembered by the author.

Clark is a retired entrepreneur with six successful startup companies to his credit. His eclectic background includes truck driving, heavy equipment operator, lounge singer, dish washer, sales clerk, aerospace engineer, rocket scientist, miner, rancher and actor. Degrees include BSFA (Theatre Arts), BSEE, and JD with accompanying degrees in math and physics. Hokee Wolf is his second full-length novel.

View other Black Rose Writing titles at www.blackrosewriting.com/books and use promo code **PRINT** to receive a **20% discount** when purchasing.

BLACK ROSE
writing™